The Ruffled Owl

Sean Peter

Edited by 'Twicky Vicky' Sadler.

ISBN: 978-1-916820-09-8

Chapter One

Early days

The river was brown and sinuous, as it wound its way east. I stood in the early morning sunshine listening to the bush, the familiar cicadas chirruping and the hollow call of a hoopoe echoing above the other background bird calls; I stood motionless in the warming air and was rewarded with the distant sound of meshing gears and the steady rumble of a heavy diesel engine.

It was still way off, but from experience I knew how long it would be. I moved further back into the thorny bush and acacia trees, where I could see the thin graded strip next to the river where no vegetation grew, it was kept this way by the government as a precautionary method to pick up footprints to or from the river.

I lay down behind a rotting tree just as up the hill came the labouring troop carrier. In front walked a small nut-brown San bushman, his eyes intently scanning the track. The San were peerless trackers, and I was thankful that I had not ventured towards the river. I held my breath as the heavy armoured vehicle hove into view and the bushman came to a stop. For some unfathomable reason he stared over in my direction and my heart missed a beat as I thought he might have seen me. I forced myself deeper into the undergrowth hardly daring to breathe. After an age he resumed his pace and the vehicle growled on behind him.

I heard it slowly moving off and I peered over the log, watching them crawl along the river. These were the men of the Seventh South African Infantry Battalion, highly trained and very able. I remained motionless and thought on how drastically my life had changed.

Only a few odd months previously I had been roaming the streets of Swaziland on my motorbike, with my first girlfriend, Wendy, my 'brother' Sven, and his fiancée Jenny. It had been sublime and even though I no longer had a veterinary career, I had thought that I would be able to obtain a position in one of the game parks in Swaziland, or across the border in South Africa. Unfortunately, I had underestimated the reach of the South African Bureau of State security (BOSS).

Their first strike had been at my 'adopted' family by advising them that any assistance they gave to me would have repercussions for them when entering South Africa, and that they should dissociate themselves from me. I was mortified and packed my belongings and left the house on the hill. Mia was devastated and tried to persuade me that things could be worked out, but I knew that there was no way after all the family had done for me, that I would allow them to suffer. I moved back down to the house in the Enzulweni valley. Grand-pere Jacques was also approached with similar threats but as his only investment across the border was the farm in Marble Hall, he engaged a manager and brought his new wife back to Swaziland. I felt terrible but there was nothing much I could do so I accepted Grand-peres decision.

Wendy was initially supportive but as the weeks had rolled on, with severe pressure, I presume from her family, she phoned me, in tears, and told me that they had had a visit from members of the security services, informing them that I was a dangerous activist. Consequently, she felt it best I did not contact her again. I had been distraught but could do nothing to alter her decision, so accepted it with unhappy grace.

The options of working in one of Swaziland's game parks were limited. I had applied to Londolosi in South

Africa, who had offered to employ me previously, but they informed me that they could no longer avail of my talents as I had a conviction. I spoke to Sambulo and Mandla to see if they could help in securing me a position in one of the Swazi Parks, both had been sympathetic and made enquiries for me but unfortunately there was a long waiting list for these sought-after positions and 'indigenous' citizens would always be offered employment first.

I consulted my mentor, Dr Dlamini (the Witch Doctor), who was a little surprised that I was still allowed to travel to South Africa and surmised that the security services hoped I would lead them to bigger operatives. I was non-plussed as realistically I had no affiliation to any subversive organization at that time and told him so. He looked at me knowingly, saying that 'time would tell'!

I had applied to the S.A. Department of Nature Conservation in the hope that they might offer me some sort of employment. At that stage I was prepared to accept anything. Amazingly they offered me an interview, so I travelled to Pretoria, their headquarters, with all my qualifications in anticipatory hope. This was dashed as on arrival I had to complete an extensive application form where one of the questions was whether one had any convictions. Consequently, my interview was cut short, and I left the building and found myself on the hot pavement of one of Pretoria's busiest streets.

It had been another disappointment and I had strolled down the Jacaranda embellished street a little disheartened. I decided to look for an outdoor café as it was a glorious summer day, and the heady scent of the Jacaranda blossom could be appreciated. Walking slowly along I had failed to notice an African man next to me, it was only when he spoke to me in Zulu that I had taken note. He strangely had asked how my life was going? I had been slightly perplexed but replied that things were calamitous. He had nodded sagely and had proposed we have a coffee together.

Once the coffees had arrived, we talked, well he did. He told me his name was Elias Makoena and said did I know I was being followed? I was astonished as I had not been taking much notice of my surroundings, as my then dire predicament occupied most of my thoughts. I asked him, why did he think I was being followed? He smiled and replied that when the security services kept someone under surveillance he was interested. When I enquired who he was and what his interest was in me, he had smiled, then informed me that he was a member of the then banned African National Congress (ANC). I had been ambivalent as I had bigger concerns, namely a job and a future, and told him so. He had nodded, then said that if I wanted any information on the organization, I should return to the coffee shop owner and leave my contact details. I had looked at him incuriously, but he simply drained his cup, shook my hand, and left.

I returned to Swaziland dispirited and at a loss to know what to do with my life! I discussed it with Grand-pere and though he had assured me that I would always have a home in the valley, and he would find some meaningful occupation for me on the plantations, but it was entirely up to me. If ever I missed the comfort of my adopted family, it was then.

I had thought long and hard on my dilemma and after discussing it with Grand pere, he had suggested I seek the advice of Dr Dlamini, so I arranged to meet him in the bush. It was a beautiful day in the Ngwempisi Wilderness area South of Manzini, where I found him. He had been dressed in his traditional garb and, I always felt in awe as he exuded mystery and idiosyncrasy, which I suspect was his intention.

We sat on a massive bolder in the sun with the 'brio' of the bush surrounding us. I had told him how things were conspiring against me, I had lost my 'family,' my girlfriend and my career. I told him of my meeting with the enigmatic man from the A.NC. He had surveyed me with deep, dark eyes and then stared off into the distance. "Isikhova (owl), you are like the Impungushe (Jackal) that is being cornered, you must realize by now that those across the border will never relent! You acted, initially, on what your conscience dictated, you must now do the same and stand up for what is right! It won't be easy, but you will find friends and support in unexpected places. 'Hamba ngokuthula isikova (Go in peace Owl)". Following this advice, I contacted the coffee shop in Pretoria and arranged a meeting. I was interviewed, accepted the A.N.C. constitution and within time was a card-carrying member of a banned Organization across the border. Grand-pere had been extremely worried, but Mother had been apoplectic!

I informed the organization that I was not prepared to be a 'combatant', as in endangering' lives of people, but would be prepared to help in any other way. I was assigned to a cadre in the Asian township of Lenasia, just north of Johannesburg and accommodated above the local Cinema. The leader of my Cadre was a kind, benevolent Indian Sikh who told me that eventually I would need to attend a training camp in either Angola or Zambia. I was not over enthusiastic about the prospect but, in the interim, I was given the mission of driving prospective recruits to the armed wing of the A.N.C–umkhonto we siswe- (The Spear of the Nation) to these camps. I was given a small covered 'bakkie'-pickup- with the livery of a roofing company. I simply had to convey these young men across the borders, either into Botswana or Zimbabwe.

I began and soon became proficient at avoiding the security and police services roadblocks. The border at Ramotswe just south of Gaborone in Botswana became a regular access point but I was careful not use it too often. The border into Zimbabwe had the added complication of being the Limpopo River which did not help as many of the young recruits were poor swimmers. I normally crossed the river just north of the small town of Masisi, where it kinked on its way East. I would swim across and tether a thick rope to a sturdy bush tree on the opposite bank, then recross the river leaving the nylon rope to sink into the water. Once I was sure that a patrol was not imminent, I would get my people to cross safely using the rope.

I strained my ears to make sure I could hear only the cicadas and the myriad animal and bird calls. I watched a Slate Grey Lizard Buzzard fly up from the grass with an Agama lizard in its talons, its breakfast secure. I moved back towards the river until I reached the graded bit of track beside it, this stretch had not been graded recently and the vegetation was beginning to re-assert itself. I crossed the red dirt trying to make as insignificant impact as possible but knowing that any decent tracker would pick up my spoor. I stood on the bank and removed the stainless-steel signalling mirror from my pocket. It was small but nevertheless quite sufficient to send a flashing signal from the sun across into Zimbabwe. I flashed the signal a couple times but received no response, this was not unusual as seldom did meeting up with my counterpart on the other side go smoothly. I had once or twice had to wait two full days before contact was made. This was because of the great distances involved and often my returning trainees had travelled many days and nights through two countries, so I was prepared for most eventualities. There was no movement on the opposite bank, except for a hebetudinous crocodile sunning itself in the early morning heat, so I decided I would return to the vehicle.

I slowly made my way back through the bush-veldt and reached the van in a couple of hours. I had left it at the small rural village of Gumbu. Even though it didn't have many vehicles, the tiny village was still the best choice compared to leaving the van in the bush where, if it was discovered, it would arouse suspicion. The people here were of Shangaan decent and spoke Xitsonga, which unfortunately I was not proficient in. Nevertheless, I had been given contact details of a notable induna, by my cadre, who was sympathetic towards the organization. Dzunani was aged and his face weathered like the trunk of an antediluvian tree, but he was proficient in the Nguni language, so we were able to communicate.

I retrieved my stash of Biltong (beef Jerky) from the vehicle as well as a pouch of rolling tobacco and made my way to Dzunani's thatched hut. He was sitting outside in the mid-morning sun, I made the customary greeting and offered him the tobacco, which he gratefully accepted, then I asked after his wives and family. Once these formalities had been completed, he got down to telling me what contact he had had with the security services recently. The situation was not without peril for him or his villagers as the members of the intelligence section of the South African Police services were extremely adept at obtaining information, either by coercion or by offering monetary inducement, and because most in his tiny village were poor, they often succumbed.

He sat on his haunches and happily puffed away on his pipe. "They have been here last quarter moon," he updated me, "asking if we had seen any strangers in this area. "We told them that we do not have many 'womuntu'(human) visitors here but plenty of 'isilwane' (animal) ones" he chortled. "The Impisi (hyena) and Ingwe(leopard) are regular visitors, they steal our 'izinyoni'(poultry) and in the case of Ingwe often our dogs" he added. I asked if they had made enquiries about me or my vehicle. He shook his head and went on to say they had told him to be vigilant and report anything he or any other villagers thought out of the ordinary.

Khana, one of his wives, brought us two large enamel mugs filled with dark Red Bush tea laced with condensed milk, it was strong and heavenly. I sat sipping the hot tea and marvelled at how happy they seemed, sure they had no electrical appliances and relied on their maize crop for the main part of their sustenance, supplemented by hunting Helmeted Guinea Fowl, Kori Bustard, the small Dik Dik antelope and the larger antelope such as Impala and Eland. These were people who could do without the likes of me bringing the problems of a conservative, racist government to their 'doorstep' and I knew that should the security services discover that they had been helping me, the consequences would be dire.

I thanked Dzunani and gave him the rest of the tobacco and told him I would hopefully be bringing my 'people' back later that night but would try to be as unobtrusive as possible.

I headed Northeast into the bush, moving slowly under the midday sun. I was walking slowly along thinking on how different Dzunani and his people's lives were to those that lived in the squalid townships. They rarely experienced the abhorrent apartheid system in their remote village, in fact they weren't even aware of it. I was in a deep reverie and almost bumped into an Aardvark. It was rooting around a moderately sized ant hill so was surprised to see me. I was puzzled to see it, as these termite eaters are nocturnal and usually avoid other animals and humans. I presumed it had excavated the termite mound during the previous night and was still trying to get the rest of its 'spoils'.

It squealed like a pig, lay on its back, and prepared to defend itself with its 'pickaxe' like claws, so I quickly moved off leaving it to get on with its dinner.

I slowly made my way back to the river and as I got closer, I listened carefully, for any vehicle noise.

I reached the river but hung back in the bush quietly watching. It was mid-afternoon and I was not sure whether there had been any action on the other side of the river. Nothing moved except for a corpulent Hippo wallowing in the shallows of the river. I decided to have another attempt at signalling, so removing my soft leather 'veld-skoens'(boots), I padded across the hot graded sand. Once on the riverbank I signalled with the mirror but received no response. I considered my options. Eventually I would have to swim the river and tether the nylon rope, so surveying the river for any dangers, seeing that the Hippo had moved off downstream and there were no crocodiles visible, I decided that now would be as good a time as any.

I put my boots in the canvas backpack on my back and fully clothed entered the river. I was about to strike out swimming when I picked up the sound of the patrol coming back. This was disastrous as they would be sure to notice me in the river. My only option was to return to the bank and try to conceal myself in the reeds. I slithered into the reed bed just as the vehicle came up. I heard the bushman shout and knew he had discovered my footprints in the sand!

The situation was now perilous as I was stuck in the river. Once again, I was grateful for my early life in Swaziland and my brothers Mandla and Sambulo, as they had taught me how to cut a reed, hollow it out and then lie submerged amongst the reeds. This was still not without risk as the reed beds were also the haunt of crocodiles.

I crawled deep into the reeds and lay breathing through my makeshift 'snorkel' trying to keep my reed as still as the rest around me. It would now depend on how serious the patrol investigated the footprints. Thankfully, the footprints were going out of the country, as the soldiers considered insurgent entries into the country far more important than those exiting. They switched off the heavy diesel engine and I heard them discussing the footprints with the Bushman. I was only just submerged so should they start investigating the reed beds I was sure to be discovered. I lay still taking small breaths through my tube and heard them deliberating on the bank close to me. I could hear them as the water carried sound effectively and I could understand the soldiers' Afrikaans, but not anything the bushman said. Ominously, after a lot of deliberation, I heard the unmistakable cocking of R1 rifles. These were extremely accurate copies of the European FN rifles manufactured locally, and not a good sign!

I was now terrified and getting ready to emerge and give myself up instead of being shot. I was considering this when I heard the engine start up again. I breathed a little easier but continued to lie very still. I felt something 'investigating' my toes and almost jumped up out of the water as I couldn't see what it was, the water being murky. I calmed my racing imagination and tried to think logically. If it were a crocodile or a constricting python it would not, simply be 'tasting' my extremities, but would have either grabbed me physically and dragged me off or coiled around me. So, I considered it had to be a fish or some other smaller aquatic mammal.

I lay still in a state of great perturbation breathing rapidly through my reed while the investigation of my toes carried on. I was doing my best to listen to what was happening on the bank, I could hear the throb of the diesel engine but could also still hear the bushman. The minutes stretched out infinitely, but finally the voices disappeared, and I realized the engine noise was becoming a lot fainter. Had they left, or had they just moved off a short distance? My mind was in turmoil as I tried to weigh up the risk from them and the 'entity' trying to masticate my toes. Finally, I threw caution to the winds and sat up, removing my reed breathing tube. This action precipitated the flight of my tormentor. I managed to make it out, it was a small black billed Terrapin just over six inches long. This is what I had thought had had me on its menu!? The relief that flooded through me was misplaced as I still was not aware of where the patrol was, but I burst out laughing and yelled at it "Ufudu oyisiphukuphuku" You stupid tortoise)! At this insult it scuttled off obviously very aggrieved.

I stood up cautiously and then crawled up the bank, staying as low as possible, all the time listening intently for any sound of the patrol. I scrutinized the bush but could see no sign off anyone. I lay in the riverbank undergrowth letting the sun slowly begin to dry my clothes and counted my blessings. I had been fortunate, things could have gone terribly wrong. Instead of now lying blissfully in the afternoon sun, I could have been confined inside the hot troop carrier after receiving a harsh beating from the soldiers, as they were not renowned for their clemency towards what they would consider a terrorist.

Inexorably I had to move and get across the river to tether the rope, so I once more scanned the river for any dangers, then slid in and swam slowly across. The river was sluggish, so I was able reach the other bank without too much trouble. I emerged and after surveying the bush on the Zimbabwe side, I found what I was looking for, a sturdy Mopane. It was not too far from the bank, so I took the strong green nylon rope from my backpack and secured it to the trunk. Then spooling it out I once more retreated to the river and swam across with it tied to my waist.

Once back on the S.A. side I searched for a passable rock and then, tying the rope to it, submerged it in the shallows of the riverbank. I did not tie it to a tree on this side as I was not sure when it would be needed, and I needed to be sure any subsequent patrols did not discover it. I was now satisfied I had done all I could for the moment. So once more I crossed the sand, only this time walking backwards to insinuate to a perceptive tracker that I was heading towards the river, leaving and not entering. I was not sure that this was effective, but I had to do my utmost to avoid detection.

It was by now late afternoon, so I found a suitable 'Umbones' (Red Bush Willow) tree with good foliage to climb into and conceal myself. I was tired, a little thirsty and hungry but above all exhausted and stressed. It had been a difficult day so far. I wedged myself into the junction of two boughs and amazingly fell asleep.

I was impolitely awoken by two Brown headed Parrots squabbling over some larval meal. I eased my cramped limbs and noted that the sun was sinking low on the Western horizon, a big red ball, the air was filled with birds getting ready to roost and animals gearing up for nocturnal foraging or hunting.

A Black backed Jackal called out in a plaintive wail as it began its nightly hunting. I slipped down from the tree, removed some biltong from my backpack and munched on it. I needed fluids but was loath to drink from the river. I recalled that I had seen some Matakaan, a wild watermelon, that though bitter were good for quenching thirst. I needed to move fast as the light was fading quickly, so I set off at a swift trot. Fortunately, I found them in time, they were not as many as earlier and some of them had been split, but I was able to cut one or two open and eat the soft wet flesh. It was bitter but it quenched my thirst. I decided to take as many of the rest as they might come in handy.

I made my way back to the river and reached it in the dark. It was close to a new moon, but the heavens were illuminated with innumerable stars. I heard a cackle of Hyenas from across the river in the distance as I went to the bank and once again sent the signal with a flashlight. Thankfully, it was still serviceable after its soakings. I was amazed to get an acknowledgement at once which eased my misgivings. I found a substantial tree and tied the rope to it and then combed the stretch of river for the tell-tale retinal reflection of any crocodiles. I took my time to search as unless you shine the light directly into their eyes you could fail to see them. The advantages were now all with the saurian because their night vision is excellent.

I could see none, so grabbing the nylon rope I made my way across to Zimbabwe. I found my contact Joseph who was a Ndebele, descended from the Nguni Zulus as were my friends from my 'home' Swaziland. He was tall and strong and a good operative and greeted me enthusiastically. "Ngithemba ukuthi uyaphila Izikova" (I hope you are well Owl?) he asked. "Ngiyaphil (fine) I replied. I then asked him how his journey had been and how the returning men were? He shrugged his shoulders, smiled, and said they were eager to get back home as the 'training' camps were not much 'fun'! I nodded and then shook the hands of the four men, in fact they were no more than adolescent young men, two of whom I had moved up a few months before. They were a bit thinner but otherwise seemed happy to see me. Joseph now took his leave saying he hoped to see me soon, I 'fist bumped' him and said "Hamba ngokuphepha umfowethu." (Go safely my brother), and he melted off into the night.

I now gathered my 'flock' who in general were from township environments and so had little experience of the bush. I explained to them what to do and above all that until we were in the vehicle and on the road, they should not talk or make a noise. They nodded as I explained about the rope and how they were to cross the river. The two I had previously brought across assured the other two that if they listened to me all would be well. They looked at me, the whites of their eyes large in the dark night. I asked if any of them could swim to which they shook their heads! I reassured them that as the river was not flowing strongly, they would be fine if they just pulled themselves across on the rope. They were apprehensive but agreed willingly.

I once more surveyed the river with the torch, to make sure that no 'visitors' had arrived, and satisfied that it was potentially safe I sent the first man across. He struck out and was soon on the opposite bank. The other three followed him in quick succession and soon all four were safely on the other bank. I untied the rope on my side and swam rapidly across as by now, with all the 'action' in the river, every inhabitant would have been alerted and me ending up as a saurian skinny supper would not be a good end to the enterprise.

Thankfully, it was a hot night as we were all soaked through, but I told them to cross the sandy strip carefully then crossed myself. Once in the bush I broke off a branch from a tree and using it as a makeshift besom swept it across the graded track, hopefully obliterating all our tracks. I knew that in the harsh light of day any decent tracker would note our presence, but by then hopefully we would be halfway to Johannesburg.

I navigated my way back to Gumbu using the stars and we were soon at the pick-up. It was past midnight so thankfully the villagers were asleep, only the odd dog barked at us. I put them all in the back where there was a makeshift seat, amongst the pots of subterfuge paint and other accoutrements of the roofer's trade, and we set off. I negotiated the rural dirt roads until I was on the R525 heading for the N1 motorway and the nearest big town of Louis Trichardt. I planned to stop there early morning to buy us all breakfast.

The journey was monotonous and the steady rumble of the tyres on the tarmac soon sent my 'charges' to sleep obviously, they hadn't had much sleep over the past days. I too was a little somnolent but knew that putting as much distance between us and the border was imperative.

Early morning found us parked up in the town of Louis Trichardt, waiting for the roadside café to open. I finally saw the lights come on in the café and then waking my charges, I distributed the roofing company overalls and a small amount of cash to buy food. Looking like suitable workers we went ahead to the café. The proprietor was a portly Portuguese gentleman who was extremely happy to take their orders. After being in a bush training camp and only being fed limited rations, the young men were keen to order a township favourite 'Bunny Chow.' This was a half loaf of white bread hollowed out and filled with either a vegetable or beef curry. The bread that had been removed was then used to dip in the curry. It was both delicious and filling. Once they had all bought their food and bottles of Cola, I herded them back to the van and we set off once again heading south.

Once we were a few kilometres from the town, I searched for a suitable stopping place. I found a lay-by shaded by a large 'Imported' Eucalyptus Tree and parked the pick-up underneath it. I told the 'crew' that we would stop for thirty minutes and that they were to do the 'necessary' as I didn't plan to stop again for several hours. They all disappeared into the Lowveld bush. I lay back in the seat and dozed off. I was awoken by them returning and then, as they sat under the tree, I nipped into the bush. On my return I asked if they were all ready for a few hours driving as unless something untoward happened such as a Police roadblock, I would be pushing on to the Witwatersrand and Johannesburg. They all smiled broadly as I suspect they were glad to be returning to friends and family in the townships.

The drive was hot and tedious, but we were soon in Edenvale one of the outer suburbs of Johannesburg and the small industrial estate, the head office of the roofing company, and my hand over point. I drove into the yard and then into the covered warehouse. It was filled with a stock of tiles, corrugated iron sheets and rolls of waterproofing materials. I parked the van and went into a small office on the side. A middle-aged gentleman, Solly, sat at a desk who, when he noticed me, rose and greeted me enthusiastically.

"A successful mission Owl?" he queried? I sank down in a chair and told him his 'cargo' were safely in the van and would appreciate food and the use of the 'facilities'. He went to the door and called out instructions to someone I presumed would see to them. Solly now asked if I would like coffee or tea, I thanked him, and he called to his secretary to bring me coffee. Solly was my immediate superior in the cadre and a more incongruous operative one could not imagine. He was balding, had a pronounced paunch, and wore braces and on a large 'proboscis' was a set of thick rimmed bifocal glasses. Nevertheless, beneath the bushy brows was an intellect as sharp as a rapier and he genuinely cared for all people, which was borne out by his deep commitment to the organisation. I both admired and respected him.

I sat relaxing in my chair sipping my delicious filter coffee while Solly enquired how things had gone. I told him everything, as often he was able to make suggestions which might save my life and those of others in the future. He sat back in his chair after I had finished my report, tented his fingers in his customary manner, and I could see by his furrowed brow that he was pensive. Presently, he stood up and paced around the office. "I think my boy" he said "we may need to find an alternate crossing point into Zimbabwe next time! The security services are very astute, and I would hate for you or your charges to walk into an ambuscade." I nodded saying that the problem was the time, as I often had to wait in the area before contact was made. He looked at me over his thick lensed glasses and commented "Leave it to me Owl, I will think on what to do, but for now you go back to your digs in Lenasia, and we will discuss it in a day or two."

I left in a small non-descript white hatch back saloon and made my way back to my small garret above the cinema in Lenasia where, after a hot shower and a simply delicious curry from a local vendor, I fell asleep and slept until late the next morning. I awoke refreshed and after a decent breakfast I decided to give Grand-pere a call. I found a public telephone and phoned the plantation offices; I was put through to his secretary who connected me. It was good to hear his characteristic accent and he greeted me enthusiastically, asking how I was, but then before continuing, suggested that I call him on a different number in ten minutes. I was a little surprised but took the number down and called him back as asked.

He answered the phone, and I queried the change, as I had always used his office number and had it consigned to memory. He sighed and told me that he had a suspicion that calls coming into his pulp company offices were being monitored, as there seemed to be an anomaly in the international calls. Additionally, he had been informed by Mr Faulkner that they suspected the same. This troubled me deeply, not because I had phoned my old household, but at the ability of those who were obviously interested in my affairs! Grand-pere told me that Mia had called him on several occasions enquiring as to my health and wellbeing. He suggested I contact her somehow, not by phone obviously, but through an intermediary. Mother had also called him and asked him to please try and persuade me to stop being a 'total idiot' and return to Swaziland and settle down at any menial occupation Grand-pere could provide. Other than that, they were all well and Nolwasi (my old nanny) sent her regards. I told him I would think on how to contact him and Mia without it being an inconvenience to either of them or let him know. He told me to look after myself and to be careful.

I put the phone down and was deeply troubled, once again I had underestimated the prowess of the Intelligence service! Realistically was I safe where I was? Could it be that even now I was under surveillance, my imagination ran riot, surely not! I was of no importance; I was a little fazed and decided that I needed to discuss matters with Solly, so after collecting some effects from my garret I drove to the company in Edenvale. Unfortunately, on arrival I was told that he was out and would only be returning early afternoon, so I decided to visit a small picnic area in Bedford view, a few miles away.

It was a glorious African day with only a few cumulous clouds, the area was next to one of Johannesburg's kopjes and the Juskei river ran through it. I bought a soft serve ice cream and strolled along with the other visitors, mothers pushing prams or push chairs. I ambled along in deep thought, thinking how I had affected the lives of those close to me. Sitting down on a bench next to the small river, I watched the people strolling by, there were no dangers here from anyone! No one seemed worried at the vast differences that existed between the 'haves and have nots' or the fact that much of the country's people had no vote or could not live in certain areas! Was it any affair of mine, or was it, as my mother alleged, nothing that should concern me?

I watched the people strolling by and then noticed a familiar face. It was Wendy, her glorious 'mane' of dark hair cascading over her shoulders, sauntering along arm in arm with a good-looking blonde man. My heart clenched and I felt bereft! Obviously, she had simply moved on and who could blame her? Luckily, she didn't see me, and I was able to slip away. I made my way back to my small car; the clouds had moved in, and it was building up to the customary afternoon thunderstorm that occurred on the Highveld. I drove back to the company in Edenvale in poor humour.

I found Solly at his desk, with a crumb decorated chin from a bagel he was eating. "Well, Owl what brings you back here so soon, I have no commission for you at the moment" he said, wiping his mouth with a serviette. "I know" I replied sighing, "but I think I might have a problem!" I then explained Grand-peres' concerns to him. He inspected the rest of his bagel, and I could see he was evaluating the information. Finally, he looked at me, "Well I expected nothing less, they obviously would like to know how you are occupying your time and they have only a few options open to them, namely your family and friends." He explained "You must know they control all the telecommunications infrastructure in the Southern African region?" I was a little surprised as I thought Swaziland had its own phone system and said this to him. "Don't be naïve, Owl, the S.A. government helped set up the Swazi system, so they are bound to be able to intercept calls to a known incoming line and as your grandfathers' company is well known, it would be a simple matter for them. The best means you have of communicating with them is in person, but I would recommend discretion," he mused. "Your best way is to leave with your passport, but then return surreptitiously as you are by now proficient at crossing borders illegally. "You have a break at the moment so now would be the time to take a trip back home" he finished.

"Right" I said, "that's settled. It will be good to get back home for a while!" I got up shook his hand and headed for the office door. "Please don't be more than two or three weeks and when you return contact me as soon as possible, so I can plan", he said as I was leaving.

I drove back to my 'digs' feeling a little elated at the thought of returning home and a little bit of normality. Additionally, I would see Grand-pere and Mia and the family.

I packed only my toiletries as most of my clothes were in the house in the Enzulweni valley and as I was making the journey by taxi, baggage would be an obstacle.

I dropped the small saloon's car keys with the owner of the cinema and took a local taxi to Johannesburg. The taxis were minibuses, that stopped when you made the correct hand signal. Often the drivers were surprised to see me hailing them as few Europeans used them because they were, in most instances overcrowded and the whites were not comfortable sharing with non-whites. I enjoyed them as one met all sorts of people; Africans, mixed race or what were locally called coloureds and Indians. The trip into town was uneventful and once we reached the 'rank' in the centre I swopped to one heading East to the town of Middleburg. I had to wait an hour or so before there were enough people aboard but then we were finally on our way, the diesel engine emitting volumes of blue smoke as we wound our way out of the city centre. I did elicit some attention as many of the Africans were surprised to see me, but in their characteristic way they accepted me graciously, especially once they realized I spoke their language.

It was a hot and long trip as the minibus stopped at all the local towns on the East rand on our way, dropping some off and picking others up. My travelling companions varied from grandmothers who had been to visit families in the Townships to young men heading to the coal mines in Witbank in search of work, even though the government tried to prevent this with the odious passbook system. Overall, I was able to avoid any probing questions by simply telling the truth and saying I was returning to Swaziland, which they accepted with 'knowing' nods of their heads.

We arrived in Middleburg finally in the late evening, and I was able to stretch my cramped legs. I made my way to the local cafe and had a delicious Steak Burger and chips and thought on where I would spend the night. I found a cheap B & B, and after having a refreshing shower settled into a well-used but extremely comfortable bed and fell asleep.

I awoke to the smell of frying bacon, washed, and found my way to a small dining room where the sun was streaming in through an open French door. The proprietor, a middle-aged attractive lady appeared from what I presume was the kitchen, smiled at me and asked what I would like for breakfast. I thanked her and ordered cereal and a small fried breakfast. I finished off the meal with some strong black coffee and asked her, when she came to clear up, if she knew the bus times for Mbabane. She smiled and replied that she wasn't sure but directed me to the bus station. I complimented her on her 'homely' B&B and left.

I found the bus stop of the Eastern Transvaal bus Corporation, and the bus heading east to Swaziland. I asked the driver, a young 'bronzed 'muscular Afrikaner, where I could buy a ticket. He replied that I could buy a ticket from him as long I was in possession of my passport, and picking up a clip board he requested it. I noted that all the details of the other passengers (as this was a white only bus) were recorded with their residential addresses and passport numbers! I made a show of looking to retrieve my passport from my backpack then exclaimed saying that I had left it at the Bed and Breakfast. The Driver laughed saying " Magtag !, jy better hardloop terug na die tuishuis , want ek ry in twintig minute." (Good Grief! You'd better run back to the B&B as I am leaving in twenty minutes!) I smiled and jogged off. As soon as I was out of sight, I stopped running and walked back into the centre of town. I knew there was no way I was going to give any governmentally controlled transport service, even if it were only a small provincial one, my details. It would be folly in the extreme, so I decided I would wait for the bus to leave and then hitchhike to the M4 and then onward to Belfast, Carolina, Warburton and the Oshoek /Ngwenya border post.

I went to a local news agency chain and bought a piece of stiff white card on which I wrote 'Mbabane' with a black marker pen. I then made my way on foot to the access road on to the M4, where I stood displaying my cardboard sign. I was picked up by a pick-up with a load of potatoes on the back and my luck was in as it was headed for Carolina. The driver, a middle-aged Zulu, introduced himself as Amos and after I had introduced myself, he headed off, driving fast.

I discovered Amos was a driver for a large Afrikaans farmer near Carolina. He said he loved his job and lived on the farm with his wife and two children, and he maintained his boss Stoffel was kind to him and his family. I had found this a lot in country and farming areas where most of the 'Boer' farmers treated their workers well and with respect. I tentatively asked him what he thought of the A.N.C and other liberation organizations? "Aish" (sorry) he tutted "Ziyiziwula eziyingozi" (they are dangerous fools!) I nodded as I didn't wish to offend him, but asked how he felt about not having any say in who governed his country? He smiled and replied "Kungani kufanele?" (Why should I?) and went on to explain that he had a decent job, enough food for him and his family and his children were being educated at the local African school. "Azobangela inkatthazo" (They will only cause trouble), he asserted. I nodded, thinking this was a person happy with his lot, he had no perception of what it was like for his 'brothers and sisters' in the townships in the cities. I decided that it was pointless to persuade him otherwise and swopped the conversation to that of soccer which all Africans were passionate about. I learnt he supported Witbank black Aces avidly and we enjoyed the rest of the trip talking football.

On arrival in Carolina, I thanked him as he dropped me off, his farm was a few miles southwest of the town. I did offer to pay him, but he just laughed and said he was happy to have helped, I fist bumped him and he drove off. I walked through the town until I found a small shop. It was like most rural shops in that it sold everything from food and provisions to bicycles and yes, even a kitchen sink. The man behind the counter wore a Kurta and was Indian. He greeted me enthusiastically and asked what I wanted. I asked for a Coke which he readily produced from the fridge behind him. I paid him and opened the bottle sipping it gratefully, he looked at me and then asked "You're not from around here, are you?" "No" I replied, "I am on my way to Swaziland." "Ah" he nodded, and I told him I was hitchhiking but would happily take a minibus taxi if he knew of one going there. "What part of Swaziland do you want to go to?" he enquired. I hesitated for a second, but then decided there was no harm in telling him that I was going to Grand-pere's pulp company. "Oh" he asked "do you know Monsieur Levesque?" "But of course," I replied, "he is my grandfather!" At this he came from around the counter and pumped my hand effusively, obviously Grand-pere's name meant something to him. "I am happy to meet you" he said. "I am Mohammed Sayed and I buy a lot of kindling from his company, in fact I was planning to go there this afternoon with my truck to collect the logs. I would be happy to take you with me." This was fortuitous, and I happily thanked him, adding that I would be grateful for the lift.

In the early afternoon 'Boetie' (Mohammed's nick name) and I left the shop in Carolina, after he had said his goodbyes to his wife and daughter who were now in charge of the shop. The truck was an old drop side Mazda, a bit battered, but it seemed serviceable, and I was on my way directly to glorious Swaziland.

Chapter Two

Acclimation

The trip to the border went smoothly as we skirted past the small towns of Warburton and Lochiel and arrived at the Oshoek Border Post early evening. 'Boetie' drove as fast as the old truck would manage as he wished to return that night to his shop. Luckily, there were no delays either side of the border. I was vigilant to see if there was any reaction when I produced my passport, but it was obviously not 'flagged' as they simply stamped me out without any trouble, and I breathed easier.

Once thorough the Swazi side we motored on past Ngwenya and onward to Mbabane, which we passed on the MR3 and further on, took a right turn on to the MR19 heading for the Luphohlo dam. The road curved round a hair pin bend above the dam, and I was able recall happier times when as a young 'lungwaan' (small white person), I had first met the Anthropomorphic Dr Dlamini, our Isangoma with my good friends Mandla and Sambulo. I would need to look them up and see how things were going for them. We drove on along the M19 and soon arrived at Grand-pere's company.

Nosibusiso, his secretary, greeted me warmly and buzzed Grand-pere who came bounding from his office saying "Mere de Dieu, Sean it's good to see you!" He hugged me to his tall frame. Once I had extracted myself from his ursine grip, he noticed 'Boetie'. "Ah, Monsieur Sayed is it not?" he asked, grasping Boeties' hand, and shaking it with enthusiasm. Nosibusiso now intervened asking if either of us would like tea or coffee. "Oui, oui get them drinks" said Grand–pere as he led us through to his office. "How did you get here Sean?" he asked. I told him that 'Boetie' had kindly given me a lift as he was coming for firewood anyway. "Ah, Mohammed that was good of you, I am most grateful. Let me get my store man in here so he can sort out your order as quickly as possible, as I imagine you want to return to your shop before the border closes?" "Thank you, that will be a significant help" Boetie responded gratefully. Once we had finished the coffee Boetie left with the fore man and Grand-pere told Nosibusiso that he was leaving, and we drove home.

I woke up the following morning in the house in the valley. I could hear someone singing down the passage and I strolled down to the bathroom and then found Nolwesi, in the small kitchen, brewing coffee. "Sanbonani usisi (Morning sister)" I called out above her singing, as she hadn't noticed me enter. "Hewu , isikhova esincani nguwe uqobo"(Wow, little Owl is it really you"!?) she exclaimed and hugged me. I sat down at the old wooden kitchen table that had been there since my childhood days, while she poured me a large cup of strong dark coffee and asked what I would like for breakfast. I replied that a bit of toast and a couple of boiled eggs would do nicely. She smiled, and I was amazed at how little she had changed over the years. I knew that she was now married and had a few children, and as she bustled around, we caught up on each other's news.

She told me she was happy and that 'Lokuduma' (Voice of Thunder), Grand-pere, had found a 'Umfazi Omuhle' (a lovely wife) as he had been lonely when Mother, myself, and my sister had all left. She said Hetty was a kind, gentle person, and a good mistress. After she had given me my breakfast, she sat down opposite me, and we chatted away like old times. I watched a red beaked green and blue

Turaco land on the grass outside and begin searching for the odd earthworm. I sipped my coffee and listened to Nolwesi chat away about people we both knew.

I heard the screen door bang and Hetty came in and I smelt the delicious aroma of freshly baked bread, she smiled at me and greeted Nolwesi who asked if she would like some coffee? Hetty said happily that she would love some, and would we like hot rolls. While Nolwesi got the coffee Hetty busied herself with plates, butter, knives, and jam. Once everything was ready, she sat down saying that even though Grand-pere had gone to the forestry office early, he was coming back shortly for 'brunch' and to chat to me.

Hetty was a petite, Afrikaans lady with auburn curly hair that surrounded her small face. I estimated that she was in her late fifties, but I was an extremely poor judge of ladies' ages. I knew that she had been a widow when Grand-pere first met her, but other than that I didn't know much about her. I had met her on Grand-pere's farm in the Marble Hall district when I had gone there during university vacation time. I had found her pleasant to be around and she obviously adored Grand-pere, who could be a little austere on occasion.

Nolwesi came back, just as Grand-pere crashed through the screen door and sank down in the chair next to Hetty, stretching out his lanky legs. Nolwesi brought his coffee, and, then he asked. "Well Sean, how are you this morning?", while attacking the fresh rolls with gusto. I in turn took a roll and began munching on it. Hetty, buttering a roll said. "Let him eat first Jacques, he needs it."

I discovered I was quite hungry and after my second cup of coffee, Hetty told me that she had seen Mia in town a couple of times, and she always asked after me and was worried as I never called her or got in touch. Grand-pere added that Sven too had asked after me and what I was doing with my life? Mother and my sister, Cheri, also wondered about my lack of communication.

I sat back, contemplating how to respond! I had purposely gone out of my way to avoid contact, as I felt it would be better for all if they had no knowledge of my dealings across the border. In the case of my 'adopted' family, I didn't wish to complicate their lives. In respect of my mother and my sister, I feared their censure! Grand-pere added that my 'brothers' Mandla and Sambulo enquired, periodically, what I was doing.

Hetty remarked that it was really none of her business, but she did worry as of all of them she was aware of just how dangerous the security services could be. I sighed, then told them that I understood their concerns, but even though I had no deep commitment to any ideology, I did feel that the apartheid system was inherently wrong, and most Africans lived in poverty. "Well, we feel the same, but some things are best left to those involved and do you really think you are making a genuine difference?" Grand-pere asked, raising an inquisitive eyebrow. I sighed and admitted that I really didn't know, for on reflection I wasn't sure that my work for the organisation was vital.

I understood their reservations and I knew that Grand-pere was apolitical and believed the South African system was seriously inadequate. His opinion was that as we didn't live there, it wasn't our affair. Hetty, who however was Afrikaans born and bred, commented. "I agree with you Sean, I know that things need to change. But I am not sure that the violence that the A.N.C. advocates is the way to go." I responded by telling them I avoided any involvement in 'guerrilla' attacks on the European population, as in bombs and other incendiary devices that they planted in the restaurants and shopping malls. I looked at their expectant faces, hoping I would elaborate on what I did do for the organization, but I knew it was best if they didn't know!

"I was coerced into this, the S.A. authorities made my life as difficult as possible, they destroyed my professional career and then made it impossible for me to practice anywhere. So as Dr Dlamini said, I had to fight back!" "Oui (Yes), I understand" Grand-pere affirmed. "Unfortunately, you may be making matters worse and eventually you may find your position more untenable and a life as a fugitive living in the shadows can't be overly attractive. These are powerful and dangerous people who I think you have gravely underestimated! Anyway, you are now home for the time being, and I suggest you catch up with the Faulkner's and your friends and we will talk about it again later."

He got up saying that he needed to get back to his office and would see us all later. Nolwesi, got up to get Hetty and myself more coffee and I sat back in my chair, thinking on what had been discussed. Hetty asked what I planned to do that day. I looked out of the window, it was a bright blustery day and thought I might go for a sail on the Luphohlo dam, if I could find a towing vehicle. "Do you know where Grand-pere has stored the catamaran?" I asked. "Well," she replied, "I think it might be at the plantation offices in one of the storerooms, but if you want to borrow my car, I am sure you could 'liberate' it!" I gratefully accepted her offer. Hetty, handed me the keys, smiling, and saying she hoped I had an enjoyable sail.

I found her Toyota estate outside in the yard and went to my room to find my sailing gear. I decided as the weather was warm, not to bother with a wet suit, so only picked up an old life jacket. Hetty's car was obviously new and still had that unmistakeable smell, but what mattered most was that it had a tow hitch. I arrived at the offices and went in to see Nosibusiso, who happily arranged for me to go a mile or so down the road to one of the company's warehouses to collect my boat.

The lumber yard was bustling with large semi articulated vehicles bringing in logs and others transporting them to the pulp factory. I found the foreman who directed me to one of the warehouses where I discovered my boat covered in dust and cobwebs. I used an old broom I found lying at the back to get as much dust off as possible. Luckily, the sail bags were all stored in a box on the trailer. I soon had the trailer hitched up to the Toyota and was whizzing up the road to the dam.

I arrived and parked the car as close as I could get to the water, there was obviously no slip here as few people used it as a boating venue. I undid the straps that secured the sixteen-foot catamaran to the trailer and attaching the stays, rigged it. I then manhandled it off the trailer and dragged it to the water, no mean feat as it was usually a two-man operation. I sat on the trampoline of the boat getting my breath back, when I noticed a group of 'Dassies' (Rock Hyrax) meandering their way towards the water's edge. I found these small red brown mammals endearing so I kept still and watched as their leader, obviously a large male, led them to the bank. I at first thought they were going to drink, but then I noticed they were foraging for grubs.

They made extraordinarily little noise as they went about their business, but suddenly one of them called out in a high-pitched trill! They scattered, I presumed to their nearby little rock cavity, but not before a Martial eagle had managed to decimate their number by one. I watched as the white spotted plumage of the Eagle powered skyward with the poor unfortunate 'Dassie' in its talons.

Well, I decided it was getting late and the wind was starting to drop, so I pulled the boat into the water, sheeted home the sails and was soon skimming along on one hull. The thrill and vibration of the tiller in my hand cast away all thoughts of the poor Dassies fate. I put the catamaran on its best point of sail and in no time was nearing the opposite bank. So, easing off the sails I was able to broad reach back to towards the centre and make better use of the large dam.

I recalled my earlier forays on this dam when with Mandla and Sam, we rowed on an old up turned Morris Minor roof and had first met our ' Batakati'(witch) at one of the inlets to the dam. I chuckled at how overawed they had appeared and how naive to their culture I had been. I had since come to respect the 'iSangoma' - Dr Dlamini and relied on his uncanny prudence. I decided to make a return visit to the culvert that we had discovered in those early years. It was a way off, but I now had a wind efficient and fast catamaran, so it would not take long. I noticed the cumulous clouds were building up in the West and I foresaw an electrical storm brewing, so I wouldn't want to be on the open expanse of the dam when the lightening started. The sailing was exhilarating, and I soon arrived at the culvert and dropped the main sail.

I managed to moor it in a fashion to the reed beds close to the culvert. The yellow and verdant weaver birds nesting in them didn't appreciate my intrusion but that couldn't be helped, and it would only be transient. I entered the shadowy culvert and even though it had been many years since we met the Witch Doctor here, I felt apprehensive! I walked deep into the interior, and nothing seemed to have altered even after all the years, the floor was still strewn with fine golden sand with many bird footprints.

I crouched on my haunches and recalled his question to me about 'time and the future,' how intuitive he had been! I could almost smell his leopard skin cloak. Was he able to foresee the future? It was a conundrum. I almost expected the sudden flash that had accompanied our first encounter, but all I heard was the rippling of the water as it cascaded over the lip of the culvert and onwards down the tunnel and the mournful moan of the wind outside. I shook myself and stood up, he certainly knew many things that were inexplicable, but could he realistically anthropomorphise into a leopard? I walked slowly out of the culvert back into the occluded sun, as the clouds had built up and the storm was imminent, and I needed to get back across the dam as soon possible. The jib sail was furiously flogging itself against the mast as the wind had strengthened, so I quickly secured it and pointing the bow of the boat into the wind I managed, with difficultly, to raise and secure the main. I let the main out on its traveller and the boat bucked and jerked on a fast run. The wind was now 'singing' in the rigging as I powered away, I could have sworn I heard "Ngiyakubona"(I see you!). I looked up seeing a Harrier Hawk with its bright yellow face bank steeply as it fought the wind, had I imagined it?!

I hiked out on the back of the frame of the trampoline, trying to keep the bow of the boat raised as I raced along heading for the car, the rain now began falling in huge drops splashing off my face and body and making the water 'boil'. The wind was gusting and lightening flashed off in the distance with accompanying thunder. I scudded along doing my best to keep the catamaran stable so as not to pitch pole. I reached the bank where the Toyota was and ran the boat a little way up through the reeds. I jumped off and turned it into the wind letting the sails fly. I struggled to get the sails down as the wind whipped them often from my slippery fingers. Finally, they were bagged and stored, and I was able to drop the mast, winch the boat back on to the trailer and secure it.

I got in the car wet and dishevelled as the thunderstorm raged on outside. I started the engine and slowly headed back towards the plantation storerooms. Driving along my brain was in overdrive as I tried to rationalise my thoughts. Had I genuinely heard anything, or had it just been the wind and my emotional state? I burst out laughing!

I returned the boat to the storeroom, and then made my way back to the house in the valley. Later, as we sat down to dinner, Hetty asked how my day had gone. I decided that overall, I had had a good sail, with plenty of wind and it had been enjoyable, so I thanked her for the use of her car.

Grand-pere, said that he had spoken to Mia, and she was desperate to see me. He had suggested to her that I meet her in a restaurant in Mbabane the following day and I nodded happily. I missed her, and the rest of the family and it would be wonderful to catch up on their lives.

It was another glorious Swazi day when Hetty dropped me off in Mbabane town centre. I strolled along enjoying the bustle of the capital. I found the restaurant and as I was early, ordered a good breakfast and sat watching the locals come and go. Suddenly a strong hand grabbed my shoulder from behind, I jumped up in alarm only to hear a loud chuckle as Sven released my shoulder. Mia then came up and enveloped me in a giant hug! I could smell her familiar perfume as she crushed me to her body. "Let him go Mum, you'll smother him." Sven said, sitting down opposite me. I untangled myself as Mia slid onto the bench next to me and Sven beckoned the waiter over.

"You have lost weight!" She said accusingly, her grey eyes examining me diligently. I nodded saying "Sometimes I just don't get the opportunity to have regular meals, as often there are more pressing things." "What sort of things?" Sven asked, pointedly. I sighed; I had thought about how much I was going to tell them about my 'new'- life but had decided that, as with Grand-pere and Hetty, what they didn't know couldn't hurt them. "Well, you know," I dissembled, "often I am busy doing things and just forget to eat!" "Things?" Sven said, raising an eyebrow. "What sort of things?" "Hopefully, nothing that is endangering your life" Mia exclaimed, looking worried.

I was embarrassed but reassured them that I was not engaged in anything that threatened any one's life. "Well then, what exactly do you do?" Sven pressed. Luckily, their orders were delivered, and I was given time to produce a suitable answer. "I drive around delivering information to different people, as the organisation doesn't trust the telecommunication system or the postal service." I lied glibly! "Oh," Mia smiled wanly, "well that's not too dangerous, I imagine?" I agreed, saying that yes most of the time it was extremely boring.

Sven sat back wiping his chin with a serviette and staring at me knowingly. "So, you are telling us that you studied all that time to become a vet, and now drive around in a rusty little 'bakkie'(van) as a glorified errand boy?" he questioned derisively. I nodded, "It's not that simple. "Obviously, I must try not to be followed and make sure that the 'stuff' I am delivering gets given into the right hands." Mia looked at me over the rim of her coffee cup, eyeing me speculatively. "What sort of 'stuff'?" she challenged. "Oh, you know, letters, and propaganda pamphlets." I replied.

"So not armaments or explosive devices?" Sven questioned pointedly. I bridled thinking did they imagine that I might have turned into a phlegmatic, vicious person? If this was from people who knew me well, what were others thinking. "Let's not discuss this awful topic anymore," Mia cried, and I could see that it was upsetting her. "Agreed," Sven said smiling for the first time. "It is after all your life, and you must do what you think is right for you!"

I asked how Suzanne and Luke and Colin were. Mia, now more relaxed, brought me up to date with all the goings on in the house on the hill, with the odd interruption from Sven. Suzanne and Jenny were still flitting between the world's capitals working in the fashion industry and Suzanne still had a steady stream of suitors. Mia didn't seem over enthusiastic about the latter but as she said Suzanne was now an adult and seemed responsible. Luke was now a full-time photographer for one of South Africa's prestigious daily newspapers and was living with Dick and Sandy in South Africa. Otherwise, things remained much the same with everyone in good spirits. "We haven't forgotten you," Sven said, calling the waiter over and asking if I wanted more coffee. "Yes," Mia interjected," even Masia asks after you, and Suzanne often asks if we have heard anything, especially since Wendy told her what happened between you! You must understand they hardly knew you, what were they to think? Obviously, they were bound to be wary!" I nodded, obviously the police had left no stone unturned to discredit and isolate me from any support.

Mia asked how long I was going to be in Swaziland and suggested that I should not go back to S.A but instead go and work for Grand-pere where I would be safe. I looked at her and so wanted to put her mind at ease, but I knew that as in Luke's gospel- 'no one after putting his hand to plough' should look back. I had taken a course of action and even now if I abandoned the A.N.C. the security services would not just leave me be. I had crossed the line! "It's not that simple," I said, "I am now a 'person of interest', and I am not so naive as to believe that they do not have an inkling of how I have been occupying my time! No, I am sorry Mia, unfortunately I now must do the best, with the cards I have been dealt, to the end of the game!"

"Well, that's your decision but I wish you could just come up to the house!" she pleaded! I sighed and voiced my reservations. "I understand but I am wary that even here I may be watched, and I would hate to complicate your lives." Sven stood up saying, "But you are here for a week or two, so why can't we go for a bike ride around the country on Sunday, like we used to?" I nodded happily, agreeing. Mia stood up, and hugging me said, "That's good, at least you will have time to think things through." I thanked them for coming and said we would meet soon. I sat back down and after ordering some waffles, pondered on what a liability, I had become.

I left the restaurant and strolled through the streets of Mbabane; it was shaping up to be a sweltering day. I found a branded clothes store and decided to augment my sparse wardrobe. I was looking at shirts when someone called my name, it was Dr Tom. "Well hello Sean, I am surprised to see you, I heard you had left the country?" he questioned. I shook his hand and asked how things were with his practice and his family. "Ah! Not much has changed, I still do my best to look after the local 'pet population' nothing ground-breaking, you know the normal 'bread and butter' of a small animal practitioner," "he replied, "just consultations and routine surgery. I think the last time anything exciting happened was when you were bitten by the rabid corgi!" He chortled, "Indeed you did provide some entertainment." I nodded, smiling. "If that's what you call it," I responded. "I heard, via the veterinary grapevine, that you had gone to the UK to practice, but that was obviously not true, so what are you doing with yourself?" he asked.

I shook my head. "There would be little chance of that as I would have needed the sanction of the S.A. veterinary council and that would never be forthcoming. As you know I have a conviction and they consider me an embarrassment to the profession," I replied. "Really!" he uttered. "So, then what are you doing with yourself?" I decided that I had already had enough interrogation for one day from my adopted family and to explain things to Dr Tom would be counterproductive, so I replied, "Oh this and that, I am a delivery driver for a roofing company." "A delivery driver, surely not!" he exclaimed. "What? After your education?" "I am afraid so," I answered. "What else is there for me to do?"

"Well surely you could, with your qualifications and talents, work for an animal charity or similar institution, or a zoo or game park?" he challenged. I looked at him a little puzzled, was he unaware of how things worked across the border, where once you were 'on the radar' of the security services, there were very few opportunities! I decided that he didn't quite understand things, so just shrugged saying. "That's life, one must go with the flow." "Ah, well if you would like to spend a day at the practice with us, just to keep your hand in, we would be happy to have you!" he suggested. I was surprised, as I presumed that I was a total anathema to the veterinary world but said I would gladly spend the day with them and thanked him profusely. "Right, that is settled then, give me a call and I will arrange for a day when we have a fair bit on, as you don't want to be standing around," he said, shaking my hand, then sauntered off.

I bought a few items then left the store and wandered around the town until Hetty picked me up. On arrival at the house, it was mid-afternoon, and we settled down for afternoon coffee with Nolwesi. I asked Nolwesi if she knew how my 'brothers' Mandla (Tom) and Sambulo (Sam) were doing? Of Sam she knew little. except that she heard he was a lawyer in the 'Idolobha' (City), but she had regular contact with Mandla as they were distantly related. She said he was now a well-respected 'Induna'(headman) and had a fair number of cattle and two wives. I was suitably impressed as in Swazi culture cattle and wives were a sign of success. "Why don't you walk down the valley and see him, his house is next to that of his mother, Agape, and I am sure you will find him there later," she suggested. "Right," I replied enthusiastically getting up, and went to my room to change into bush trousers and boots.

So, as the sun was dipping to the western horizon, I made way along the old familiar path towards Mandla's kraal. I walked along the well-used dusty path. Most of the birds were getting ready to roost down for the night and the air was alive with different calls. I felt euphoric and surprised a Kori bustard who was foraging for the last few caterpillars and bush crickets before night fell. It emitted a strange grunt like bark and then with a hasty run it careered off down the path trying to get enough speed up to launch itself on its ponderous dusty brown wings. "Iya ngobumnene Inyoni" (Go quietly Bird) I called after it as it finally became airborne. I kept my eyes on the path as I was loath to stand on any small creatures such as lizards or spiders that could also be travelling on this 'highway.' I watched a Black File snake scuttle off the path.

I arrived at Mandla's kraal just as the cattle were returning from grazing with a couple of 'abafana' (boys) in attendance, and was surprised to see the old Induna – watchman, from my youth, still counting the cattle as they came in. "Kusihlwa ubaba Omdala" (Evening old father) I called out to him. He squinted through wrinkled mahogany eye lids for an age but then smiled. "Ini leyo isikhova esincane" (What is that the little Owl?) he shouted. "Ikona" (It is!) I said, going up and shaking his hand and arm in the traditional fashion. He was genuinely pleased to see me, and I was happy that he had remembered me. I asked after his family and extended family, and he launched into a detailed account of their lives. I listened intently but as I knew very few of them it was out of politeness. He was jabbering on when Mandla himself came up and seeing me yelled out "Isikhova nguwena ngempela" (Owl, is that really you !?).

He was tall and muscular and exuded confidence as he came up and clasped my hand in his massive one. "Umfowetu"(brother) it is good to see you, I thought you had deserted us," he cried. I shook my head saying, "Never, I just have been across the border misbehaving!" "Aish Ini (What!)" he exclaimed, " Kungani" (why?)" I shrugged, saying it was a long story. "Well, I have time, come," he gestured and led me to his house.

We entered the thatched house, and he was overwhelmed by two young children, a boy who he called Ndumiso, and a younger girl called Sophie. They were both trying to get their father's attention and hardly noticed me. He disentangled himself and picking up the tiny Sophie led me to the kitchen where two Swazi ladies were busy cooking. Mandla introduced me to his wives, Senti and Thula. Senti was tall and statuesque, while Thula was a little shorter and stouter. They both smiled and shook my hand, saying they were happy to meet me. It always amazed me how adept the Swazis were at speaking English, while a lot of the Europeans didn't attempt to learn any eSiswati.

Mandla asked if I would like to stay for supper, to which I readily agreed, only asking if it would not inconvenience his wives? They both laughed saying that it was not a problem if I ate 'Sishwala' (maize porridge), 'Slaai' (Avocado salad) and Ostrich Steak. Mandla answered for me, "The Owl is 'umuntu wendawo' (local person)" I nodded saying that I would be satisfied with whatever they produced.

He led me through to the sitting room where it was obvious that the children had been watching cartoons on television, and I saw that Wiley's coyote was still vainly trying to catch the road runner. Mandla settled in a chair, and I sat down, the children went back to Wiley and his ingenious attempts to catch the road runner.

"So, 'Umfowetu'(brother), tell me what sort of trouble you have got yourself into," he questioned, just as Thula brought us in a couple of beers. I sat back sipping my beer and decided that I could trust Mandla with my life so told him all that had happened to me since I had last seen him. "Aw wa!" he uttered, "that sounds like you have the 'inyoka' (snake) by the tail, and eventually it will wriggle out of your grasp, and you will be bitten!" I smiled wanly, saying. "Well, I am not really harming anyone, I am just helping those that want to effect change in some small way." "I am not sure those in power over there will be inclined to see it that way, they can be vindictive," he commented. I was about to reply when Senti called all into supper.

Sophie was put in a highchair, but Ndumiso had a place at the table and while their mothers supervised them, I asked about their families and where they were from? Like all Swazis they were happy to talk about family and I learnt that they had both been to the same school in Mbabane, though Senti had been a year or two ahead of Thula, they were obviously good friends, and I was happy for my long-time friend.

Conversation drifted to what he was doing, and it turned out he was now a government official in charge of the local area as well as his cattle farming. Agape and his father lived a little way away and were still both healthy and comfortable in their old age. In Swazi culture senior citizens were revered and never cast aside and put into a home.

I asked after Sambulo, and Mandla laughed saying, "Ah, that one, he has become very self-important! You know he is now a lawyer and has swanky offices in Mbabane and Manzini?"

I said I wasn't surprised, as he had always had delusions of grandeur. Senti added that he was married to a cousin of hers and yes, he thought a lot of himself and had avoided the traditional Swazi way of life but invested in stocks and shares and the bank. Mandla chuckled, remarking that he hadn't been such a great man when the three of us had roamed the bush trying to hunt a 'batakati' (witch).

I laughed but thinking back I too had not been that enamoured at hunting a 'Witch'!

Thula and Senti both then asked what had happened and were slightly in awe as Mandla elaborated on our exploits.

The meal was enjoyable and the company ideal, and I spent time catching up on all the news from Mandla and his family.

I finally took my leave of the family and headed home. The night was dark and alive with the nightly chorus. I had borrowed a good flashlight from Mandla, but I didn't switch it on but waited for my eyes to adjust to the low light. I was comfortable in the dark and I walked along slowly and quietly, a Spotted Eagle Owl called out close by ' Hooo hooopoooo,' I was particularly fond of this Owl as I had been given the Siswati name of 'Isikova'- Owl by our Isangoma (Witch Doctor). I stood still, hoping it would call again. Instead, it was answered by another Eagle Owl in the distance. I smiled, an Eagle Owl didn't have to cope with the 'rights and wrongs' of life, his days and nights consisted of hunting and procreation and all on a glorious set of wings above the bush.

I was ruminating on this as I meandered along when I heard a sound that made me uneasy, it was undoubtedly the raspy growl of a Leopard. I stood still, considering whether it would be better to retrace my steps back to Mandla's kraal, as it was a lot nearer than the house in the valley, or vainly hope that it had not detected me. My befuddled brain failed me, but my primal instinct took over and I sprinted back up the path.

"Ungabaleki Isikhova"(Don't run Owl), a soft guttural voice called out.

I stopped, not sure if I had heard anything, but then in the darkness I could just make out the tall Isangoma.

"Aish! You scared me!" I squealed.

He was dressed traditionally and carried his 'izikhwama'(bag). "I am sorry," he replied, "I should have maybe called out to you."

"What are you doing out here in the middle of the night?" I asked a little breathlessly.

"I was helping an elderly man who believes he has been bewitched" he chuckled, "he has obviously been told that one of his enemies has used an 'Umthakathi'(witch) to put a 'weakening' spell on him."

"Really!" I exclaimed, "were you able to help him?"

"Come," he answered, "I will tell you about it as we walk back to your house."

He set off able to see his way clearly despite the darkness. I trotted next to him as he explained. "Our people and our culture believe in many inexplicable things, I reassure and protect them, even you Isikhova are 'under my eye'."

I gulped and whispered, "I see, so that is how you knew I was in the bush tonight?!"

He burst out laughing. "No, I heard you had gone to visit your 'brother' tonight and as I was returning the same way I stopped in at his kraal and asked after you!"

"Oh!", was all I could muster in reply!

"So, you have returned to us then?" he asked. "But I don't think you have achieved your aim?"

I, as always, felt that he was reading my thoughts. "I am not sure that I am doing anything worthwhile, and I am obviously making things difficult for those close to me," I responded in a small voice.

A jackal yowled sadly close by and then it heard us and alarmed it scurried off into the stygian night. "Isikhova, sometimes it is difficult to see a purpose in what we do but trust me, even the lowly worker 'amasimu'(termite) is an integral part of the colony, believe me occasionally the most insignificant person can be the difference between success and failure" he said.

"What," I uttered "don't you see, I don't want to hurt anyone directly and yes, I understand that I am facilitating in the training of activists who may go on to commit awful atrocities on the Europeans, but I am a coward!"

"Ah, you must understand Isikhova that the 'Uju lwezinyosi' (Honeyguide) leads the Honey Badger to the hive to benefit by obtaining many larvae. So, it is with you, you are a tiny cog in the machine" he commented.

I told him what Solly has advised. To return to S.A. unofficially, crossing the border illegally. "Ah, that would be the best then, as the less those in control know of your movements, the better it will be for you," he agreed. "When you are ready, come to me. I know many paths in and out of this country and be assured, with me you will be unnoticed!"

Our journey was now almost complete as I could just discern the veranda light of our bungalow. I thanked Nhandla and he shook my hand saying in his low raspy voice "Do not worry Owl you are never alone; I am always aware of your course and what path you are walking. Look for me when you get into a situation you feel you are unable to handle!" He then strode off into the night.

Chapter Three

Abeyance

Over the following days I morphed back into a little of my old life as Nolwesi and Hetty spoiled me. On the first Sunday I went roaming around old haunts with Sven on our Honda's, from down in the deep Southeast towns of Lavamisa to Nsoko and Big Bend to the Mhlume and Pigs Peak in the North, it was great and relaxing.

On the Wednesday of that week, I went to Dr Tom's surgery and his assistant James greeted me like a long-lost friend. James was indispensable in the surgery and had been with Dr Tom since I first began seeing practice there. He was calm and professional, and I admired his knowledge and skills. I spent the day watching consultations and surgery and enjoyed it. I was overjoyed when Dr Tom said I could pop in any time while I was around.

On the second weekend, Suzanne and Sven's Fiancée, Jenny, were home and Sven was keen for them to come biking with us. I wasn't quite sure if Suzanne would agree to that as the only other time, she had ridden pillion on my bike, had ended in disaster, with her being unceremoniously dumped on her dainty derriere!

We met at the house on the hill, but I was loath to go into the house, even though Mia came and said that after the day in the countryside I was to come back for supper. I said I would consider it but if I came, I would come alone after dark on foot. She tutted but accepted my compromise.

Sven came around from the back on his bike and then Jenny and Suzanne joined us, looking cool and attractive.

Suzanne asked with a smile "So Sally, how's the life of a dissident?" I grinned and replied, "It's not all it's cracked up to be, but it is what it is." "Well, I am looking forward to a good day out today and thank you for having me along," "she responded, and I noted just how much she looked like Mia, the same tilt of the head and sparkling grey eyes. She swept back her curtain of strawberry blonde hair and put her helmet on, then as I put mine on, she climbed on the seat behind me and with Sven and Jenny we roared down the road.

It was a typical Swazi day, warm and sunny, as we headed north to Piggs Peak and the Pophonyane Falls reserve. The roads were clear, and we were able to race along, Suzanne squeezed my waist and shouted that I should go faster. I nodded and edged next to Sven who then grinned and opened his throttle further. The ride was exhilarating and a little fool hardy as we wound through the tortuous bends along the MR1 with Suzanne clinging to me like a limpet.

We slowed down as we went through Piggs Peak and then arrived at the Pophonyane reserve just on lunch time and were able to have a lunch and drinks at its outdoor restaurant. Over lunch Jenny said, "let's walk up to the falls as it's such a wonderful day." The forest floor was cool and welcoming after the harsh sunlight, as we walked along on a carpet of discarded leaves with Jenny, Suzanne and Sven talking about the last time they had been there. Sven, looking at Suzanne, asked "It was when you were with that crazy Neanderthal Gary, wasn't it?" "Ah, yes it was, what a boring guy he turned out to be! "She replied. "Well at least he was probably good 'in the sack'". Jenny quipped. "Not really, he was all show and no action!" Suzanne commented. "Ah, that would be because he was taking steroids." Sven noted. "What do you think Sally, as you are a medical trained person?" Sven asked looking at me for conformation. I was a little taken aback but muttered that indeed steroids could influence one's libido. I was out of my depth as in truth I had no experience in relationships or sexual encounters, as my first and only had been cut short when Wendy had ended it.

I was saved further comment by a troop of Vervet monkeys, that appeared above us weaving through the canopy. Suzanne cried out ecstatically her small heart shaped face lighting up. "Oh! What gorgeous little animals they are, what type are they Sally?" she asked. I watched as one of the inquisitive juveniles came down to 'investigate' us, its grizzled grey coat off set by its little black face. "They're Vervet Monkeys," I told her, "And I believe they are 'Old World' Monkeys". The juvenile was now joined by a few of the other younger monkeys, even though one of the 'mothers' gave the alarm call to warn them. I explained to them how the mothers shared all the young. "I think that's a marvellous system," Jenny commented, "I would happily embrace motherhood if I knew I had the support of other mothers". "Yea, we could share children," Suzanne said to her, laughing "although I think Mum would demand a lot of input as well." "Bloody hell Suz" Sven exclaimed "you would need to settle down with a husband first, instead of playing the field!" "Sven, that's not nice!" Jenny admonished him. Sven chuckled," But it's true."

I looked at Suzanne thinking that she would be offended but she was so absorbed in watching the monkeys, that the jibe didn't register. She turned to me and asked if one could keep a monkey as a pet. "I am afraid not," I replied, "it is an indigenous species and outlawed by the game department." "But if you worked as a ranger or vet for one of the parks, we could surely have one?" she said turning to me with inquisitive eyes. To say that we were all shocked is an understatement and before I could think of a retort Jenny asked, "What do you exactly mean by 'we' Suz?" Suzanne, unfazed, replied "I meant that if he worked at one of the parks, he would have some sort of accommodation included and then I could visit and help with orphaned animals." The sun filtered through the foliage of the trees casting shafts of light which illuminated some of the troop, making their slivery fur gleam. A few of the bigger adults now positioned themselves between us and the youngsters, obviously evaluating us to see if we were a threat, or possibly if we could be a source of food, as Vervets were accomplished opportunists and often harassed people for sandwiches and sweets. In a strange standoff, we stared at them and they at us, then with a call from the alpha male they all moved off, effortlessly swinging through the trees.

Suzanne was disappointed "I wanted them to stay," she said whimsically, "they were extremely cute." The rest of the trip to the falls was done in a strange silence as I think all of us, especially me, were thinking of what she had said. Over the years Suzanne had treated me with ambivalent disdain and now and then had been openly dismissive of my existence. The falls were small but still quite noisy and we sat down on some rocks close by and taking of our boots dabbled our feet in the cool water below the rushing falls. A Red beaked Grey headed Kingfisher flew down in a flash of blue tipped wings and landed on a fractured tree stump close by. "Oh, how beautiful, look Suz," Jenny whispered, grabbing hold of Suzanne's arm! "Wow!" Suzanne cried, then looking at me asked, "It's a Kingfisher, isn't it?" "It is," I replied" and we were all silent as we watched it sitting on the stump inspecting the pool for any fish. It finally decided our presence was not conducive to its hunting, so it flew off, its blue tipped wings bright in the sunlight.

"Well, if we're going to get another drink before we head back, we better get going," Sven remarked, so we retraced our steps down to the outdoor café. We sat in the mid-afternoon Sun, having cooling drinks. "So then, Suz, you have decided to map out Sally's life. He is to give up the life of a dissident and get a job in one of the parks, so that you can visit him and look after baby animals," Sven questioned mischievously. "How do you think his future wife or girlfriend will feel about that?" Suzanne, smiled and replied, "Well at least he wouldn't be in danger of going to prison or worse and as to a girlfriend or wife, where are they?" At this they all looked at me and Sven chuckled "Yes that's true, I bet you haven't even lost your virginity yet!" he quipped. "Sven!" Jenny burst out "That's a bit personal!" Suzanne now gazed at me intently, "Is that true?" she asked. "Surely you 'had it away' with the lovely Wendy?" I watched a large Tortoise negotiate his way along a sandy patch close by, avoiding all their questioning faces. Finally, I answered quietly, "I will opt for the fifth on that." Sven burst out laughing. "So, we will take that as a no then," he tittered. "Good Grief! Leave him be" Jenny chided, "Sean is just waiting for the right girl to come along!" "More like any girl that will 'put out' for him" Sven chortled. Suzanne now weirdly took my hand and said, "Well she is going to be a lucky girl," again shocking us all, and I once more saw the 'Mia' in her. "The sun is on the move," I murmured "and your mum is preparing supper, so we better be getting back!"

The ride back was almost better than the trip up as we didn't speed, as Sven seemed to have other things besides speed on his mind and soon, we were at the house on the hill. Sven and Jenny drove around the back to put his bike in the garage while I put mine on the stand and Suzanne alighted. She took of her helmet and shook her 'cloud' of blonde hair into a semblance saying "You are coming back for supper, aren't you?" I hesitated for a moment, so she shook my arm adding, "I won't accept no for an answer, and neither will Mum, so you better be here!" I removed my helmet and docilely admitted that I would come back on foot as soon as it was dark and thanked her for a lovely day. She smiled and kissed me on the cheek saying "No, thank you! You have been a proper gentleman and that's your problem." With that she skipped up the driveway and disappeared through the front door.

I started my bike and slowly drove down the hill, my mind a confused jumble of thoughts. This was not the Suzanne I was accustomed to. I reached our bungalow and climbed the few steps up on to the veranda. Hetty and Grand-pere were sitting on an old wicker bench clearly finishing off their afternoon coffee. "Good day?" Grand – pere queried and before I could answer Hetty giggled saying "I would think so by the lipstick on his cheek." "Oui exactament" (Yes exactly) Grand-pere laughed. I touched my cheek, and my fingers came back with the rose red lipstick that Suzanne wore. I simply smiled and said, that it had been an enjoyable day.

I left them mulling over this and went inside for a shower. I dressed in dark clothes and went out onto the veranda where Hetty and Grand-pere were seeing in the evening in true Swazi style. The sun was sinking, a big orange ball in the West and the wildlife was getting ready for its nightly cacophony; advertising territory or just the joy of existence. I sat down in a comfortable wicker chair. Hetty asked if I would like a drink or anything else and if I was in for supper. I thanked her and replied no, I would be going up the hill. Grand-pere Jaques raised an eyebrow saying "Ah, is it the return of the 'Prodigal Son'?" I shook my head and answered, "I think not, but Mia was insistent, and I don't want to disappoint her!"

Dusk found me on the main road to Mbabane waiting for a minibus taxi, which shortly arrived. I greeted the driver and told him my destination, paying my small fee happily, then sat back and waited for my stop. Once in Mbabane, I walked up the hill. Nearing the house, out of habit, I diverted into the trees behind the pool and garden and stood in the dark, knowing that if anyone had followed me, I would hear them. The moon that rose was only a thin sickle as I entered the garden and pool area and made my way to the back door. I was almost there when Jessie the Faulkner's German Shepherd, began barking. I quickly entered, shutting the door behind me, and patted her reassuring her that it was me. She was overjoyed to see me and cavorted around me like a puppy, even though she was now getting on for eight. I was just disentangling myself from Jessie when Luke came into to the kitchen. "Bloody hell Sally, you scared me!" He gasped. He hadn't changed much except that he now sported a scraggly beard. This was the 'reporter look,' I guessed. I apologised and was about to ask how things were with him when Colin (Mr Faulkner) came in and seeing me looked little a shocked. "Oh, I didn't hear you arrive," he said. "How did you get here?" Then added, "Not that it matters, the main thing is that you are here, and I am glad to see you." He shook my hand saying, "We are all in the dining room. I sent Luke to get a corkscrew for the wine and as he didn't return, I thought he had been side-tracked as is common with him." Luke now grabbed my arm and ushered me into the dining room.

"Look who I found lurking in the kitchen," he said, "it's the wayward Sally!" Mia tutted, "Take no notice of them, I am glad you have come. Sit here between Suzanne and myself!" I sat down and Suzanne said "I warned him that if he didn't come, we would be upset." I felt a bit awkward but was saved any comment by Colin returning with the corkscrew, who after opening the wine, began extoling its virtues. The dinner was enjoyable, and the conversation fortunately was about the upcoming Swazi Reed dance the country's premier festival where the king would choose a new maiden wife. In the lounge after supper, we watched the evening news on the television. It was in general 'parochial' with a few items from around the rest of the world with input from the BBC. The news over, Sven channel hopped in a desultory way, but finding nothing that wasn't a repeat, he switched it off. I asked them when Sandy and Dick would be coming next. Mia answered that they were coming the following weekend and asked if I would still be in the country. I nodded replying, "Yes, I think so, I don't have a fixed date to go back yet." Mia said, "Well they would love to see you and often ask why you don't go over and see them on the East Rand." I smiled sheepishly saying, "I am worried that I will bring trouble to their door, as I am sure that my movements are on occasion monitored." "What!" Suzanne voiced "Surely not, why would they do that?" "I am afraid that is more than likely the case" Colin remarked. "I wouldn't for one minute underestimate their intelligence service, they are clever and well informed because they believe their cause is just!"

"What I don't understand is why you are doing this" Suzanne asked me quietly. "Why can't you just come home where you're safe and work for your grandfather. It's really not your affair you are Irish." "I agree," Mia echoed, "it's only going to end in you getting into serious trouble or, God forbid getting injured." "See I told you," "Sven said to his mother, "Suz has decided to reform Sally's life. Earlier today she even told him that she was going to live with him when he gets a job in a game park."

Mia burst out laughing "Really darling is this true?" "Oh, don't pay any attention to him Mum. I simply said that if Sally worked in a reserve or a park, I could visit him and help look after orphaned animals!" "I think you're being horrid to Suz," Jenny said to Sven, "I know what she means, we travel the world but it's not that much fun. It's strange hotels, Dickensian fashion house directors and often over presumptuous guys! Sure, the money is good, but it won't last forever. I am just waiting for you to make an honest woman of me!" "Yes Sven" Mia now jumped in, "When are you going to get married. You have been engaged awhile when are you going to set a date?"

I had seldom ever seen the sharp-witted Sven at a loss for words, but now he sat there with his mouth open. "Well, I have told you several times Jen that whenever you want to set a date, I will be happy to comply," he said to the diminutive Jenny. "Excellent!" Mia exclaimed. Let's do it right now!" Luke guffawed, "That didn't turn out so good did it bro? One minute you were on Suz's case and the next it's your 'nuts in the vice'!" Mia, Suzanne and Jenny excitedly started making nuptial arrangements, so I offered to go and brew the coffee.

I brought the coffee in and then Mia said there was Devil's Food Cake which she had made earlier. Luke was up in a thrice and soon returned with the cake. Talk now drifted back and forth about the possible date for Sven and Jenny's wedding. Jenny was obviously overjoyed that she could plan her wedding and now Mia asked her if she would continue to work in the fashion industry once she was married. Jenny smiled and said, "I might in the short term, but we talked about starting a family as soon as possible." Mia seemed pleased, as even though Sandy and Dick had been married several years, they had yet to produce a grandchild. "So, you are going to leave me then!" Suzanne grumbled. "No not immediately Suz, but I am a little older than you and am frankly getting a little tired of the lifestyle and would like to settle down," Jenny replied. Sven now added that he would also prefer to have her close by and not travelling to foreign climes all the time. "Anyway Sis, you are not short of admirers and surely one or two of them has proposed?" he asked.

Suzanne, curled up like a cat on the chaise lounge languidly curling her fingers around a lock of hair, looked at him and replied sardonically, "Yes, I have had my fair share of proposals, but I don't take any of them seriously. I find most men quite shallow and narcissistic and those that have asked are not the type I would ever consider to be tied to 'till death do us part!" "Oh," Mia commented, "I don't think you can generalize. Admittedly a lot of the men you have brought home left a lot to be desired and in most cases I suspect were entirely driven by their hormones. I imagine in the world that you and Jenny frequent, men will either be overtly masculine or 'the other way'!"

"The other way?" "Sven burst out laughing, "You mean gay!" "Well, yes" Mia conceded, "I think a lot of men in the fashion industry are inclined to be egocentric and metrosexual." I have to agree with your Mum, Sven" Jenny remarked "a lot of our male models actually fancy other male models and the others in many cases think that the world would not spin on its axis without them!" "My God!" Colin exclaimed. "What a damning judgement that is on the male population involved in the fashion industry!" "Seriously Dad," Suzanne interjected, "those that are not homosexual are rodomontade and quite frankly very boring." " Uum, I wonder how they feel about you. "Colin asked. "Frankly, I don't give a damn, as I have a plan," Suzanne said with an enigmatic smile. "Oh," "Mia burst out, "that sounds intriguing, what plan is that?" Obviously now wanting to know what devious scheme her daughter was incubating. "What sort of future son-in-law would you like Mum, surely not someone self-centred and conceited like most of my boyfriends have been?" she asked, her tone now serious. Mia sat back in her chair obviously trying to produce a suitable answer. "Wow!" Sven commented, "This is becoming interesting. I have never heard you talking like this Sis, but that is a moot question as I think the guy that would be on top of Mum's list of prospective sons-in-laws is bound to be Sally. The 'cuckoo' has always been her favourite," he said, looking at me meaningfully. I stared at him, not knowing how to react! "Of course, he would be," Luke concurred laughing. Mia tutted, "Don't be stupid Sven, I don't have favourites. But yes, he would be perfect-son-in law material. He is kind, clever and above all loyal!"

I didn't know how to react, except to go a shade of vermilion. I gulped then and said in a quiet voice, "Thank you, but I am also the only person present with a terrorism conviction, something I am not proud of." "Well, be that as may," Mia added, "that doesn't change the fact that you would be a good partner for any lucky girl, once you have got this thing out of your system!" "I agree," Suzanne said, which not only shocked me but the rest of the room. "What!?" Sven gasped, "I am amazed, as I recall you have on occasion almost half killed Sally!" "Yeah, Suz, I think Sally would be safer with those across the border than being your partner". Luke concurred.

"Well, if nothing else Sis," Sven continued, "you would be able to 'educate' him and as Sally is, I suspect, a virgin you could programme him!" Everyone, including Suzanne, found this hilarious, well everyone except me. I could have happily slunk away! "Well, I find that refreshing," Mia said smiling "and to be fair he has had many other things occupying his time, studying and doing other things." I tried light heartedly to divert the conversation away from my lack of sophistication by saying, "I really don't think I would make good husband material as I don't have anything to offer. My veterinary career is defunct, and I am 'Persona Non Grata 'across in S.A." Suzanne looked at me, then said, "I think you would be particularly good husband material. I have seen how you care for animals and so I think you would be a good father and you are not selfish, so yeah, I think I might just decide to marry you!" Mia burst out laughing and remarked, "Oh, and I suppose poor Sean doesn't have a say in this, he must simply comply with your plans?" "Well," she countered smiling, "I think he will be getting a good deal; I am a 'sought after commodity' or so I have been told by many!" "Sis" Sven rebutted "guys are very fickle and if they think they are going to 'bed' you then damn sure you are sought after." "Not true," Jenny said, coming to Suzanne's defence. "I know that Suz has had numerous proposals." "Thank you, Hun," Suzanne replied, with the natural poise that most confident and attractive people exhibit, "I know that those that have asked me to marry them are not suitable to be the father of my children. So, I think in the absence of a more suitable candidate, Sally will have to be the one."

"Oops! Well Sally, it looks like your numbers up," Luke cachinnated from the depths of the sofa. "Welcome brother-in-law!" "Hold on, hold on," Mia interrupted, "this is getting serious, and I won't have you lot railroading poor Sean into committing to something he would rather not do. Much as I would be overjoyed to have him as my son-in-law! Please don't feel you have to listen to these crazy people Sean!" I sat in stunned silence. What was happening? Suzanne was without doubt lovely and I had always thought that she felt me pathetic. Or was she just mocking me? "So, Sally, what do you say?" Suzanne challenged me, fixing me with a look from her grey-blue eyes and I could see that she was serious. I swallowed, but in a flash of sagaciousness, I realized that I would never get another offer like this in my life. So, I said in soft voice, "I am flattered and overwhelmed that you would even consider me and yes off course I would happily be your spouse. So, as it is supposed to be the man who proposes, I am now asking you?" The room went deadly silent, and I could see that even Sven was shocked. "Shit Sally, we were only messing around. Weren't we Suz?" he asked, staring at her intently. "No, I wasn't!" Suzanne asserted in a sincere voice "and yes I will marry you, when you are ready to settle down, and it better not be too long as none of us is getting any younger!" Mia fixed me with an enquiring stare, then said to Suzanne, "I hope you are not making a fool of all of us. Believe me, Colin and I would be happy to see you settled down and Sean would be my choice. But this is all so sudden?" I stood up, a little unsteadily, astounded at how the night had turned out. I had simply come for meal with my adopted family, hoping for a quiet evening and a catch-up on all their lives but unbelievably I was now engaged to the vivacious Suzanne! "If, you change your mind Suz, I will understand!" I said breathlessly.

Suzanne leaned back in the chaise longue totally relaxed, as if it was every day that she got engaged. She lifted her left hand and said, "Well, I will expect some sort of ring as soon as! It doesn't have to be much, but it will make my life so much easier if I am wearing your ring!" Mia stood up and hugged her daughter exclaiming, "I am so happy for both of you!" Jenny jumped up and hugged Suzanne, "Oh that's excellent Suz, I had no idea you that you even wanted to get engaged never mind to Sally." Sven came over to me and shook my hand vigorously, remarking, "It's going to be interesting to see how this works out!" Colin peered over the top of his glasses and the papers he was reading and noted, "I know you well enough Suzi. If you have decided to marry Sean, then I believe you will. You have always known what you want, so all I can do is wish you both well." Luke and Carmel also now 'disentwined' themselves from the sofa and came over, congratulating us both.

A little later after much discussion, I got ready to leave. It was now after midnight, and I needed to return to the bungalow in the valley. Sven offered to drive me down, but I said it would be best if I made my own way in the dark. Mia made me promise to come over on the weekend when Sandy and Dick would be over. I promised, and after saying goodbye I made my way to the back door and was about to leave when I turned to see that Suzanne had come with me. She suddenly pulled me into her arms and kissed me deeply. To say I was shocked would be an understatement. The curtain of her strawberry blond hair enveloped me in a bouquet of apple scent, and I was stunned. After we breathlessly separated, she stood back, and I could see the amber flecks in her eyes. Then she turned and whispered in my ear "Until the week-end fiancé." "Then she slipped back into the lounge, and I went into the dark starry night, knowing that inexorably my life had changed.

Chapter Four

Entanglement

The night was exquisite as I silently made my way down the hill, the lights of Mbabane a soft glow in dark. I decided I would go into town and see if I could still pick up a taxi down to the valley. I arrived in town just as a bunch of revellers were leaving a tavern and I sauntered behind them, lost in my own thoughts. Never in my wildest imagination would I have believed that Suzanne had any intention of marrying anyone, especially not someone like me. I was pondering this when I heard my name being called. " Isikhova uyaphi"(Owl where you going)?

I turned and just behind me was an overweight Swazi gentleman who at first, I didn't recognise. But then something in his deportment sparked recognition, it was Sambulo, who with Mandla was my life long ' abafowethu begazi' (blood brother). He smiled and put his substantial arm over my thinner shoulder. "Sam," I cried " Unjani" (how are you)? "Just fine brother and you?" He asked.

I was about to answer when a young, pretty, Swazi lady came up. "Ah," he said, removing his arm from my shoulder and instead wrapping it around the girl's waist. "This is Sandile, my wife." I shook her proffered small hand and said I was glad to meet her. "So," Sam questioned. "What are you doing here and more importantly where are you going this time of night." I told them I had been up to see my 'family 'and was now making my way back to 'ikyalami' (my home). "Where is your car then?" Sam inquired. I told them I had come by taxi and was thus looking for one to return me to the valley. "Ah!" Sam responded "Come we will give you a lift."

Sam took Sandile's arm and set off down the road, leading me to a large expensive German sedan. He opened the passenger door and put Sandile in, then gestured for me get in the rear. The vehicle was the latest model and very opulent. "I am suitably impressed Sam, and I am glad that you are doing well," I remarked with sincerity. "Yebo (Yes) I am doing ok. I have a practice in Mbabane and luckily have exclusive clientele. What about you? "He asked. I reluctantly told him that I was not doing much, only doing what little I could for the A.N.C. "Really," he observed, "you must give up that ideology. Those across the border will eventually cause you nothing but problems. I have dealings with a lot of them and they are not to be trifled with!"

I concurred demurely, saying that I knew it was a difficult 'path to walk,' but I would try and see it through. "Well, ' umfowethu' (brother) you always were a little too brave for your abilities. But I hope it all works out for you. If you ever need any legal help, I am here for you."

I thanked him and skilfully diverted the conversation to more mundane topics such as the weather and happenings in Swaziland, which Sandile was then able to comment on. In no time at all Sam drove the car into the drive of the house in the valley and I alighted, saying "Ngiyabonga(Thank you), you are a good friend." Sandile said goodnight and Sam shook my hand through the window and gave me one of his cards, reiterating. "Remember, any time you need me, just call." Then he drove off back in the direction of the city.

I showered then lay in bed feeling strangely pleased, not only was I now engaged to a lovely girl, but I had also connected with both my 'brothers'. I drifted off into a sweet slumber.

I awoke to the smell of freshly brewed coffee and wandered into the kitchen where I found Hetty and Grand-pere sitting having breakfast. Hetty asked if I wanted anything, but I replied that coffee would be fine and that I would help myself to that. Grand-pere, enquired how my visit to my 'family' had been. I sat down and reflecting on the pervious nights events quietly replied, "It was one of the best nights of my life, not only was I happy just to be with them but I got engaged! "Engaged!" Hetty echoed, "What, as in to get married?" "Yes." I said smiling, self-satisfied. "Oh, congratulations Sean, that's wonderful news. Do we know the girl?" Grand-pere looked totally dumbfounded and looked at me as if I were delusional. "Mon Garcon (My boy)", he blurted out, slipping into his native tongue, "how can you be engaged when, as far as I am aware, you haven't ever been in a relationship?" I grinned. "True, but I did go out with Wendy a while back," I argued, feeling quite the libertine. "Oui," Grand-pere responded, "but if I am not mistaken, she dumbed your sorry arse!" "Jacques!" "Hetty cried, "Leave the boy alone so he can tell us all."

I sipped my coffee and peered over the rim of the cup at them. They were obviously waiting for me to disclose more information, so I took my time feeling like a 'man of the world,' when in fact it was as Grand-pere had said. I was totally without experience when it came to the 'fairer' sex. "Do you love the girl?" Hetty needled, plainly exasperated at my reticence. This shocked me back into reality. Did I love Suzanne? It was a tricky question and one I knew I could not answer. I decided the best answer would be the truth, "I am not sure that either of us considered that, I think Suzanne simply decided that, if she is to have a spouse it might as well be me and for my part, I am undeniably flattered. Let's be honest, I am no catch!" "Oh!" she said,

"Don't put yourself down. You might be a little unpredictable, but you genuinely are a good prospect."

"Mere de Dieu (Mother of God)" Grand-pere bellowed 'a little unpredictable' that's putting it lightly. The boy is a walking disaster." He stroked his chin, perplexed, then looked at me under bushy eyebrows, saying in an amused voice, "You know, I think it would be the best thing for you. I know Suzanne is a little difficult and yes, she is undeniably pretty, but besides that I think she has her mother's astuteness, and I don't think she would make any decision rashly or lightly. If she has decided you are her best prospect, then my boy you are fortunate. So, she must see something in you. Lord knows what it is?!" I chuckled, then replied, "Well, be that as it may, and as we are not planning any nuptials just yet, I imagine she might change her mind sooner or later, when she thinks things through in the 'cold light of day'. But I will savour my status as her fiancé for as long as I can."

"Well, I hope you will think about this and not go back and stay here and work with Jacques where you are safe," Hetty said smiling. "Oui (Yes)," Grand-pere agreed "I am sure I could keep you occupied."

I felt besieged, knowing that I was obligated to return to Johannesburg and Solly, to explain what I planned to do. So, I placated them saying "I will return to S.A. and discuss my plans with my cadre superior Solly, to give them the opportunity to make alternative arrangements. But thank you." Hetty and Grand-pere looked suitably satisfied. Hetty asked why this was necessary and why couldn't I just phone him from here, but Grand-pere understood my reasoning. He got up saying that he needed to be places and he would see us later, then left. I told Hetty that I would be going to see Tom Stockdale at the practice and see if I could be of any use to him, as I was at a loose end. Hetty offered to drive me there, which I readily accepted, so she left to get ready while I 'foraged' for some breakfast.

I spent the next couple of days helping Dr Tom and James with the anaesthetics and general tasks. Dr Tom decided that it would be helpful for me to keep my 'hand in', so he arranged with the local animal welfare organization to bring in a collection of cats and dogs for me to do routine surgery on. At first, I was a little rusty but soon I was in my stride and enjoyed it immensely and after a few days he commented that he was happy with my technique, and it was a shame I wasn't in practice anymore. I also observed consultations and he involved me as much as possible by asking my opinion prior to make a diagnosis. The clients didn't seem to mind. In a few days he called me into his office and said that even though he knew I was banned by the council, he could still use me on an occasional basis when James needed time off, or just as an extra pair of hands. I was gratified and felt that I did once more have a purpose to my life.

The weekend arrived and I surreptitiously made my way back up the hill. I had done my best to make my visit as unobtrusive as possible by using a circuitous route and entering the property via the road behind.

Sandy and Dick greeted me happily and Sandy smiled saying "You are a dark horse Sally, we never even suspected that you might fancy Suz." I coloured, feeling like a total charlatan, replying self-consciously "Neither did I." "What!" Dick responded, "So you two haven't been secretly seeing each other?" I was saved from having to find an answer by Mia coming in. "Ah, my prospective son-in-law" she tittered and hugged me. "Come, Colin is getting ready to 'braai'. Would you like a drink."

The afternoon was hot, as it often is just below the tropic of Capricorn, and we spent the afternoon swimming and lounging around. Suzanne still treated me as before and even though we both received a fair amount of tormenting from Sven and Luke, she just smiled and maintained that she still intended marrying me and unless I had changed my mind, she saw nothing unusual in this. I insisted that 'No' I most certainly had not changed my mind and that I could not believe my good fortune. I did insist that if she ever felt that she wanted to opt out I would understand. Colin commented that it was the strangest engagement he had ever seen, but he expected nothing less from his atypical daughter.

The night drew in and the time came for me to take my leave. I told my 'family' that yes, I would be returning to Johannesburg within the next few days, to inform my A.N.C supervisor of my intention to scale down my involvement and to return to Swaziland and work with Dr Tom as a 'gopher' and Grand-pere when he needed me. Mia was overjoyed and smiled knowingly. Sven looked at his sister and commented, "Well Suz, your prowess has no bounds as you are already reforming Sally!" Luke guffawed and added, "He would be better off working for his freedom fighter brothers." Suzanne treated her brothers with her usual derision, but Jenny came to my defence saying that they were just being stupid.

I said my goodbyes and once again Suzanne came with me to the door. She gave me her contact numbers and said that I was to please stay in contact. Then she kissed me fleetingly and was gone. I made my way back down a couple of side streets to where I had left Hetty's Toyota, and then drove back down to the bungalow.

The following day I phoned Dr Dlamini's -the Isangoma's - office and asked to speak to him. Unfortunately, he was unavailable, but his secretary said she would ask him to contact me. I spent a further day with Dr Tom and James and then, on returning home that night, Grand-pere informed me that Dr Dlamini had phoned him, and I was to meet him at the falls on the following evening.

The moon was waxing and almost full, so the night sky was light as I made my way through the reserve towards the falls. The night was alive with those animals that were hunting, and others simply trying to stay alive. This was the joy of Africa. I felt exhilarated, knowing full well that I was just another 'animal'. I had said my good-byes to Grand-pere, Hetty and Nolwesi, promising to keep in close contact. I had promised to return as soon as possible once I had sorted out my position with Solly.

A rustling and a hissing made me pause. I saw a spotted coat and first thought it might be a juvenile Leopard but the I noticed its ringed tail; it was a large Spotted genet. These mongoose type animals are prolific and crepuscular and hunt small mammals, rodents and often birds. I stopped and waiting while it sidled away into the night.

I made it to the falls in suitable time and was contemplating calling out to see if there was any response when a quiet deep voice close to me said "Ah, Isikova I see you have arrived." I was startled and responded hoarsely, "Oh, Dr Dlamini, I hope I haven't kept you waiting." He was standing close to me and once again it astounded me how he always appeared without any sound or warning." No, I have only arrived myself a few moments ago," he assured me. I thanked him again for helping me, but he brushed it aside saying, "Come we have a way to go, and I wish to get you across the border before daylight."

He was dressed in bush clothes and his customary Leopard skin cloak, we set off at a blistering pace in a westerly direction. I followed, doing my best to keep up. "So, I hear you are planning to give up the cause across the border and settle down to a normal life with us here," he asked quietly as we strode through the bush "and you are to take a wife!" I was dumbfounded, how had he come to know all this. "How did you find that out?" I asked breathlessly. "I have many sources Isikova , and many of them are not known to you," he replied. "I do need to tell you that you need now to be extra wary, as many things are coming to culmination. Your aptitude and fortitude are going to be tested severely, but know this, you are not alone.

When you need me, I will know and be there." I was a little puzzled, but he didn't elaborate but and pushed on at a furious pace.

Soon we were out of the reserve and crossed the MR 19 road without incident and then the small village of Mhlamanyatsi to the south. I was not sure where he was headed for but trusted him implicitly as he walked on quietly and with purpose. In time we came to the small Metfulo river which we followed without any trouble and the gradient became steeper as we ascended onto higher ground and the bush was not as dense. In time the river transversed the Swazi – S.A. border without any indication that we had left one country and entered another.

Relentlessly we pushed on as the moon crept across the night sky. In time we came to the small village of Magoqo, a dog braked as we neared one of the small houses, and from it appeared a wizened old mother. I could tell by her accoutrements that she was an Inyanga or healer. She greeted Dr Dlamini with profound respect and looking me over asked if I was the 'umlungu' (white person) that needed help? "He is," Nhandla replied in isizulu saying "Can you get him to the 'idolobha' (Town) of Amsterdam as soon as possible please?" " Inkambo (of course)," she replied deferentially. She called out to someone in the house and a tall muscular young man came out. "This is Moses my 'umfundi' (apprentice)" she said, "He will drive you to the idolobha." Moses bowed to Dr Dlamini, who greeted him and thanked him for helping.

Moses went around the back of the small house and soon we heard the 'purr' of a diesel engine, and he came round in a little Nissan pick-up. Nhandla took my hand and looking directly at me with atramentous eyes said "Now I take my leave of you Isikova but know that I will know how you get on. It is not going to be an easy time for you, but you must believe that when you need help it will be there for you. 'Hamba uthule' (go quietly)". I had no inkling what he was talking about but thanked him profusely for getting me across the border. He nodded then went into the house with the old lady and I was left to get into the pick-up. Moses drove along the tiny dusty streets carefully so as not to draw any attention to us. He didn't ask any questions but simply paid attention to his driving, as the roads were corrugated and pitted with holes. In no time at all we were on the tar road of the A33 and heading for Amsterdam. Dawn was beginning to lighten the sky in the east as we drew into Amsterdam. Moses asked where I would like to be dropped off? I told him that anywhere in the main street would suffice, I knew that I could get a bus later to Carolina via Warburton. He smiled and drew up outside the Post Office. He shook my hand and said "hamba ngokuthula" (go in peace). I thanked him and alighted. He drove off and I walked down the street looking for a place to get some breakfast.

The sun slowly rose above the eastern horizon a magnificent orange ball, the air was crisp, clear, and thin. I walked down the empty street until I came across a small Vetkoek (fried bread dough) shop off one of the side streets. It wasn't open yet, but I could see lights on in the interior and the mouth-watering smell of the cooking made me hungry. I stood outside and pressed my face against the steamed glass, trying to see if I could attract anyone's attention. I was so busy doing this I didn't hear the footsteps behind me until someone said "kan ek u help Meneer" (can I help you mister?) I jumped, feeling like a peeping tom caught in the act. It was a small middle-aged woman, so regaining my composure I asked, "I was wondering when the shop opened?" "It's my husband's shop," the lady explained "and we won't be open for another hour or so but if you like you can come in and have coffee until the vetkoek are ready." I happily accepted her offer, so using an extraordinarily large set of keys she used one to unlock the door.

Entering the shop, she shouted out "Henny, dis net ek en a skraal client (Henny it's just me and a thin client)" ""Wat (What!)" A shout came from the back of the shop and then a large man, wearing an apron, came from behind a beaded curtain, his hands covered in flour. My door keeper then gestured for me to sit at one of the red and white table clothed tables, while she went on to explain that she had found me leering into the shop and that I was after breakfast. "Ag ja, die koffee is aan en die vetkoek is amper gaar (Oh yes, the coffee is made and the vetkoek are almost cooked.) Henny responded, looking me over surreptitiously, then added "wel Alicia, hy lyk as of hy baie honger is (well Alicia he looks like he is very hungry)." Alicia, my door opener, now told him I was English and as she was going to get me coffee, would he like coffee as well. "Nee dankie (no thanks)," he responded, then he came over to my table, clapped his hands together to rid them of the flour, then offered a still floury massive 'paw,' saying that his name was Henny van Wyk. I shook his hand and thanked him, introducing myself just as Sean. "Well Sean you are obviously not from these parts," he noted. I thought quickly and told him no, but that I had been hitchhiking through Natal and was on my way to see friends in Carolina. "Carolina hey," he said wiping a still snowy hand across his forehead. "Alicia's people are from there, perhaps they know your friends?" Clutching at straws I told him that my friends were Frik and Marie. "Frik, the horticulturist you mean," he said beaming. I nodded, thinking that I wasn't quite sure Oom Frik could be called a horticulturist, but nevertheless he was a good friend who had given me succour and I liked him and Tant Marie.

"Wel ek sal sien hoe dit lyk met die Vetkoek (Well I better see how the Vetkoek are doing)," he proclaimed and went off behind the beaded curtain again. Alicia now came in with my coffee. Putting it down she then busied herself in getting ready to open the café officially, checking the tables for condiments and making sure everything was as it should be. I sat back sipping my coffee with zest as the sun streamed through the window.

Henny now returned with a plateful of steaming vetkoek that smelt divine. "Enjoy" he said in English "they are the best Vetkoek in all of the province," he continued smiling, and obviously waiting for me to pass some comment, pulled out a chair on the opposite side of my table and called to Alicia to bring him some coffee. Alicia tutted, saying that she asked him previously but nevertheless bustled off to do his bidding.

Hennie leaned his bulk in the chair and studied me more closely, while I eat his delicious vetkoek. "When last did you see Marie and Frik, Marie and Alicia are cousins you know?" Luckily, I had a mouth full of vetkoek so could consider my response. "It's been a while," I said, trying not to say much. "Well, if you hang on till after the morning rush, I am sure Alicia will take you along the road to their farm," "he added drinking his coffee. I was overjoyed as not only would it see me along my journey, but I would also be happy to see Oom Frik and Tant Marie.

The morning wore on and I moved outside to one of the patio tables under a gay yellow awning, drinking copious cups of coffee which Alicia kept bringing me. Around mid-morning the customers tailed off and Alicia came to me, saying that she was ready and was just going to get her car. I went into the café and approached Henny at the till, I queried what I owed him for all the coffee and Vetkoek. He obviously found this amusing and replied, "Nee vat, jy is n'vriend van Alicia's familie , daar is gun koste (No way, you are a friend of Alicia's family, there is no cost)." I shook my head saying that friend or no friend I wanted to pay. He scrutinized me for a second but then named a nominal amount which I happily proffered.

Alicia brought her small car around and we set off for Carolina. Alicia talked up a storm telling me about her grandchildren and their exploits. I nodded and tried to exhibit as much interest as possible, asking pertinent questions now and then. In no time we were pulling up outside Oom Frik and Tant Marie's farm, we stopped outside the wrought iron gates and Alicia used the hooter to attract their attention. The first to arrive at the gateway was Leeu, the massive Boerboel. He stared at us with large amber eyes. Not far behind came the diminutive Tant Marie, smiling she used a key and rolled the big gate open. Alicia drove through and up the driveway to the farm bungalow. I got out as Leeu came trotting up and I was amazed that he remembered me, he jumped up on me and gave me a happy dog smile. He had aged a bit as there were a few grey hairs around his muzzle, but he was his normal massive muscular self.

Tant Marie arrived from the gate and greeted Alicia with a hug, then looked over at me not recognising me, but then her green eyes softened, and she beamed "My magtig, is dit jy Sean (Good grief is it you Sean)?" I walked over and she took my hand and said in English, "Let me have a look at you, you have grown a bit, but I see you have an anxious look about you," I swallowed but smiling gave her a hug and asked after Oom Frik. "Wel Frik is net in die veldt maar is netnou hier (well Frik is just in the fields but will be here shortly)," she affirmed. We all three made our way to the kitchen where Marie put the kettle on the big Aga stove and asked what we would like coffee or tea? Leeu sat next to me, his floppy tongue hanging out of the side of his mouth, his amber eyes searching my soul. I patted his broad head, and he rested it on my knee, but not for long as he suddenly jumped up and headed for the door and I heard Oom Frik saying "Wel Ou vriend , dit lyk as of ons gasta het (well old friend it looks as if we have guests)." Frik came in dusting his bush hat on his trousers, he greeted Alicia and then looking surprised said, "Sean, man is it really you, I thought that you had forgotten Marie, Leeu and myself?" He came over and slapped me on the back with his large rough hand. Marie now put large steaming mugs of coffee in front of us. "So, Sean, what brings you to our neighbourhood. I thought you were hiding out in Swaziland?" he laughed?

I paid attention to my mug of steaming hot coffee, then replied that I was returning to the East Rand. Tant Marie was the first to ask the obvious, was I so hard up that I didn't have a car. I laughed and said that I did have a car but that it was in Johannesburg, and I was returning from a trip to Swaziland, after having gone there with Grand-pere Jacques. "Ah, and how is Meneer Levascue, I haven't seen him in an age?" I replied that indeed Grand pere was in good health.

Tant Marie asked if we would be staying for supper. Alicia quickly acquiesced, but I was a little hesitant as I wanted to get on the road to Johannesburg and hinted at this. Oom Frik, after a moment said, "Well I was planning on going to the Rand tomorrow anyway, so if you want to stay the night we can set-off early tomorrow." This was fortunate, and I gratefully accepted.

I spent an enjoyable evening with them and Alicia, listening to the stories of their protracted family and who had annoyed who and who was currently 'in favour' and who was causing worries for their parents or relatives. It was quite amusing, and I imagine they were a microcosm of most closely knit families. Finally, Alicia took her leave to return to Henny and I thanked her profusely for her and his kind help. Once we had all cleared up the dinner dishes and fed the ever-attentive Leeu, Oom Frik and Marie retired, and I once more curled up with the massive tawny bulk of Leeu on the sofa. It was a good feeling, his warm bulk close to me. Early the next morning after a big breakfast of bacon, egg, and sausage Oom Frik and myself took our leave. Tant Marie gave me a big hug and one of her smiles that transformed her from being moderately attractive to beautiful. She made me promise that I would come again soon, and I agreed saying I would do my best. I patted my faithful sofa-sharing, friend Leeu on the head and we set off.

Oom Frik was in good humour and chatted away about the business of buying and selling Aloe plants. The plants were controlled by the government and all plants had to be traded with a certificate to stop any illegal trade. But I knew from previous experience with Oom Frik, that he was not averse to digging them up on the kopjes clandestinely at night with his horticultural partner, who provided I presume the necessary paperwork. Nevertheless, it was obviously profitable, but more importantly I suspected he enjoyed it!

In no time we were on the M4 and heading West with Oom Frik regaling me with tales of how they had evaded the authorities on moon less nights. "Man," he expounded "the plants grow like weeds on the kopjes, so what's the problem?" I presumed that some of them were rare and so the S. A. Department of Flora and Fauna were trying to ensure their continued existence, but I certainly didn't voice this opinion. I of all people was the last to point a finger and Oom Frik was not really harming anyone.

Oom Frik made only one stop and that was to top up with diesel and buy a soft drink. It was coming up to mid-morning when we reached the outskirts of Pretoria and where the motorway diversified into several directions, and I needed to stay on the M4 to get to the Rand and Edenvale. I asked Oom Frik to drop me on the off ramp to the motorway East while he carried on into the city centre. Even though stopping on the motorway was illegal, he pulled the bakkie over to the side of the motorway and I gratefully shook his hand and jumped out. He sped away yelling through the closing door that I 'shouldn't be stranger'!

I quickly walked off the motorway and on to the on ramp of the M4 which fed to the motorway for the vehicles from Pretoria and finding a spot where a vehicle could stop to pick me up, I began hitch hiking. It wasn't long before I managed to get a lift with an Afrikaans pastor who spoke with a mild voice and who's only concern was my salvation. I assured him that indeed I 'had seen the light' which satisfied him, and he dropped me off at the warehouse in Edenvale, giving me a farewell blessing.

I strolled into the yard and then on into the warehouse, making my way to Solly's office. Solly was sitting behind his desk, his glasses hanging off his robust nose. He looked up as I closed the flimsy prefabricated door saying, "Ah Sean so you have returned. How was your visit?" Not giving me a chance to reply, he went on, "I'm glad you are back as I have an urgent little job for you!" I sat down in the swivel chair opposite and sighed. I had come to tell him that I was intending suspending my endeavours and was considering how to word it. Solly went over to the door obviously checking to see we were not overheard. Sean, this is extremely important. I have news out of Lesotho, from no less than Comrade Chris himself, we have a vital mission for you to undertake which needs to be actioned as soon as possible. I swallowed. This was not how I had envisaged this conversation going. I asked tentatively what was so vital? He once again sat down in his chair and getting a brown folder from the drawer, he slid a newspaper picture across to me. It was faded and slightly indistinct but portrayed a tall, bearded military figure in a camouflage jacket. He had a swarthy complexion and was either Mediterranean or of Hispanic descent. "This is Col Santiago Perez, and he is currently waiting in Botswana for transport to Johannesburg and MK high command. I want you to try and memorise his likeness, as I can't allow you to take this article. Not only would it cause dire consequences for you, but also for the organization." I looked at the faded picture and realised that the Colonel had a remarkable resemblance to Che Guevara and decided that would help me when I met him.

I got up and looked out of the Perspex panelling of the office, down below to where the vehicles were coming in from the days roofing jobs, because this was a genuine business. I paced a little, building up my courage, then blurted out, "I will get the Colonel and bring him across the border, but then I think I will be calling it a day Solly!" Solly leaned back in his chair, his large hands clasped around his copious belly and replied, "We can discuss your decommissioning once you have delivered the Colonel to MK, but you need to move fast as the Comrade Colonel is waiting at a house just across the border, near the confluence of the Taung and Ngotwane rivers. The house is owned by one of our supporters, Comrade Bapiri who is the local cobbler, but his position there will not be tenable for too long. I would appreciate it if you could leave as soon as possible. I have the van all prepared so what else will you need?" I asked if he had a map of the Northern Transvaal, as the area he mentioned was a little more easterly than where I normally moved the outgoing or incoming conscripts.

Solly went over to one of the metal filling cabinets and returned with a large map of the Transvaal which he spread on his desk. I looked at the map, the area was far north of my normal crossing point, and this was a good thing as it didn't pay to use a route too often. The closest area to where I would need to cross was a small mining town east of the Town of Zeerust. I studied the map comprehensively trying to get the topography into my head, there was a lot of open country, but I noted that it was sparsely populated and was in the main Lowveld bush country.

Solly rubbed his partly bald head and asked, "Can you leave as soon as possible?" I nodded, saying that I would just collect a few things from Lenz and then leave. "Thank you, my boy, you have 'saved my bacon.' I thought it was an incongruous comment as I knew Solly was a devout Jew. He shook my hand and wished me the best and all the blessings from Yahweh in Hebrew. I could see that he was worried. I found my 'bakkie' and drove out of the yard into early rush hour traffic.

I hardly noticed the trip back to my digs above the cinema, my mind was trying to come to terms with what I had to do. Without doubt this was a lot more precarious than moving a few MK recruits across the border, I had no doubt in my mind that the Security Services would have informants in Botswana and have an inkling as to some of MKs plans, they were astute and had good intelligence! On reaching my digs I ran upstairs and collected what I thought I would need, a powerful torch, signalling mirror, a couple of changes of Khaki shirts and trousers and a sturdy pair of 'bush boots'.

I left Lenasia and meandered my way through the suburbs of Johannesburg taking the road past Randfontein and heading for the Magaliesburg mountains and my stop for the night in Rustenburg. Once the other side of Randfontein the traffic petered out and I was able to make good time. I reached Rustenburg around midday and stopped at a local roadhouse to get a quick burger and chips, as well as information on a non-descript motel or boarding house. The proprietor of the Son-op (sun up) roadhouse was most loquacious on the merits of the local establishments and gave me a full run down of all their features. He was obviously of Portuguese descent and carried around a lot of excess avoirdupois but nevertheless he was a font of information. He directed me to a small rambling bungalow on the outskirts of the town. Unfortunately, he was also intrinsically inquisitorial, which worried me, asking what my stay in Rustenburg entailed. I told him I was only passing through on my to Swartruggens, where I planned to give a roofing quote. This appeased his curiosity but while my order was being prepared, he chatted on about the locals who he told me were overall very conservative. I nodded at the appropriate times and thankfully my food soon arrived.

He asked if I wanted to dine at one of the small outside tables but thanking him, I said no I would, like most of his patrons, be eating in my van.

I ate quickly as I was famished, then flicked my lights so as to attract the attention of one of his waiters to come and remove the tray. This done I drove out in the direction he had given me and soon found the boarding house. The owner, a tall gaunt Afrikaans gentleman, made me sign the register, gave me keys, towels, and a few small bars of soap, and told me what time breakfast would be available. Thankfully, he was taciturn and not inclined to indulge in small talk. The room was basic but clean and after taking a shower in the communal bathroom I fell into bed and slept like a surfeited warthog.

I awoke the next morning to the sound of a profusion of bird calls and after a quick shower went downstairs and had breakfast. Once again, the landlord was reserved, which suited me, so consuming my breakfast quickly I thanked him and collecting my bag made my way out to the bakkie. I took the road to Swartruggens which I reached in a brief time. I decided not to stop but pushed on and was soon in the Groot Marico area. It was an expanse of savannah and grassland with wetlands and Dolomite formations. I drove along the lonely road with the window wide open to help with the heat that was now rising off the tarmac. I watched as twenty or so Red Hartebeest or Kongoni grazed on the grassland. These are large attractive antelope that I had not seen often, so pulling up on to the side of the road I got out and watched them with my binoculars. The sky was its beautiful pale blue with a spattering of small cumulus clouds building up.

I spent a little time just enjoying their uniqueness but unfortunately time wasn't on my side, so with a sigh I once more pushed on for Zeerust. I reached the Town just after midday and decided to stop and get a drink and pasty, which proved to be delicious and unbelievably fresh. I drove on through the Groot Marico, watching a few Ostriches pecking their way along the Savannah. I suspected that these were not wild Ostriches but more likely farmed birds. I turned north for Supingstad, it was only a short hop, and the small village soon came into view. There was not much of it, but it would suit my purpose.

I found a rooming house where the rooms were situated away from the main facilities of the dining room and bathrooms. This was perfect for my purposes as I needed to slip out in the dark to cross the Ngotwane River into Botswana. I registered and told the young proprietor that I would need the room for a couple of days because I was going to canvases for work in the area. She was a little perplexed as it was not a big place, but I allayed her concerns by saying that I planned not only to tout for business in the small town, but also was going to try to get business across the border in Gaborone, adding that I was basing myself at her hostelry due to their competitive rates. This pleased her and giving me my key, she asked if I would be having any meals. I smiled and said that I might. Smiling she wished me a pleasant stay and I made my way to the room. It was a typical African thatched bungalow, with a small kitchenette, a toilet and wash basin. It was perfect and I settled down in a well-used lounge chair for a few hours' sleep before nightfall.

The night was resplendent with a myriad of stars and the moon had not yet 'shown its face'. This was not ideal but as time was of the essence, I slipped out of the bungalow after putting the 'do not disturb notice' on the door handle, hoping this would circumvent any undue attention. It was a glorious night, and the night life was in full chorus, frogs and toads called out and owls hooted exuberantly. I set off with a brisk pace, my compass in hand, although I didn't have to refer to it much, as I could find my way by the stellar constellations. Soon the moon aided my passage, and I was able move quickly, avoiding inadvertent ground roots that might have slowed my passage.

I covered the few short miles to the river in an hour or so. As with the border into Zimbabwe, this river was also patrolled by the S.A. defence force, and I suspected these would be members of the 3rd Infantry Battalion stationed in Potchefstroom far to the southwest. They would have a mobile headquarters closer by, but these were committed soldiers and I never underestimated them. I approached the river and noted the sand track where their vehicles patrolled. I decided I would wait and observe when and how often they patrolled. I settled down a little way off in the grass as large trees were exceedingly rare. The night was 'alive', and the calls and sounds were now magnified, with the noise of my scuffling through the brush no longer dulling them.

I settled down and listened intently for the sound of any vehicle, but I only heard the calling of frogs, crickets and strangely a soft snuffling, scarifying, ripping sound not far off. I slowly crept towards it, not knowing what the cause could be. As I got nearer the sound stopped except for the soft snuffling. I parted the thick grass stems and there in front of me was an old acquaintance of mine, an Aardvark. I recalled how Mandla, Sambulo, and I discussed what sort of termite we would have been to avoid ending up being 'snuffled' by an Aardvark. I chuckled. Then, I had been enjoying glorious days of sunshine and friendship. Never in my wildest dreams would I have thought I would be hiding in the dark, awaiting an army patrol.

I watched, fascinated by the animals' actions. It used its curved claws to dig under the ant hill and then, as the 'defenders' appeared to try and repair their habitation, (he or she, as I was not an expert) sucked them up. It suddenly froze and then turned and scurried off. At first, I thought that it had perhaps either discovered my presence using its olfactory senses or detected a slight noise I might have made, but then I heard the rumble of a heavy diesel engine and realised the Aardvark had heard it as well.

It was not long before two bright lights illuminated the track, and I could see the armoured vehicle approaching. It was moving quite quickly, so I presumed that in the dark they were not using a tracker. It passed no more than fifty feet from me, and I saw one of the soldiers head above the vehicle hatch, only due to him having just drawn in on his cigarette. I watched as it rolled on into the night and then moved slowly towards the river. The river here bent back on itself in a serpentine loop. It was not overly wide but was deep and fast flowing and not wasting any time I launched myself into it and swam strongly across. I was driven a fair way downstream before I reached the opposite side and struggled up the slippery, muddy bank.

Streaming with water, I quickly put as much distance as I could between myself and the river border. I was now in Botswana. I tramped on sodden, but I soon started to dry off. I looked up at the stars and then at my compass as I headed northeast, hoping to find the Taung river at its confluence with the Ngotwane, as my rendezvous with the Colonel was close to that. I hiked on into the night musing on how much time and money had been spent on my education and skills for me now to be creeping covertly around in the night like an ostracised Hyena. The time the austere Christian Brothers had spent teaching us etiquette and comportment to fit into what they determined 'civilised society'! I chuckled. If they could see me now, it would confirm what they believed of me all along, namely that I was by nature a wild feral creature. I imagined that the majority of those that had matriculated with me were now likely upstanding members of society and would frown on my endeavours, and many would no doubt believe that my ideology was dangerous and subversive. I was in deep thought but was brought back to reality by the prompting of my bladder. Out of modesty I looked for a suitable tree to relieve myself behind. This stemmed from some long forgotten primeval instinct that all men have. I perceived a suitable dark form and approaching it and unzipping, sent a hot stream against what I thought was the trunk of a tree. The 'tree' suddenly grunted, and I am not sure who was more surprised, me or what I now saw was a Hippo grazing on the sedge close to the river. It turned and I could see its globular eyes glimmering in the dark, as it tried to evaluate what had 'sprayed it'. Thankfully this enabled me to turn and run as fast as my spindly human legs would allow me. I heard it thundering behind me and it was so close the ground trembled. I searched for a suitable tree which if I had been paying attention before, I would have seen. This was bushveld so large trees were rare, but I had to take what I could get as there was no doubt the ' Imvubu' was gaining on me. I scrambled up a scratchy thin-branched tree just as it was on me but, due to its exuberance to pummel me into the turf, it over shot. Turning, it came back using its outstanding sense of smell to find me. It approached my feeble tree and looked up at me, I think not comprehending what manner of 'creature' had the audacity to disturb its grazing!

I tried to stay as motionless as possible as it circled around below me. I knew that if it wished it could quite easily use its bulk to either shake me from my spindly perch, or in fact quite easily demolish the tree. It grunted and stomped around like a petulant adolescent unable to get its way, then fortunately decided that as it was no longer under attack from some type of scent marking entity, it wandered off back to its sedge browsing.

I spent ages just trying to control my shaking limbs, then I burst out laughing as I envisaged my epitaph if I had been found trampled into the Southern Botswanan bushveld-Isikhova esimanzise uMvubu (The owl that met the Hippo).

I took a while before climbing down off my pathetic puny perch and it was more that the thorns were causing me discomfort that made me decide to jump back on to the ground. I silently crept along now, paying far more attention to my surroundings and thinking how foolish I had been. My 'brothers' had taught me many lessons, but one of the most important was never to underestimate Africa and its animals. Most just wanted to get on with their lives, avoided human contact and didn't take interference sanguinely.

I soon came across what I believed was where the Taung river met the Ngotwane and forded it easily. I now turned slightly west, heading for what I hoped was the map reference for my rendezvous with Colonel Perez at Comrade Bapiris house. I made suitable time, and the false dawn was not far off when I picked up the sounds of a generator meaning some habitation had to be close by. I decided to wait for dawn because it would be highly suspicious for any of the locals to meet a small European wandering around in the night. I drew close to what I presumed was the village, but it was only a couple of small houses, some traditional walled and thatched ones and some made of corrugated iron sheeting. A dog barked close by as I watched the sky lighten in the east. I walked up the dusty street that was obviously the hub of the small settlement and noted that there was a general store. It had the obligatory metal advertising boards, depicting the banal everyday necessities such as tobacco, tea, and detergents. I went to the door to see when it might open but there were only faded bits of old advertising decals. I decided this would be the best place to make enquiries about the local cobbler Bapiri when it opened, so slowly carried on through until I was once more in the surrounding bush. Finding a suitable old stump of a long dead tree, I settled down to await the new day.

Chapter Five

Audacity

I entered the small store just after eight and I was greeted ebulliently by an Asian gentleman dressed in a thawab so recognising this I greeted him in a respectful Islamic manner saying, "As Salaam alaykum." He smiled broadly and replied, "alaykum salaam" and asked in perfect English how I was. I nodded saying quite well but would be better for a little coffee if possible. He clapped his hands and within moment a tall Asian lady came through a small door at the side of the store. "Miriam," he said addressing her, "this man would like some coffee." She bowed slightly, then asked in a soft voice how I liked my coffee. Thanking her I gave her my preference and she once more disappeared through the small door into what I presumed was their living quarters.

"Well now," the shop owner responded, "we don't see many white people in our small community. Did you come from Ramotswe by taxi or bus?" He caught me a little off guard and for a moment I hesitated but having become out of necessity a consummate liar, I replied that indeed I had come across the border at Ramotswe and was hiking through Botswana.

Luckily, Miriam now returned with a tray containing my coffee and happily also a plate of biscuits. I thanked her and once again she retreated behind the small side door. "I am Suleiman," the shop owner acquainted me as I sipped my strong coffee. "I am the proprietor of all you see here" he said happily, "and if you are hiking on through Botswana, where is your backpack?" I took another long sip of my coffee, giving me time produce a suitable reply. "I find it easier to travel light and buy what I need as I go along and then just dispose of the old stuff."

He clapped his hands again in enthusiasm, obviously thinking that this was 'manna from heaven', a customer he could sell copious goods to. Poor Miriam, thinking she had been summoned, came rushing through the door. He shooed her away with a wave of his pudgy hand and then looking me over decided that I was in dire need of a new set of clothes, as the necessities of swimming across rivers and escaping from an irascible Hippo had certainly not enhanced my appearance.

Taking a one-sided ladder, he placed it against the one wall of the shop that was stocked up to the roof with boxes. Pulling a box down he once more surveyed me. "Right, I suspect you are a twenty-eight-inch waist and a fourteen-inch collar," he asserted pulling shirts and trousers from the boxes and coming over to me to present them. I finished my coffee and thought why not, I had Botswanan Pula in my pockets, supplied by Solly, for incidental expenses. Buying clothes, which may provide me with the information I wanted, could be considered an 'incidental expense'.

I tried on a pair of serviceable bush trousers and a lighter olive shirt which astonishingly fitted, as normally I had to have my clothes adjusted. Suleiman was in his element, obviously believing that here was a fortuitous opportunity, an affluent European who needed a new 'ensemble'. I now lifted my boot, asking if he knew where I could find a cobbler. "Cobbler?" he echoed, "Why no, I could just as well sell you a lovely pair of good boots that would be far better than those old Veldschoene you are wearing," he asserted. He rushed over to the other side of the shop, coming back with a couple of pairs of heavy leather boots. I shook my head saying that no, I needed a cobbler to sort out my Veldschoens as I was attached to them.

He looked at me and I could see that he was deeply wounded that I had rejected his obviously more suitable boots. "Well, I suppose there is a man here called Bapiri who is an average cobbler. He might be suitable." I smiled to myself 'pay dirt' then nonchalantly asked where one might find this Bapiri. "Ah," Suleiman acknowledged, "I know him well and will take you there once we have concluded our business." I bought two shirts, a pair of trousers and a small olive coloured canvas haversack, which appeased the innate marketing skills of Suleiman.

It was now getting on for mid-morning and I needed to hurry things along to get to Comrade Bapiri. I suggested to Suleiman that he could take me to the cobblers place of business. "Right," he acceded to my request with a pained look, as I suspect he was just getting into his stride and would rather have sold me the entire clothing stock in his store. "Miriam," he bellowed once more and in a matter of minutes the beleaguered woman made her appearance. I suspect she waited resolutely for her 'masters call' all too frequently. "I am taking this gentleman to Bapiri's house as he wishes to get his boots mended. Even though I have offered him the most comfortable and durable boots in the whole of Botswana, he would rather mend his own!" he acclaimed with a heavy sigh.

We left his shop and entered the now more bustling sandy street. Suleiman was greeted by several people, and it was obvious that he was a respected member of this small community. Bapiris house was only a short distance away. It was a small, neat traditional building with a thatched roof and a small yellow sign with a picture of a boots and shoes on it, which advertised his occupation. Suleiman didn't knock but just opened the door and called out, "Hey Keletso, I have a customer here for you". I followed behind him into a small front room that was clearly the cobbler's workplace, as there were all the tools of his trade around the room. A lanky Tswana man came in from the back of the house wiping his mouth with the back of his hand, he had obviously just finished his mid-morning cup of coffee and biscuits.

"Ah khotsong (Good morning)," he said coming over and pumping Suleiman's pudgy hand. Suleiman smiled happily and pointing to me said, "Here is someone needing your help. Even though I have offered the best boots in Botswana, he still insists he would have you mend his disreputable pair of old Veldschoens!" I sheepishly now offered my small hand and said I was pleased to see him and using the code word provided by Solly I said, looking at him meaningfully, "My boots were manufactured in Cuba, so I am quite attached to them." "Cuba," he intoned, looking puzzled, "really that is indeed rare!" I could see he didn't connect me with the person he was expecting, possibly because he was expecting an African. Suleiman, after patting me robustly on the back, said he had to get back to his shop, as poor Miriam was alone. I smiled, thinking that she was enjoying the respite. He shook our hands, saying that if I changed my mind about the boots, he was open all day. I thanked him and replied that I would bear that in mind and if I was ever in the vicinity again, I would no doubt patronise his shop. He bustled his way back out into the street, like a Black Rhino on the trial of Marula fruit. "Now," Bapiri said, "how can I help you with those Veldskoone? I must admit I have never come across Veldskoone that were made in Cuba!" I stared at him and then said, "They are a favourite with the Cuban military, most particularly the officers." "Ah!" he exclaimed, banging his forehead, "You are here for Colonel Perez?" I nodded, feeling relieved. "Come, come, you are most welcome. He is very impatient and expected you a day or two ago. In fact, he said this morning that, had you not come, I was to contact someone and find out what was going on."

He led me to the back of the house, to the kitchen where, at a small wooden table, sat a tall muscular swarthy man in green bush fatigues. "This is Colonel Perez," he said, "and this, Colonel, is your contact who will be taking you across the border and on to Johannesburg." Then looking at me he added, "Sorry I didn't get your name?" I looked at the Colonel and could see he wasn't overly impressed but, not waiting for him to say anything, I informed them that I was simply Comrade Owl." "I can see why," the Colonel iterated in a derisory manner. "There is certainly not much of you but nevertheless, I hope you know your job as I am in a hurry to get to Johannesburg, and I have wasted enough time here already." Comrade Bapiri came to my rescue by asking if I would like coffee and something to eat. I thanked him, replying that I would love some coffee and anything to eat as I was famished. Bapiri went over to his small coal stove, put the kettle on, then asked if a bit of maize meal and meat would suffice? I nodded gratefully saying that would be fine.

"Sit, sit," Bapiri said, pushing an old wooden chair my way while he hurried around getting my fare. The Colonel now asked, "When can we leave, wasting time is not one of my best attributes." I gulped down some of the coffee then replied, "I would think just after dark, the border is not too far, and we should hopefully be at the vehicle by the morning, all being well." "Mmmmph," he replied, "why can't we leave after you have eaten? I am quite ready?" I looked at him for a second or two and thought that this was not going to be easy. The Colonel was used to giving orders and having them obeyed without question. Bapiri brought the food, and this allowed me to plan.

I asked comrade Bapiri if I could use his facilities to wash my hands and he led me to a small clean bathroom where I was able to do a rudimentary wash. I returned to the kitchen and began to eat. I noticed the Colonel watching me assiduously, as I eat using my hands in the African manner. Undoubtedly, he was unimpressed, but I didn't care. I wasn't overly impressed with him either.

I finished and thanked Bapiri and suggested that I could wash my bowl and spoon. He laughed saying that "No" his wife would do it and did I want anymore. I shook my head but did ask for another cup of coffee. I could see that Colonel Perez was by now getting quite agitated and suddenly he burst out, "Listen I have been patient. But enough is enough! Do you people think the punctiliousness of life should be adhered to? No, I have no time for that. I say we should leave right now. I have valuable information and planning strategies that I need to impart to MK high command."

I nodded saying I understood his anxiety, but it would be foolhardy for two white people, to be seen leaving and walking off into the bush. I added that it was never wise to underestimate the S.A. intelligence services, as they had many agents in many of the neighbouring countries. He looked at me as if I were a bit of faeces that he had unfortunately stepped in. He tutted saying, "You are all hopeless fools. This is a war and procrastination often costs lives. You are not even a soldier, but an inadequate civilian!" I sighed and conceded that I was not military trained, but I was all he had, adding that if he wished to take his chances on his own, I would give him the keys to the vehicle, tell him where it was in South Africa, and he could leave as soon as he liked. Comrade Bapiri snickered but then said, "Comrade Colonel, I encourage you to listen to Comrade Owl. They would not have sent him if he were not capable, and he is right, there are many informers. You must understand that. I say relax, then as soon as it is dark you can leave." The Colonel was not overly pleased but seemed to accept Bapiris advice, as he got up and stormed off into the other room. Comrade Bapiri looked at me apologetically saying, "He is evidently an important man and used to getting his own way. Thankfully, he will soon be off my hands and become your problem. Can I help you in any way until then?" I thanked him and as it was only just midday, asked if there was some where I could get my head down for a bit of sleep, as I was a 'dead' tired.

It was dusk when we left Bapiri's small home and made our way into the darkening gloom. The Colonel strode out on his long legs, and I had difficulty matching his pace. But once we entered the true bush, he had to slow down to avoid tripping over grass tussocks. I tried to impress on him prior, to departure, that his incessant cigarillos would be taboo as not only was the smell distinctive but also, when he drew in, the glow would be seen for a few miles. This did not go down well, and he told me that he was not stupid and a trained military officer. I headed directly for the confluence of the Taung and Ngotwane Rivers, not wasting any time. The colonel may be military trained, but he certainly wasn't quiet. He marched along as if on the parade ground and worryingly disturbed a couple of Bustards that had settled down for the night. They thumped along emitting their customary bark-like 'Ca-caa-ca' alarm call. I stopped in my tracks and held up my hand for the Colonel to stop, but he carried on heedlessly, not perturbed in the slightest. I hissed at him to stop, as by now the birds were airborne and making a considerable cacophony. He stopped and turned around ordering me to 'come on'! I sat down in the grass and refused to get up until he came back to me. "What is the problem now?" he seethed. I told him quietly that bumbling through the bush was no way to go about things and by now every animal or human in the vicinity would be aware of our presence. "Y que (so what)," he interjected in Spanish, "there is no one about for miles, so what does it matter." I sighed, explaining to him that that might be the case, but we couldn't be sure and as the border was not too far distant, there was always the possibility that we could be heard by the Infantry patrol. "Rubbish," he admonished, "I haven't seen or heard anything." Exasperated, I replied,

"Undoubtedly you won't have, as you are making such a commotion that plainly you wouldn't hear anything. Please, I understand you are in a hurry, but getting caught will not help your cause and will inevitably be disastrous for both of us."

Fiddling in his bush jacket he found another cheroot and lighting it with a flare from his match drew in on it, contemplating me while I remained on my haunches. "Ok, I will try to be quieter" he conceded. The rivers flowed into each other gouging out a deep pool. So, moving a little more west along the Ngotwane, I found a place where even though it was wider, it was shallower. I asked him if he could swim, hoping beyond hope that he could. In a gruff voice he assured me that he was a proficient swimmer. I suggested we wait for the patrol on the other side of the border to pass by before we forded the river. "Hmm, do we really need to do that?" he asked. "Most definitely," I replied, as it would be reckless to be caught crossing the river with no cover. He accepted this with bad grace, so we sat quietly waiting and thankfully he had extinguished his cheroot.

The gnarl of the engine resounded in the night and the darkness was ruptured by a powerful search light as the patrol came along. I was slightly disconcerted as I had expected it to be headed easterly, but it was heading westerly. I lay flat on my stomach trying make myself invisible. Colonel Perez, on the other hand, just stood motionless. I gestured for him to at least crouch down, but he ignored me. The search light panned the section next to the river on the opposite side and I prayed that they would not scan our side, as without doubt they would see the Colonel. Slowly but inevitably, they moved on and I stood up. "Well, they have gone. Let's get on with it," Colonel Perez grunted. Without further hesitation we ventured into the river and were soon on the other side. I suggested to him that we cross the vegetation-less sandy strip on our toes, to try and leave as little impression as possible. But once again, he simply ignored me and strode purposefully towards the bush on the other side. Once there he questioned which direction we should take, but I ignored him and instead found a small branch and tried to obliterate our footprints. I re-joined him and using the stars we set off at a rapid pace. It was just after midnight when we reached the bungalow and were able to creep in. I made us a quick cup of coffee then suggested he use the small bed to get a bit of sleep. Once again, he questioned why we couldn't leave at once. I explained that, not only did I need to check out the next morning, but that driving away in the middle of the night would undoubtedly raise suspicion. Staring at me for a moment he shook his head in a dismissive manner, but then draining his cup he thumped it down and headed for the bed. In a matter of minutes, I heard the sonorous sounds of slumber. I curled up in the chair and awaited the dawn.

The sky lightened and I went to the bed and shook his shoulder, he awoke with a start uttering some Spanish expletive but then quickly got up. We used the small kitchen sink to have a wash then, after coffee, I smuggled him into the pick-up, stressing that he should try not being conspicuous. I waited till I saw lights on in the main dining facilities and reception, then quickly went across with the key. The lady seemed a bit put out as she said she presumed I would be staying at least a week and had anything been unsuitable? I thanked her profusely and said that to the contrary, everything had been fine, but I had received news that necessitated me moving on. I didn't elaborate but paid her for an extra day then left, even though she said breakfast was not far off.

Once on the road, with the Colonels lanky frame crammed into the passenger seat, I brought up the subject of his attire explaining that, as we were supposed to be a roofing company, it would be expedient if he would at the first opportunity change into one of the company overalls. This did not please him, and he voiced his objections. "I am an officer in the Cuban Military. I will not wear any of your ridiculous overalls. Not only are they demeaning but they smell." I couldn't dispute that some of the overalls did smell but then again, they were meant to be work wear. I tried in vain to reason with him, but he was adamant that he was perfectly comfortable as he was. I pointed out that the Police positioned regular roadblocks on the main roads, especially those that led to and from Botswana and Zimbabwe, and as he had no Identity documents it would be a considerable obstacle. At this he shrugged saying, "I thought you were an expert at moving people, why don't you just avoid those roads?"

I sighed and replied, "It is not that simple. We have to use these roads, as there is no other way to get to the 'Rand' "The 'Rand'" he asked, raising an eyebrow, "where is that?" The 'Rand' I explained was short for the Witwatersrand and that includes Johannesburg. "Si," he acknowledged in Spanish "well I think it best you just drive as fast as possible and get us there. I am really quite sick of this journey, it has already been over a week!" I bit my tongue and thought he was not the only one who sick of this journey. In all my time moving recruits and comrades across the borders, I had never met anyone so objectionable.

I pushed the small pick-up to its limits and soon we were in Zeerust where I stopped at a service station for fuel. Luckily, it also had a reasonable takeaway, so we were able to get some bacon rolls and coffee. Once more on the road heading through the Groot Marico towards Swartruggens, the day was hot and even though we had all the windows open it was stifling. I pointed out a few antelope species to him thinking he might be interested, but he feigned indifference. I was a little bewildered that he showed no interest, as just the joy of seeing them always brightened my day.

In Swartruggens we stopped again for drinks and to use the facilities and then pushed on, I decided that the road to Koster would be the better bet than going via Rustenburg as it was a less well used road. It would get us to Randfontein, which was not too far from Johannesburg, and our ultimate destination Edenvale.

It was late afternoon, and we were around ten miles short of Randfontein, when ahead I noted a bit of congestion. I slowed the vehicle down and then saw the presence of armoured police vehicles. This was a problem as there was no way we would be passed through without Colonel Perez producing some sort of identity, either the conventional Identity document or a passport. I noticed a small gravel road heading off in the direction of the small holdings surrounding Randfontein and decided this was our only hope, so I took it. The Colonel, who had been snoozing, now awoke with a jolt at the change of the motion. "What's going on?" he asked in a gruff voice. I brought him up to date as to our predicament. "What!" he shouted, "Madre de Dios (Mother of God), they have put me in the hands of an imbecile. Why did you not use a safer road?"

I ignored him as I was too busy looking in the mirror to see if we had been followed, but due to the dust being raised by the pick-up I couldn't see anything! I was just beginning to think we had gotten away with it, when a police vehicle overtook us and began forcing the little pick off the road and I had no choice but to pull over.

I turned the engine off as two armed police officers approached us. I wound the window down as they came up, one on each side of the vehicle. "Wel nou, waarheen is julle op pad (Well, where are you going)?" The thick set police officer asked. I noticed he wore a flak jacket and carried a loaded semi-automatic weapon. I sat very still trying desperately to think of a plausible answer, but in the end simply said, "Ons het verdwaal (we are lost)." He looked at me, raising a very lavish ginger eyebrow, "Identity books asseblief Meneere (Identity books please gentleman)," he said, with an outstretched hand. I leaned over and rummaged in the small glove box, all the time hoping the Colonel would keep quiet until I retrieved my ID document and then handed it over to 'ginger eyebrows'. "Wat van jy(what about you)," he said, directing his look at the Colonel. I replied saying "Hy's dom (he is dumb)," praying that the Colonel would remain mute. "Wat, jy se he kan nie praat nie" (what, are you telling me he can't speak)?" he queried. "Hey moet nogtans 'n ID document besit (he must still have an ID document)." I shrugged adding that I had met him on the road where he had been hitchhiking. 'Ginger eyebrows' flipped through my ID book then clicked on his radio and spoke to someone giving my details. I now knew that we were in deep trouble.

In an unbelievably rash move, the Colonel suddenly wrenched open the passenger door, taking 'Ginger Eyebrows' colleague by surprise and knocking him backwards. The Colonel foolishly ran hell for leather towards the bush. Chaos ensued. The Police shouted for the Colonel to 'halt' unfortunately they did most of the yelling in Afrikaans which the Colonel couldn't understand, so inevitably they resorted to their semi-automatic weapons, firing shots over his head. I sat rigid in my seat, not believing what was happening but the Colonel, in his belief that he was impervious to nine-millimetre shot, carried headlong on with his insanity. The end of the fiasco was never in doubt as 'Ginger eyebrows' now took accurate aim with his semi-automatic rifle and disabled the errant 'escapee' with a judicious shot in his leg. The poor Colonel crumpled and fell, yelling profanities in Spanish. I sat dumbfounded this had all gone so terribly wrong!

Chapter Six

Retribution

The police truck smelt of sick and urine in varying degrees. I was alone, as the Colonel had been taken off in an ambulance after citing the Geneva Convention. I hung on for dear life, trying my best not to wrench my wrist where they had handcuffed me to the rail on the side of the vehicle. I had no idea where we were headed but it was taking ages. 'Ginger eyebrows' had not been ambiguous when loading me into the truck, by saying that I was in for 'Groot Kak' (big shite), and unlike the Colonel I could not claim protection from the much-vaunted Geneva Convention. I struggled to maintain my equilibrium on the metal bench as they drove at breakneck speed around the bends.

Finally, the truck pulled up and I noticed that we at a set of barb wire festooned gates. The driver spoke to the guard on the gate, and it was rolled back manually, the truck drove through and arrived at a second set of gates and again the driver had to offer some sort of validation before being allowed through. Once through we drove a short way to a conglomeration of buildings, which had barred windows. The driver and his passenger now came round and with a copious amount of clinking of mortises, the back door was opened, on squeaking hinges, and one of the police officers climbed in to liberate my stick-like wrists from the hand cuffs. I clambered down, half falling on to the rough ground of a compound. It was bathed in bright orange light from on high security lighting.

I was hustled over to a long concrete building and then along a narrow corridor, before being put into a small cell. The cell was strangely clean with a small iron bedstead attached to the floor and a plastic covered mattress and two grey blankets. In the corner was a toilet and a stainless-steel basin. The door was locked, and I sat on the bed, trying to evaluate where I might be. I had been in the truck for an hour or two, so I presumed I must at least be a hundred miles from where everything had gone wrong near Randfontein. I was still contemplating this when I heard the lock on the door opening and a small mixed-race guard asked if I would like any food, coffee or tea? I was pleasantly surprised and replied that yes, I would like a coffee and whatever food he had to offer. In a short while he returned with a pie and some curled up dry chips, floating in a sea of gravy, along with a large tin mug of steaming coffee. I thanked him in Afrikaans and sitting on the bed I ate every scrap.

An hour or so later he returned, taking the tin plate and mug, and asked if I wanted more coffee. I thanked him, agreed to another coffee and decided to chance it by asking him where I was. He burst out laughing "Wat jy weet nie waar jy is nie (What you don't know where you are?)," he seemed to find it amusing. I shook my head genuinely puzzled and countered, "Nee, ek het gun idee" (No, I have no idea!) "Man," he grinned, with a few missing upper incisors, " jy's in Vlakplaats!" (Man, you are in Vlakplaats !). Chuckling he went off to get my coffee. I slumped onto the bed 'Wow!' I was in serious trouble, as the Vlakplaats farm was used by the Security Services as one of their interrogation centres. My second coffee arrived, and I asked my 'cheerful turnkey' what he thought would happen to me?

"Wel ek weet nie wat jy gedoen het, maar ek glo hulle sal seker eers more-oggend jou ondervra" (Well I don't know what you have done), but they will only question you tomorrow morning), he replied locking the door and went off whistling a gay melody through his gapped teeth. I finished my coffee and had a small wash, then curling up on the mattress with my blankets went to sleep.

I awoke to the sound of the key rattling in the lock, it was my amenable warder. Breakfast was the standard maize meal with coffee. Then after my ebullient jailer went off, I performed my ablutions because he had brought me my toilet bag that had been in the pick-up, so I was able to do a reasonable job.

I waited a few hours in intense apprehension, with diverse scenarios playing out in my fatigued brain. I jumped when I heard the lock turning expecting my gaoler, but instead a familiar dreaded acquaintance stood outlined in the doorway, namely my old interrogator Colonel van Deventer.

"So, Sean, we meet again as I always suspected we would," he smirked, "come, I need some facts from you." He turned and walked away. I wasn't at first sure if I should follow him as I expected some sort of restraint, but down the passage I heard him say, "Well I haven't got all day!" I stumbled down the passage after him, following him through a maze of corridors, the place was a warren. Finally, we came to his office and entering he sat behind his desk and gestured for me to sit opposite him. He shuffled several papers, then looked at me piercingly. "Ja nee (Yes), you have been busy since our last meeting and as you were of interest, we have been watching you." He laughed, "Ja, we knew you were up to something and to be honest were not worried that you were crossing the borders frequently, you were just truly fortunate, or you have become more proficient at going unnoticed." I swallowed but didn't comment. Was he aware that I had been moving other people as well, I thought desperately, and did, he know about Solly? I gazed surreptitiously around the room to see if the hideous Blue Barrel was present, as I knew I didn't intend going in it again! Lightning a cigarette he continued, "No, we were never over worried at what you were up to, but now you are bringing dangerous individuals into this country! The Cuban colonel you have inadvertently delivered to us is certainly of major concern." Blowing smoke over towards me he squinted and added, "You are certainly endangering the lives of many in this country, and this is a gross act of destabilisation and blatant terrorism."

I sat immobile, silently beginning the 'De Profundis'. Was I going to face something worse than the Blue Barrel filled with soap and water?! "So," he went on, "your man Colonel Perez has demanded his rights under the Geneva Convention, which he is entitled to, but they don't apply to you as, even though you are an Irish citizen, you are also a naturalized South African. So, you will face the full penalty of the current terrorism and treason laws. What I need to know are only a few salient facts. Firstly, where were you to deliver him to. Secondly, who gave you your orders, as I doubt your handler Solly is that high up in your subversive organisation?"

I sat dumbfounded, if he knew about Solly this was worrying. I wasn't sure what else he might know. "Don't be shy, Sean," he smiled, but the smile was not reflected in his eyes. "I know many things about your Cadre and its structure." I sighed inwardly, this meant that there were informers in the organization. "I need to know," he resumed, "who gave the instructions for you to collect Colonel Perez?" I knew that there was no way I had the courage or the stupidity to lie to him, so I replied that I had not been told. I explained that I had just recently returned from a break and had been instructed to liaise with the Colonel at the earliest.

Leaning back in his chair and making a steeple with his hands he looked intensely at me, then added, "You know, I believe you, as I don't think they would have trusted you with who had requested your involvement. But assuredly it would have come from a very senior person in your seditious organisation." I shrugged and said, "No name was mentioned, I was just told where to contact the Colonel and to bring him back to the Rand as expediently as possible."

"Ah! Very well, I actually feel a little sorry for you as you have been used and this time there will be no simple court fine. I am afraid you are going to be incarcerated for a substantial term. But you must have known the risks involved so like everything else in life it has consequences." he acknowledged. Leaning forward he said, "I think this will be our last encounter, as you will now be put out of action by your internment. I can't say it's been a pleasure as you have been an annoying, but somewhat competent. We have often wasted resources on you as you were elusive. No matter, you can now contemplate the value of your existence from behind bars." I sat feeling insignificant, but asked in a small voice if I would appear in Court?

"In due course, certainly," he retorted "but that might take a while. You will be held at Pretoria Central Prison until then and due to your charges of acts of terrorism and treason, I am afraid you will not be allowed outside communication." I gaped at him and inquired, "So I won't even be able to contact my family?" "Not personally no, but don't worry. I will make sure they are brought up to date with your demise," he acknowledged.

Standing up he called out and in no time a tall red-haired female entered, "This is Inspector Gertrude Rabie," he said. "She is now your case officer and will be seeing to it that you suffer the full penalty of the law, so'Totsiens'(Goodbye), Sean." Inspector Rabie now handcuffed me and then taking me back to the holding room I had been in, collected my meagre belongings. Then she took me outside into the compound and put me into a small beige sedan, but not before adding leg irons onto my ankles.

She settled herself behind the wheel and drove quickly towards the compound gates.

The gates were opened expediently, and we were on our way. "So Mnr Kennedy, we are on our way to Central Prison where, as a dissident, you will be held with other deluded prisoners like yourself. Otherwise, were we to put you in with the white prisoners, you would be beaten to a pulp." she informed me. I sat awkwardly on the back seat, a million questions going through my mind but not daring to ask any of them, as she was more austere than Colonel van Deventer.

Driving fast and efficiently we were soon on the outskirts of Pretoria. She negotiated the traffic and we arrived at Potgieter Street and then the forbidding entrance to the Prison. The Inspector took me to the reception where all my details were taken. I was fingerprinted and photographed and then my clothes were taken off me. I was thrown a large orange overall, which I was forced to put on, rolling up the legs and arms so my limbs would be visible. I spent the night alone in a small cell, only being offered coffee. The following morning, I was rudely awoken at 5am and, told I was being moved.

I was met once more by the odious red-haired Inspector Rabie, unsmiling and extremely smug. We were soon on the road, and I noticed we were on the N1 heading south. Driving fast we bypassed Johannesburg and all its suburbs, still heading south. Around midday we took the turnoff for a town called Kroonstad, where I was allowed to go to the toilet, with my handcuffs off but still with my leg irons on. Once on the road she provided me with a sandwich and a drink. She had said little on the journey, but now enlightened me that I was going to a prison on west coast in Port Elizabeth adding. "We don't like having too many of 'your sort' in one prison, as your comrades might think of doing something stupid. So that's why you have been moved, it is in the middle of nowhere and you will be happy to know that your 'Comrade' Colonel is also being moved there only, because he is such a high profile individual, he is being moved under armed escort."

Driving through the night we finally arrived at the prison the next morning.

At the prison she booked me in, and I noted that she was well acquainted with many of the staff, as she was greeted enthusiastically by many of the warders. After the preliminaries had been completed, I was taken to a holding cell which had four other inmates, one Xhosa and three Zulus. The first thing they asked me was, "Wie is jy in die tronk(Who are you in the jail)?" I was a little perplexed as I had never been in jail before so couldn't answer. This didn't seem to be acceptable so the tallest, and plainly the 'leader', then said, "So jy's is n 'Franse' (so you are a 'Frans')." I still wasn't sure so thinking he was asking if I was French, I replied in a small voice, "No I am Irish." This puzzled him, so he went and conferred with the other three in Zulu. They discussed me, not aware that I could understand their discussion.

I listened intently as they debated who I might be and what was puzzling them mostly was why I, an 'umlungu' (white person) was put in with them, because European and Africans were normally segregated! The discussion was ended by the arrival of four plates of food which a warder pushed under the thick barred gate. The tall Zulu came over and took charge of all four plates, giving one to each inmate except me. My plate was taken and shared between them. I didn't object but he looked at me and said, "Franse' kry nie n bord nie , jy sal n katkop more oggend kry (Franse don't get a plate, you will get a 'cat head' in the morning." I looked at them not comprehending any of it, except that it was evident I wasn't going to get any supper. Once they finished eating, they took felt type pads that were stored in a corner and laid them out on the concrete floor. Then, taking blankets from another corner they made their beds on the felt pads. I was not given a pad but only a single blanket, as once again I didn't qualify as I was a 'Franse'. I accepted this as there was nothing else to do, so after using the toilet and splashing my face in the stainless-steel basin, I wrapped the dirty, odoriferous blanket around myself and sitting next to the door fell asleep.

In the morning, incredibly early, the door was opened, and we were ordered outside where we were counted, then given a cup of strong black coffee, thankfully sweet, and four slices of brown bread. This was the 'cat head' which I was allowed. Following this small repast, we were put back in the cell. I sat and listened to my four inmates discussing their offences and people that they knew mutually in prison and related topics, but still didn't let on that I understood them. Mid-morning arrived and a white warder came to the gate and called my name. I went to the gate he was young and seemed pleasant and appraised me of my situation. "I have requested that you be moved to the European section, but the Head of the Prison is not authorizing it, as he feels you will be harmed because you will be considered a traitor. I nodded, unable to think of anything to say. "So, "he continued, "I have found a cell for you that might be better, as it has another white 'political' in it. Unfortunately, like the rest of the inmates who have been in before, he is a 'gang member' but that's what happens here." "Gang member?" I queried. "He leaned back on his heels looking amazed, "What, didn't the 'bandities' (Afrikaans word for inmates) in your cell tell you about the gangs?" I shook my head, "They just keep telling me I am a 'Franse'," I replied. He burst out laughing and said, "Well of course you are! Anyone that doesn't belong to a gang is a 'Franse'. I will try get you moved as soon as possible if you are a non-smoker, as the cell is only for non-smokers." I assured him that I had never picked up the habit. "Well, that's all good then 'Irish', so I will make the arrangements," he said walking away.

I had a quick wash, as best I could, but noticed that I had gained a few 'passengers' in the form of lice. This suddenly brought everything home to me, my God! I was in prison and had lice. I had trouble stifling a sob and almost broke down completely, only just regaining control of my emotions when I noticed the four other inmates watching me. The day wore on into the afternoon and I sat desolate at the gate, hoping beyond hope that it was all a bad dream. I was in a semi despairing stupor when the young blonde Afrikaans warder, who I later discovered was called Officer Swanepoel, returned "Irish," he called, "come I have organised you a place in that cell." He unlocked the barred gate and told me to follow him, leading me through a maze of locked gates and corridors until we reached the section where the cell was. Taking me into the section office he introduced me to a tall Officer called "Matroos(sailor)'. "Hier is die okie waar van ek jou vertel het (this is the little guy I was telling you about)." The tall senior officer looked me over, then said "I don't like having vulnerable foreigners in my section, but Officer Swanepoel has assured me you will behave, so I am willing to have you here. You will have no bed for now as the cell is full, but the other white inmate, St Quentin, has assured me you can sleep on a mat next to his bed. He is also a political detainee, so until you are both taken to court you can go there."

Officer Swanepoel now took me down to the cell, which was in effect just a long dormitory. He got to the strong iron gate and called a name. A tall muscular Zulu came over, Officer Swanepoel updated him "This the 'Irish' he is a political detainee and I know that you have another white inmate in your cell, so I thought it best he came here, the head of section, Matroos, has sanctioned the move." The tall Zulu, whose name was Major, looked me over, saying, "We have no bed for him, so he will need to sleep on the floor. Is he a 'Frans'?" I stood mute, so Swanepoel answered for me, "Naturally, but his fellow detainee could possibly help him?" "Ja, alles goed "(yes, all good)" he said. So, Officer Swanepoel used his keys and opened the door, and I went in. The Major took me to his bed, it was right at the top of a line of bunk beds that stretched down to the end of the cell and said "We are thirty-eight, well thirty-nine, now with you so that's nineteen beds. But I will let the other 'umlungu(white man)', who works in the kitchen, explain things to you. He will be back shortly, so just sit here until then."

I sat down on an old sponge mattress that the Major had unearthed from somewhere and noted that the cell had only a few inmates in it and most seemed intrigued by my presence and asked the Major? He replied that, like the other 'Umlungu', I was a 'political' and couldn't be put in with the 'Boer' prisoners as they would injure me. All this was communicated in Zulu, unaware that I was listening intently. One or two were not overly pleased, asking why I had been foisted on them and that I was a 'Frans', and the cell was already full! The Major said he would wait for 'Spike' to come back as he was also a Umlungu but an 'Insizwe' (gang member). I understood everything except the word 'Insizwe,' but now awaited the return of the other white inmate for enlightenment.

Just after lunch the other prisoners returned and with them, Spike. He was tall, around late thirties and good looking. He was surprised to see me and after talking to the Major came over to me saying, "Well, this is a surprise, I thought I was the only European in this section. So, my friend who are you?" I replied, "I am Sean or comrade 'Owl'." Looking me over he replied " Uuum , well Sean this is not a wonderful place to end up and I take it you are not a gang member but a 'Frans '." I wasn't sure how to reply but just nodded. "So", he said "Come over to my bed then 'Owl' and I will try to explain to you how the prison works!"

I sat on his bed, while he busied himself with connecting a kettle to a couple of wires which were next to his bed. "We are not supposed to do this, but we do," he smiled, "and you will learn, if you here long enough, that many things are possible if you have the right connections. I don't suppose you have a mug, but no matter I will borrow one quickly." Going down the cell he returned quickly with a plastic mug, asking how I liked my tea. It was a bit surreal as if we were out for afternoon tea! I sipped my tea, and it was delicious. He looked at me and began by asking what I had done to end up in prison. I wasn't at first sure if I should unburden myself, but as he was a comrade, what would be the harm? So, I decided to tell him everything.

I finished my story and he looked at me and said "Well, I guess I should call you Doc." He acknowledged, as he now was conversant with my sordid history. "That's quite extraordinary and I am happy to meet an actual operative." "I must tell you, "He continued, "my involvement with the 'organisation', is nothing so glamorous. I am what you call one of the 'financial procurers'. What that means is that I arrange funds from overseas, mainly from the Soviets and Chinese, and of course I do a bit of local fraud to fill the A.N.C coffers. Unfortunately, I was let down by a so called comrade and was trapped by the awful detective Gertrude Rabie, or as I like to refer to her as 'Rabbid Rabie'." I chuckled and said. "Well, she is also now my investigation officer." "Ah," he smirked "yes she seems to specialise in us political aberrant types."

"So, Doc," he said "on a more serious note let me explain how things work here. It's a bit complicated, but you need to be careful as many of our fellow inmates are extremely dangerous. Firstly, you will need to join a gang to survive. There are three main gangs, the Twenty Sixes or 'Son-ops' (Sun risers) who deal with all the money that is exchanged illicitly in prison. I am a member of course. Then there are the Twenty Eights or 'Nogolosos' (night workers), they control the 'wives', which are not actually female but younger inmates and finally there are the Twenty Sevens. These are the most dangerous as they usually have more than thirty years to serve and consequently fear nothing!" I stared at him, asking quietly how one would go about joining his 'lot,' the 'Sixes'?

Rubbing his jaw. He replied, "Well it's not that simple. You must have something to offer, either muscle or reputation, which I am afraid it doesn't seem you have!" I thought a bit and then said, "I am an educated man and additionally speak both Nguni languages quite well so would be able to translate and write for them." "What!" he exclaimed. "You speak both Zulu and Xhosa!?" Why didn't you let them know? That changes everything. You are now undoubtedly an asset." I will speak to the Major, and I am sure it won't be a problem. You will naturally, have to 'slaan de wet' (learn the law), but for a man of your intellect it will be a doddle." He got up at once and went down to the front of the cell to chat to the Major. Shortly, I was summoned. The Major sat on his bed, then looking at me with dark eyes asked in Zulu why I had not said I understood their language and had I overheard any conversations? I answered that no one had asked and no I wasn't in the habit of eavesdropping!

"So "he said in Zulu" this umlungu (meaning Spike), tells me you wish to become a Six is this true and that you are prepared to translate and write documents for your fellow members?" I nodded in agreement. "Right" he said. I am a senior officer in the gang, so I will call a 'umhlangano'(meeting) and put it to my brother members. But I don't foresee any problems, as Spike guarantees me that you are not a Big Five (fives were 'grasses' or in Zulu (impimpies)." I assured him that no, I was certainly not an informer. "Well ok, for now you can sleep on the foam mattress on the floor next to St Quentin's (Spikes) bed and I will teach you the 'Law'. Once your membership has been sanctioned by the 'umhlangano' things will improve." I thanked him and Spike and I returned to his bed.

Around three o'clock we were let out, cell by cell, to go to the 'menasie' (kitchen) to get the only true meal of the day. This consisted of maize meal, cabbage and a small piece of chicken. I was allowed to eat it, as the Major had told the other gang members that 'I stood' with the Sixes as an initiate, so I sat with Spike and ate it all. After lunch/supper we were all counted outside our cells, then the cells were locked and 'mastered' which meant that a second solid steel door was closed over the heavily barred iron door. Spike organised for me to have a shower and bought a couple of non-lice ridden blankets for me, and we settled down for the night even though it was late afternoon. We spent it chatting and playing cards with a decrepit pack. I spent the first night, since being arrested, clean and moderately comfortable.

Over the next couple of days, I was instructed by Spike and Major in 'Die wet' (the gang law) which consisted of knowing one's place in the prison and respecting other gang members, both Sixes, Sevens and Eights, when and how to answer when questioned and to take any worries or grievances to a senior officer. Spike spent a lot of time working hard in the kitchens but was always available to help if I asked. After a week I was tested and then officially accepted as a Six. Overall, my fellow inmates treated me like one of their own as soon as they knew I spoke their language and in no time, I was put to work deciphering court documents, which were in Afrikaans, explaining it to them and writing applications for things they required, as the only way one made a request was by a written application. I also discovered that a Catholic deacon came to the Prison once a week, so I was able to meet him and attend a service.

The days went by, and I heard nothing from the repulsive red haired Rabie. But one morning I was called to the head of section Officer Matroos's office. I waited outside until I was summoned. On entering I found him with a short stout female officer. He introduced her as Officer Mzizi and told me that she ran the prison school. Mzizi smiled and said that she was happy to meet me. Under her arm she had a thick yellow folder which she put down on the desk. I saw that it had my name on it. "So, I am told that you are now a gang member," "she enquired, raising an eyebrow. I nodded, as it was pointless denying it. Picking up my file she leafed through it until she found what she was looking for, "It says here that you have two Science degrees," she queried. I looked at her, wondering what else the thick yellow folder held, but again just nodded. "Well," she continued, "I know that, as yet, you are not sentenced, and a high-risk inmate, but as the school is within the prison, I intend to make use of your talents by employing you at the school. It is exceedingly rare that we have a well-educated inmate that also speaks the Nguni languages." Matroos now butted in, "It is also a good thing if you are out working and not thinking about your situation in the cell all day." Officer Mzizi continued, "So tomorrow at seven o'clock, when they call 'school' I want you to assemble with the students and come to the school. I will get you to help with the Biology, Agriculture and Geography students." I nodded again, as quite honestly there was nothing for me to say. Matroos said, "That's all for now. Make sure you are ready tomorrow morning, you may return to your cell." I left the office and returned to the cell in deep thought. I had never taught anyone, before but then this was a new life. Three o clock arrived and with it the return of the workers and students and Spike. Once we had collected our only meal and were sat on his bed eating it, I updated him on my visit to the office. "Well Doc," he mused, "it is a good thing as it breaks up the day. That's why I took the kitchen job and as we never know when and where we are going before a judge or a court, we might as well just get on with it." I felt better as he was well informed and respected in the Prison.

The following morning, I exited with the students and after being body searched, we all marched off in twos to the school. On arrival at the school, we all assembled in a quad. I watched as different classes were called and the respective students went onto their classrooms, until I was the solitary inmate left. The warder who had been calling the different classes now called out to me, "Wat is jy dom (what are you stupid)?" He came storming over to me and I could see he was peeved, and I braced myself for a tirade. He was about to begin when Officer Mzizi called out to him, saying in Zulu, that I was a tutor and not a student! He calmed down and was notably subservient and asked me why I had assembled with the students when I was a tutor? Mzizi called us both over and explained to him that this was my first day and I was unaware of the procedures. He shrugged, saying to Mzizi that she would know where to find him and disappeared.

Officer Mzizi, smiling, took my hand and said, "Don't worry about him. Once you are in school, you will be treated with respect by both student inmates and officers. I will not have it any other way" she emphasised. "In the school you will call me Madam Sweetie as all the other teachers do. We only have one other inmate teacher, also a white man and a pedagogue in the outside world. You will meet him at break time. Come, I will show you your classroom." Leading the way, we went to a small classroom in the corner of the quad. We entered and what struck me was how quiet and disciplined the awaiting students were. Madam Sweetie addressed them, "Class this is Sean, who is to be your Biology and Agriculture tutor. He is very aptly qualified by not only having a Bachelor of Science majoring in the biological sciences, but also, he is a qualified veterinary surgeon. So, I expect you all to give him your utmost cooperation!" The students, in unison, said good morning to me in English. I replied in Nguni, thanking them, and said that I would do my best to help them. Madam Sweetie Mzizi seemed extremely pleased with this and then said that if I needed anything from her, I was to go to her office in the quad then she left closing the door behind her.

I turned to the students noting one or two familiar faces from my cell, most notably the Major. I went over to the desk at the front of the classroom and picking up the biology textbook asked where they were up to. The Major, who was obviously the senior gang member, answered that, as they had not had a regular Biology tutor, they had only just progressed past the construction of cells, both animal and plant. I paged through the book and was dismayed to see that it was the first chapter, but undaunted I began to question them to see how much they knew of the cytoplasm and nuclei? It turned out not much, but I think not out of ignorance, but because no one had explained it to them. So, I set about teaching them basic cell morphology.

The morning flew by and soon the bell rang for morning break. My students picked up their books, thanked me and began to leave. The Major stopped at my desk and looking at me said, "We have learnt more this morning about cells than we have the last couple of weeks. I will see you in the cell, as I still have a few questions." I nodded and replied that I was glad that I had managed to clarify things. "Siyabonga (we thank you)" he said and left.

I sat at the desk and eating my few slices of bread which I had brought with me, I thought that a cup of coffee would be appreciated. I was still musing on this when my door opened and a tall gangly European came in, he had a moustache and smiling stuck out his hand. "So, you must be our new Sciences tutor? I can tell you we are all relieved, as Madam Sweetie and I have struggled a bit with trying to help them. So, you are a God send. We were expecting a qualified warder anytime, but up to now there has been no sign of her or him." He noted I was eating dry bread and exclaimed, "Good Lord man, you don't have to have your break here. Come with me to the tutors room where there is tea, coffee and usually biscuits!" I followed him with alacrity, finding out on the way, that his name was Lukas and he taught English, both language and literature as well as history and mathematics.

He led me to a small room where we found Madam Sweetie and two other Officer teachers who taught the technical subjects at the school. I was introduced to all and was surprised at how readily they accepted me as an equal, even though I was an inmate awaiting trial. I had two glorious cups of coffee and a few biscuits before returning to my classroom to tackle the subjects of Agriculture and Geography.

Two o'clock came around in no time and we were called to assemble in the quad again to be counted. Only this time, Lukas drew me to one side so that we stood apart and then, only once everyone was searched did we leave the school and tramp back to the Prison. Lukas told me on the way that as he was not a gang member, he was incarcerated in the European prison adjacent to our facility and had a single cell where he said it was much more private and as I was now a tutor, I should apply for one. I thought for a moment and then said that I would think it over, but as I was still awaiting trial, I would see how things went.

I arrived back in the cell and was told that the Major needed to see me, so dropping all the accoutrements of my new occupation, I hastened to his bed. "So," he said, "as you are now my tutor in both Biology and Agriculture, I am going to give you the bed on top of your friend, St Quentin." I was puzzled as I knew the cell was full of no spare beds, that is why I was forced to sleep on the floor on a piece of sponge. The Major went on, "I would also like you, please, to help me in the evenings as we have not had a tutor for a while. I would like to pass the final exams in a month or two." I nodded and replied that I would be happy to help him once we had been locked up in the afternoons.

I went back to Spikes bed to find he had returned from the kitchens and was looking a bit bemused because the bed above him was empty. He saw me and asked me if I knew where Zitolele (the inmate who had been in the bed above him) was? I sat down with a sigh and repeated the conversation I had just had with the Major. Spike looked at me then smiled saying, "That's great news Doc, that'll make your life a lot more tolerable. Get your stuff off the floor and put it on the top bed." I did as he said but was disquieted as to what had happened to Zitotlele. Spike brewed us a cup of coffee and we sat on his bed. I asked him, "What do you think has happened to Zitotlele?" Spike blew the rising steam from his mug, then answered in a quiet voice "You do know who the Major is in the Prison, don't you?" I nodded saying that I knew he was an officer of the 'Hosh'-Sixes-. Spike nearly choked and with a hiss replied, "He is not just an officer, he is the 'Major' and there is no one higher in rank in this institution. What he decrees is what happens in this place, so I would imagine that is why you now have Zitoleles bed!" I gulped my coffee, contemplating this news, when suddenly, I heard my name being called from the door. I hurried over and found Officer Swanepoel there. He smiled and unlocking the door told me to go with him. I followed him at a trot. He led me through another section and on to a cluster of buildings, which he said was reception and the stores. On arrival he told the Officer in charge who I was, "Ah ilunga lezigelekeqe eziMhlophe "(Ah, the white gang member)", he shouted out to one of the prisoners who worked there, and they brought out a brand-new foam mattress, blankets and sheets. The officer gave them to me and Swanepoel and myself made our way back. On the way Officer Swanepoel said, "Well Irish, you have made a few powerful friends, as it is not everyone that gets new bedding from the stores. Well done you." He returned me to our cell, and I traipsed back to my bed with the new mattress and bedding.

Spike came to help me put the new mattress on the bed above him saying, "Well Doc, you will now be a bit more comfortable." Later after we had been fed, counted, and locked up, I was called once again to the Majors corner. He asked if I was happy with the new arrangements? I thanked him saying that I was, but was perturbed as to what had happened to Zitotlele? He laughed and updated me, "Don't worry, Zitotlele went to court this morning and will not be returning, he won his case." This consoled me as I no longer felt guilty for taking another poor inmate's bed. I spent an hour or so helping him with the biology homework I had set them, then returned to my now 'luxurious' bed.

Chapter Seven

Compliance

Life settled down to a routine. Only once was I contacted by the rude Inspector Rabie. She came to question me on a few details regarding Colonel Perez, but luckily Spike had recommended the best course of action, namely, to feed her spurious information which we had sat devising late into the night. Together we had invented little snippets of information which Spike suggested might lead her and the scary Colonel van Deventer astray. Strangely enough she visited us both on the same day, which helped as I was second on her list, so I had time to rehearse our plan.

Grand-pere Jacques had also sent me a letter, telling me that the Catholic Chaplin had contacted him. So at least my 'family' in Swaziland knew of my fate. In it, he told me that he was doing his best to organise me a defence but noted that finding someone in the legal profession in South Africa willing to defend me was not an easy matter. But he had contacted my 'brother' Sambulo, who was willing to do his best for me. Fortunately, he had also sent a fair bit of money to the prison for me, so although I was unable have it in my possession, it was credited to my account so I could use it at the prison shop once a week. It was a significant help as although I didn't need much from the shop, I could buy goods to trade with other inmates for such things as chicken and vegetables (purloined by prisoners from the poultry unit and the farm at the prison). The Major had an illegal electric frying pan which he allowed us to use now and then so that Spike could make use of his culinary expertise.

Officer Matroos had also 'pressed ganged' me into going to his office on Saturday mornings to sort out his paper and administration work, which though tedious often allowed me to glean bits of information which might be important to the gang, such as intended cell spot searches, allowing us inmates to rid the cell of the illicit electric cables and equipment. This not only stopped stuff being confiscated, but also prevented my fellow gang members being charged. This enhanced my standing within the gang hierarchy.

On most weekends the white Officer Swanepoel and his European officer friend Human were on duty and occupied the section office, so it was inevitable that I became friendly with them. I was surprised that they bore me and Spike no ill will, only saying that we were deluded thinking that the government would ever be brought down by a 'ragtag 'organisation like the A.N.C.! I imagine they believed the propaganda that was constantly being espoused by their European only elected democracy. Working away most Saturday mornings in the office with them was usually entertaining, as both were genuinely good people. Human sported a flamboyant beard and moustache and was married. He often made fun of his spouse and painted a picture of her being warty and unattractive and a bit of a martinet, that was until he showed me a picture of her and his two children one day. She was most certainly not as he had described but quite attractive. Swanepoel conversely was single but said that all the local eligible farm girls were boring and mediocre, so he had decided that he would import himself a gorgeous blonde Russian wife that he had seen in a magazine! The magazine was brought in so that Human could pass some sort of approbation and obviously as I was in the office, trying to make head or tail of Officer Matroos' paperwork, I was asked to pass comment. I voiced my opinion that indeed the young lady was veritably incredibly beautiful, but that didn't necessarily mean that she would be good wife material. Human, stroking his manicured moustache, asked how 'Swane' was going to communicate with this 'paragon of perfect pulchritude' that he intended to marry.

Swane smiled and replied that she only needed to understand a few English and Afrikaans words, these being – 'come to bed' and 'clean' and 'cook'. Human burst out laughing advising his good friend that undoubtedly, she would be good for one of the intended 'purposes' but not all, or that she would want to feed him good Russian food which would not be to his taste. I sat at the desk amazed at their palpable chauvinism. Did they really believe that women had only those attributes? Human now asked my opinion so, after having another look at the truly lovely Russian girl, I suggested that Swanepoel should also consider the young lady's feelings and aspirations, as she was undeniably looking to escape difficult living conditions in her home country and did, he understand that her ideology would, without question, be pervaded by a socialistic outlook. "Wat" (What!) Swanepoel burst out, "You mean she will be a 'contaminated communist'!" I nodded explaining that would undoubtedly be the situation. Human found this hugely amusing, declaring that the Department of Home Affairs would never allow her into the country as they already had problems with the likes of me. I digested this thinking that no, I didn't think I was a socialist. I knew that the 'Organisation' did have a socialistic bias, but that didn't mean I did. I had only become involved due to circumstances and all I believed in was a true democracy, where everyone had the right to make choices. Obviously, I didn't voice this.

Swanepoel now looked at the magazine again and after obviously pondering on what I had said, sighed. I could see that he was in no small way infatuated with the idea of having a beautiful, exotic foreign bride. He looked a tad devastated, so I said, "Well perhaps as she wants to come here, she might not have any ideology, but is only looking for someone to look after her and love her." Human found this amusing and added, "Swane my ou maat(Swane my old friend), it doesn't matter where they are from, all women are the same. In no time you will be dancing to her tune, especially a girl like that with manifest 'assets.' You will be putty in her hands." Swanepoel in true testosterone induced chauvinism replied, "Never! She will do as I say and be subservient to my every wish. You will see, I will teach her the important things. You are both just envious." Human looked at him, shaking his head and commented, "Oh my friend, you are so naive as to the machinations of the opposite sex. I can't wait to see the outcome. What do you think Irish?" he asked me. I looked sheepishly at him not daring to tell them that my experience of ladies was exceedingly limited, so simply said that I thought all girls and women were simply amazing. Swanepoel looked at me with genuine concern and said, "Wel dis n skanda (well that's a shame) I feel truly sorry for Irish, as it looks like you will be an old man before you are free to have contact with any of them!" "Ja nee," (Assuredly), Human commented smoothing his luxurious beard, "it is a shame Irish, but you should consider getting a prison 'wife'" Swanepoel found this hilarious and added, "Ja(yes), a young boy might be the answer after all Irish!"

I finished updating the weeks inmate movements in the register and closing it said to them, "Firstly I am not a Twenty-eight but a Six, so that would cause me problems with my gang. But more importantly it is abhorrent, and I would never ever consider it!" They both looked at me and I could see they were embarrassed, then Human came around my side of the desk and put his arm around my shoulder saying, "We were only fooling with you Irish don't take it to heart." Smiling, Swanepoel added, "That's right Irish, we were only pulling your leg. We both think you are a good man and even though you have not been here too long, you are already well liked by your fellow inmates and officers, you have a decent job at the school and are helping prisoners to better themselves. I think you must accept that this is your new life and forget about the outside world." "Ja (Yes)," Human confirmed, "possibly this is your destiny Irish, and it could be worse, you don't have any concerns on how to make a living and unlike our friend Swane, don't have to contend with women folk which, believe me, can be a blessing. Watch and see how his little 'Russian Ruby' wraps him around her little finger. Believe me there is nothing more hilarious than an infatuated man," and finding his own comment amusing, spluttered "she will have him 'goose stepping' around his house like a true Cossack!" Swanepoel smiled and replied, "Nee my friend (no my friend), the only 'stepping' to be done will be by her, straight to my bed."

I got up from the desk and asked if either would like a coffee as Officer Matroos had a kettle and cups in the office, and I often made coffee for him. They accepted readily, so I made the coffee while they carried on arguing about the complexities of women!

Later I returned to the cell in deep thought, was I here for the rest of my life? But I decided not to worry about it until I had discussed it with Spike. Later that evening after we had settled down to play cards, I broached the subject with him, voicing my concerns about the 'screws' comments. Spike gave it a little thought then commented, "Well Doc, they don't envisage the bigger picture. For them, the Nationalist government they support and have voted in is omnipotent. There is no way they can accept that it can be brought down. I do not dispute that it is unquestionably authoritarian and with the State Security Service strangle hold on all those that question the system, you and I are examples of their prowess, but inevitability they will fail as one cannot suppress the people forever." I nodded agreeing with him but asked, "So do you think that we will be here a very lengthy period?" Smiling he said, "I wouldn't worry about it Doc, we have yet to be convicted and as you know life is strange and anything can happen." Standing up he stretched his lengthy frame continuing, "For the moment we are coping, we both have reasonable jobs in the prison and are 'Son-ops' (Six gang members) of good standing, so it's best not to worry about it and just take one day at a time. We will be vindicated." I packed up the well-worn cards and we both climbed into our beds to sleep the slumber of the 'unjust.'

The year wore on, and I settled into a routine. Officer 'Sweetie' at the school had now requested my help in the everyday running of the school, so when I wasn't tutoring, I was doing her paperwork. I was now receiving regular finances from Grand-pere via the Catholic Chaplin, which went along way to making Spikes and my lives more comfortable. My 'friendly' officers Swanepoel and Human were on most weekends, and they helped me by bringing in small luxuries such as fresh fruit and toiletries, which were appreciated. I found them both empathetic and even though they were 'Screws' I counted them as friends.

Christmas arrived and the school closed, so, as I now ran the school library, I made sure I brought boxes of books back to the cell, so that we would have something to read over the break. Spike unfortunately did not get the break, in fact his shifts seemed to increase, but we still had the time from three o'clock in the afternoon when we were locked up, until five o clock the following morning, so we discussed many topics and our earlier lives, which whiled away a lot the time. Officer Matroos, now seeing that I was around in the day, utilised me every morning to do his paperwork. So, in effect I was kept busy. Christmas Day arrived and apart from it being extremely hot it was like most other days, except that instead of the usual staple maize meal all the prisoners were given rice! What joy, a rare treat and additionally every prisoner received an extra piece of fruit. On the downside we were locked up earlier but, as my two friendly 'screws' had been on over the days running up to the festive season, I had ensured that they had brought in a plethora of chocolates and sweets.

The inmates also had not been idle, many had secreted extra fruit and with the sugar which was smuggled in they brewed up buckets of 'hooch'. So once the doors had been double locked a small party ensued with many, I think, having to retire to their beds early.

The new year arrived, and it was seen in, in our cell, with even more imbibing of illicit liquor. I noted that the African psyche is more optimistic than that of the Europeans. Many of my fellow inmates were serving lengthy sentences but still they found happiness in their 'new lives.' Spike and I spent a quiet retrospective day discussing what we would have been doing had we not been incarcerated. Poor Spike had children, so I suspect it was a lot harder for him. I felt a little maudlin thinking on what Grand-pere and Hetty must be thinking of me but more importantly the Faulkner's, especially my fiancé, Suzanne. She must be rueing her decision. The more I thought on it the more determined I became to get some sort of communication through her, to tell her simply to forget about me as I was a lost cause. I had let all of them down badly and I recalled occasions they had warned me as to what could happen and now it had! The problem was that as Spike and I were political detainees we were not allowed any contact with the outside world for fear of us passing on information to our cadres. But I knew that if I secretly asked the Catholic Chaplin when he came next, he might phone the Faulkners and relay on my decision.

At the next meeting of the Catholics for a communion service I drew him one side and asked him if he could help me. He was reluctant at first but when I explained that all I wanted was for them, and more importantly Suzanne, just to forget about me, as I suspected I would not be free for many years, he agreed to it, and he took their telephone number. I thanked him profusely and returned to the cell a little more at ease and later conferred with my mentor Spike. "Well Doc," he said, "as I mentioned before, we have no idea what's going to happen so it is for the best, but life is indeed strange, anything can happen."

The new year got into its stride and the school reopened which gave me far less time to brood on my situation. Of Inspector Rabie (Rabies as we now called her), neither of us heard anything so we were in 'limbo.' I began getting my students ready for their finals which included a lot of revision and I even resorted to doing one-on-one tutoring on the weekends for some of those struggling. Officer Sweetie was impressed and thanked me for going the 'extra mile'. She felt that my knowledge of the Nguni languages had made a significant difference to a lot of the students, as the textbooks were all in English, so my ability to make things clearer was a boon. I would go around the different sections of the prison on the weekend and force officers to open gates and doors for me. At first a lot of them were reluctant, but after Officer Sweetie had used the sharp end of her tongue on them, they soon complied.

The final exams were suddenly on us, with the arrival of independent invigilators and the exam papers. Officer Sweetie buzzed around like an overzealous arthropod trying to ensure that everything went smoothly. I had done my best for the students, having looked at past papers and attempted to prepare them for what I thought would be the obvious questions. The first of my subjects was Geography which in truth I had been the most unprepared for, but my students seemed amazingly relaxed after leaving the examination room. I relaxed slightly when one of the weakest came up and thanked me saying that he had been able to complete most of the questions. A day or two later it was again my turn with the biology exam and once again I had guessed right and most of what I had told them to pay attention to appeared on the paper. Finally, a day later it was

Agriculture, this was by far my biggest subject and had almost double the number of students of either Geography and Biology because I believe many of them were genuinely interested in learning about the land and farming. It was gratifying to see them leave the examination room optimistically, claiming that there had been nothing on the paper we had not covered. It was now just a matter of time before we would be notified of the results.

One morning a few weeks later I was summoned to Officer Sweetie's office where I found her and the other tutors all present. The results had arrived. Officer Sweetie was in good spirits, so I surmised that it was good news. One by one she went through the subjects and results, doing the languages and mathematics first as these were of paramount importance. Finally, it was the turn of the sciences, and the humanities like Geography. I was overjoyed to hear that not only had all my students passed, many with above average grades, but two of my students had gained distinctions in Biology and Agriculture, one of them being the Major. Officer Sweetie came up and congratulated me giving me a massive bear hug. I was overwhelmed and told her that honestly it had had little to do with me but with the total dedication of my students. Several of the other tutors also congratulated me, saying that I had missed my calling by becoming a vet and should instead be a professional tutor. I felt a little uncomfortable because the students' success had little to do with me, but with their wholehearted attempts to improve their lives. Ironically, prison was the first place they were offered an education, when in the outside world they would have been just trying to survive on a day-to-day basis.

The new school year soon arrived, and we tutors canvassed the cells for candidates. It turned out that the success of my previous students had spread around the prison and so I was gratified to have several prospective students.

The time had flown by. I had now been incarcerated for ten months and I think had accepted my new life. This was all to be turned upside down when one morning Spike was called to court, sentenced and transferred to another prison. I was totally devastated but heard via the gang grape vine that he had received a five-year term which pleased him as he had expected far worse. I was told that once I too had been sentenced, I would also be sent to the same correctional facility in the Cape. A few weeks after his departure I received a letter from him. In it he explained that he was well and that the prison he was in was slightly better than Port Elizabeth. He had gained rank in the gang and was once more working in the kitchens but had been elevated to a position of a cook. He concluded by saying that I should do my best to get my conviction over with so that I could be moved there with other convicted politicals.

I decided that I needed to get something sorted out as I was being forgotten, so I asked the Catholic Chaplin to contact Grand-pere Jacques to nudge my solicitor into some sort of action. The result of this was that one morning I was called to the Prison admin block and to the Assistant head of Prison, Officer Jacobs, office. On entering I found him with a smartly dressed young man and a dark curly haired lady. Assistant Head Jacobs introduced them as a Mr O'Laughlin and Ms Kelly from the Irish Embassy. I could see that he was obviously unsettled by their appearance in his prison. He began by saying, "This is your man, and I am sure he will be happy to report that we are treating him well in the circumstances." All three looked at me, Assistant Head Jacobs obviously wanting me to confirm that this was the case, and the two Embassy staff also wanted some sort of affirmation. I paused, lost for words initially but then said that yes, I was coping in a manner of means due to the support of my gang.

"Gang! Jesus, Mary, and Joseph," Ms Kelly lamented, "you mean you are a gang member?" Assistant Head Jacobs got up from behind his desk in a rush, his hands fluttering like an inebriated policeman directing traffic, "Oh it's just a little thing the inmates' getup to," he explained, smiling ingratiatingly. "It's nothing serious." Nothing serious I thought, he had to be joking. Without a gang you were nothing in his institution and would struggle to survive! The two Embassy staff looked at me expectantly and I could see that explaining to them how the prison worked would not further my cause in the slightest as there would undoubtedly be repercussions for me, so I said that no, I was being looked after reasonably well by all the prison staff. Jacobs sat back down, plainly relieved that I had not portrayed his prison in a poor light.

Mr O' Laughlin asked if there was anything that they could assist me with, and did I have a good defence counsel and was I able to stay connected with my people? I assured them that Grand-pere had engaged a solicitor to act for me, but up to now I had had no contact with him. Ms Kelly didn't seem overly pleased with this and commented, "Assistant Head Jacobs, our citizen, Mr Kennedy is charged with treason. I would have assumed by now he would have at least been arraigned before a court, but now he hasn't even had the opportunity to consult with his legal counsel. Can you explain this?" Poor Jacobs seemed at a loss, and wiping perspiration from his forehead with his handkerchief replied, "Ms Kelly, we are at the mercy of his investigating officer and only act as the remand facility. I suggest you take it up with the prosecution service." Ms Kelly didn't seem overly pleased with that but turning to O'Laughlin said, "We will have to investigate this as a matter of urgency," then turning to me asked for Grand-pere Jacques contact details which I happily supplied.

"Well, is there is anything else you would like to ask Mr Keniry?" Jacobs asked once again. Standing up and plainly wishing to bring the meeting to a close, he added, "I have a busy schedule." Mr O' Laughlin looked at me and then asked if there was anything I would like to add or did I have other necessities that they could help with? I shook my head just reiterating that I would like some sort of resolution, as not knowing what was going to happen to me was a worry. Ms Kelly and Mr O' Laughlin then both shook my hand and giving me their Embassy card promised to liaise with Grand-pere Jacques. Assistant Head Jacobs, now noticeably more relaxed, dismissed me and I returned to my section.

Life stayed the same for me for another month or so, an endless repetitive regime of early mornings, school and then back to the section to be locked down by three o' clock. I now shared a lot of my evening time with the Major, either cooking or helping him with his studies.

A decent young Xhosa boy now slept below me, his name was Tembani and he was doing a twenty year 'stretch' for manslaughter. I found him to be a quiet introspective boy who was considerate and inoffensive. One night while we were sitting talking quietly, he explained how he had ended up in the prison. It was the age old 'love triangle' where he and another had both fallen in love with a lovely Xhosa maiden and inevitably it ended up tragically with a knife fight and a dead body. I listened attentively and then, asking a few questions, felt that he had been dealt with harshly as he had had no intention of killing his rival but had only tried to defend himself! I asked if he had appealed his sentence to which he simply shrugged saying that no one had suggested it. I told him to ask Officer Matroos to apply for his case docket so that I could have a look at the evidence that the State prosecution had used to gain his conviction. I told him not to be over optimistic but that it was worth looking at.

A week later a duplicate of his trial docket was given to him and over the next few nights I perused it at length. I discovered that Tembani had been in full time employment of the local council as a skilled labourer, had no previous convictions or any run-ins with the S.A. Police and overall seemed a stable individual living in the local Bantu Township. Conversely his adversary for the affections of the lovely maiden was a known recidivist who had more than one conviction for violence, but as Tembani had had no legal representation, no one had brought this to the attention of the judge. I decided that there were grounds for an appeal on the sentence. I drafted a letter to that effect, requesting the necessary forms to apply for an appeal.

The forms came and I completed them with as much legal jargon that I could glean from the few legal books in the library. I was surprised at the response, as it was only a couple of weeks before they were returned informing Tembani that the case had now been forwarded to the appeal Court. Tembani was overjoyed and spread it around the section that he hoped for a lessening of his sentence. I reminded him that he should not be over optimistic.

It took another six weeks before we heard anymore but then one morning Tembani was informed that he should not leave the section to go to his workplace, the Carpentry Shop, as he needed to attend a consultation with the Parole staff. So, when I left for school, he was happily preparing himself for the meeting. I made sure that he understood that even if it was unwelcome news and that his appeal had been dismissed, he would have lost nothing. He smiled and giving me the 'Six' salute said "Aish Lungwan (Aish small white person) I know it will be good news." I nodded but left for the school in a mildly trepidatious state.

I spent the day wondering how he was getting on as I felt that if his appeal had been dismissed, he would be disappointed. On my return to the section, I found a beaming Tembani. Before I had put my bag down, he clapped me on the back and told me that the board had told him that his sentence had been reduced by five years to a fifteen stretch and as he had already done nine of those, he would be eligible for Parole in a year or two. To say that he was overjoyed would be an understatement, he went around the cell telling anyone who would listen.

The upshot of this success was that I now had many fellow inmates requesting me to investigate their convictions, which not only took a lot of my free time, but I also discovered that many of my fellow prisoners had committed frightening offences.

In one instance a pastor had fallen out with his wife. He arrived home to find his wife and his mother-in-law sitting having a coffee and in endemic Xhosa culture he had demanded that his spouse at once see to his needs. She, feeling she had the extra support of her mother, told him to wait. This did not sit well with him and incensed he went outside, picked up the chopping Axe and returning to the house promptly killed both spouse and mother-in-law! I was naturally appalled but did not admit it to anyone as he was quiet and well liked and scheduled prayers in the cell every night. I felt that the court had been very lenient in sentencing him, giving him only eighteen years. When he approached me to appeal the decision, I tried, vainly, to persuade him that it was not a promising idea, as sentences could not only be reduced on appeal but also increased. In his mild manner he told me that no, I was to go ahead as he felt he had done nothing amiss. I was apprehensive and approached the Major, who as the senior 'officer' of the Sixes, to persuade the 'Umfundisi (Pastor)' not to go ahead as it could be disastrous. I know he did talk to the Pastor, but that also had no effect, and the upshot was that I submitted the appeal.

The resultant outcome was unfortunately as I predicted, the appeal Court increased his sentence by six years. I expected the ' Umfundisi' to be apoplectic, but he simply shrugged saying that it had still been worth it. I was amazed at his resilience!

A further consequence of my limited success in these legal affairs was that on one Saturday afternoon I was called to a council of the Twenty Sixes hierarchy. I was anxious as in most instances when a member was called before an 'umkhandla'(Council) it was for disciplinary action, which often resulted in the poor individual being given 'lashes' with a makeshift cosh. I entered the darkened cell to see six of the gang's top 'officers' seated behind a provisional bench. I noted that the Major was the senior presiding officer. Clearing his throat, he addressed me. "Well, Isikhova, it has been decided by this council of officers that you have behaved honourably as a member, by helping other members with their legal affairs. So, if you are prepared to learn more of the 'law' you will be given a junior officers rank." I was astounded but quickly accepted their decision with a muted "Thank you." That night in the cell the major began instructing me on the further aspects of 'die wet' (the law) which was expected of a junior officer.

Life continued but now I was given a lot more respect by members of the gang. This was noted by my friendly 'Screws'– Swanepoel and Human, who jokingly suggested I had sold my 'arse' for sex. I was also now on occasion called to sit with other Six officers on councils and decide on disciplinary actions, which I did not enjoy.

Early one morning I was called to the administration offices and told that I was to make myself available for an interview with the hateful Inspector Rabie. I waited outside in a small yard in the admin block, in the hot sun, until late morning when finally, I was called into one of the small visiting rooms. I found the repugnant rangy red-haired Inspector sitting smugly behind the desk with a thick file in front of her. I noticed her 'raptor' like nose twitched when I entered the room.

Shuffling through the folder, she spat "So you are getting on well in prison. They should never have let you be housed with your 'Kaffir Boeties' (Kaffir brothers), you should be in the European section where you would be getting a beating daily."

I was shocked at her audacity and the maliciousness of her tone but tried not to show it.

The Inspector continued, "I have had contact with your embassy staff and they, with your legal representative, are pushing for some sort of resolution in your case. It is making my life difficult as we intend to bring you before the highest court in the land, with your co-accused the Cuban military officer."

I stared at her as I was unaware that I even had a co-accused but obviously, to persuade the court to dispense a more severe sentence, it was logical that they would associate me with what they deemed a highly dangerous insurgent.

Sorting through the papers in my file she added, "Consequently, you and he will be taken from this prison in the next couple of weeks to the supreme court in Bloemfontein where we will start your trial. The trial will be lengthy as the state has several witnesses to call."

I sat back, again the news that Colonel Perez was also in prison was quite a surprise. He must be being held in a solitary super secure section.

Looking at me, she clearly expected some sort of response, but I could think of nothing to say. So, getting up abruptly, she left with a parting jeer, "Next time I see you, it will be in the dock. I hope you enjoy the experience!" The interview room door slammed behind her, and I waited for a screw to take me back to my section.

The following day I informed Officer Sweetie that it looked like I would be attending court in Bloemfontein shorty.

She nodded and said while there I would be held in the police cells, but once sentenced, she would request that I be returned to Port Elizabeth as I was an integral part of her teaching team.

I wasn't sure if this was a good or sad thing as I had hoped to join Spike in the Cape facility, but on the other hand I was well known in the prison and got on well with my fellow inmates. I also told Officers Swanepoel, Human and Matroos. Matroos reiterated Officer Sweeties sentiments that he would ask that I be returned to Port Elizabeth and his section. Swanepoel and Human commented that this would in all likelihood be the outcome, as the Prison was a maximum secure facility. Human jokingly added "Don't worry Irish we will keep your bed and things open for you to return to, once you have 'picked up' your fifteen years plus." Swanepoel laughed and added, "Never mind, at least you will know what's to happen to you and then get on with your sentence."

Chapter Eight

Liberation

The day arrived for the trip to the Bloemfontein Court, and I was taken to reception for six o'clock to be processed and then put in a 'cage' with the other inmates going to Court. I was surprised to see Colonel Perez in the cage, he looked remarkably well but in a foul humour. He shouted at the warders that he was not a common criminal to be treated this way, saying that he was a P.O.W and should be treated as such. The staff just jeered at him and told him to save it for the court. In all, we were four prisoners going to the Bloemfontein Court and one or two of these recognised me and asked who the other 'umlungu' '(white person) was? I told them he was a Cuban Colonel and my co-accused. "Yebo, kodwa ucabanga ukuthi ungbani" (Yes, but who does he think he is)? I explained to them that he believed he should be treated differently, as he didn't think he was like us.

Finally, the truck came and after we all had our leg irons and handcuffs put on, we were loaded. Once again, the Colonel protested vehemently but the three Policemen simply ignored him. I reckoned that it would be a lengthy trip as Bloemfontein was easily a thousand miles away. The day wore on with intermittent stops, where we were allowed one by one, shackled to a policeman, to relieve ourselves.

The truck struggled up through the Stormberg mountains and onward to our overnight stop in Cradock, where we were put in police cells overnight. The following morning, we took the road to Steynesburg and onwards through Norvalspoort. The truck ground on and I was beginning to lose my sense of direction and was in a semi stupor when suddenly pandemonium erupted. There were gunshots and the truck skidded and slewed into a ditch on the side of the road. It rolled over on its side and there were more gunshots. In the back we had all fallen on the one side and were scrambling to get our balance, when suddenly there was a gunshot at the back door, the door swung open and three Africans in camouflage dress with masks on bawled at us to get out. Chaos ensued, with a lot of shouting and threatening by the Africans in camouflage kit. We were told to lie on the road face down and I saw that the policemen were already lying prostrate on the road. One of the camouflaged gunmen asked, "Which of you whites is Colonel Perez?" The Colonel tried to stand up but was pushed back down and told to wait while another of the camouflaged men went to the policemen and demanded his keys for the leg irons and handcuffs.

I lay on the hot tarmac, my mind in turmoil. These assailants were obviously anti-government forces, so they were likely 'Umkhonto we Sizwe' soldiers or mercenaries hired by the A.N.C. With a considerable shouting of orders, one by one we were unshackled, and our leg irons and cuffs removed, but still told to remain face down and not to move. The policemen were cuffed and shackled together and put into the overturned prison truck. The leader of the group now again asked who Colonel Perez was and the Colonel stood up. The leader then told one of the others to take him to their 4X4 vehicle parked a little way off. The rest of us stood up dusting ourselves off and looked at our 'rescuers' and one of the prisoners asked what was to happen to us? The camouflage dressed leader told us that he didn't know, and he only had orders to liberate Colonel Perez and take him with them. I tried to tell him that I was integrally connected to the Colonel and was the one who had brought him across the border. He looked at me, but then started walking away to their vehicle. He turned and addressed us all, "I imagine a deluge of police are going to arrive shortly, so either you wait and be re-arrested and appear in court, or you run and disappear. The choice is yours. We only came for the Colonel!" Moving quickly, he and his squad, with Colonel Perez, got into their vehicle and with a roar of the powerful motor they sped off down the road.

I watched them drive away, thinking that they had been truly fortunate that no other traffic had been on the road. But it was good luck all round, otherwise there may have been casualties. One of my fellow prisoners was elated and clapping his hands ran off into the veld. Another didn't seem that happy and said that he would win his case and be acquitted, so he saw no reason to be an escapee and be a man on the run and went to the police van and tried to free the shackled policemen.

I had a moment of indecision, should I go on the run or alternatively face the prospect of fifteen-odd years' incarceration. It didn't take long, and I decided that I was free right now and wished to remain so, so I simply walked off into the veldt. I had only been on the move around twenty minutes and had not put too much distance between the ambushed truck and myself, when in the distance I heard the wailing of sirens and the roar of engines. Ominously, in the distance I also heard the 'wup wup' of helicopter blades. I ran as fast as I could for a clump of trees that I had been aiming for, reaching them just in time as an Alouette helicopter came scudding across the veldt moving swiftly. I recognised it as an Air Force helicopter. I had encountered them frequently patrolling the borders and I knew that unquestionably it was on the lookout either for the prison truck, or more likely one of the prisoners had helped the shackled policemen to use the radio in the truck. I reached the line of trees and tried to conceal myself from view. The trees snaked around a river, which I later learnt was the Orange river, so I sloshed through the shallows thinking that there would be a substantial man hunt for those of us that had decided to 'leg it' and the police would make use of tracker dogs.

I stood motionless under a canopy of branches as I heard the Alouette make another sweep along the road and then over the veldt. Once again, I was deeply indebted to my brothers, Mandla and Sambulo, because we had regularly hidden and tried to track one another and stealth and concealment came naturally to me. It was now getting towards late afternoon, and I knew I would need to put as much distance as I could between myself and where the incident had occurred. Consequently, it would be preferable to do it in the dark. I moved cautiously along the river, as it flowed westerly. I was grateful that as an un-convicted prisoner I had been allowed to wear my own clothes and boots to the court and not the prescribed orange attire that I normally wore in the prison. I trudged along the riverbank keeping close to as much of the concealing foliage as possible. I noticed a few farms along the way, but fortunately it was mostly fields that stretched down to the river and the farmhouses and buildings were a good distance away.

The day wore on and soon the sun slunk below the horizon in the west, and I hoped for a dark night. On and on I went not daring to stop. Of the helicopter, I no longer heard anything and thankfully the only thing to cause me any worry was the barking of a couple of farm dogs. These initially paralysed me with fear as I thought they could be Police or Defence force tracker dogs, but then I realised that they were not coming any nearer, so I deduced they were just farm dogs. I stumbled into a few small antelope, Spring buck, who had come to the river for a drink, and they went bounding off into the dark. But I was not sure who had been more scared and for a few moments I struggled to get my limbs under control.

I moved on as expediently as I could in the dark. Thankfully the moon, when it did appear, was a small sickle shaped waxing one giving off just a glimmer of light. I stopped once to have a drink from the river and then noticed that the sky was a shade lighter in the east and that dawn was not too far off. The sun rose brilliant and warming, and I cautiously made my way along the widening river. I used what tree and river foliage was available but decided that, if dogs were deployed, an entry and a long swim would be advisable to disguise my scent. The river ran north-westerly so I took off my Veld boots and, tying the laces around my neck and stuffing my socks in my trouser pockets, I waded in up to my waist and then sloshed my way along the edge of the river. It was a lot slower going, but I reasoned that while in the water I was leaving no spoor and certainly this would prevent me being tracked by any dogs.

The morning wore on in glorious sunshine, a Southern, Yellow-Billed Hornbill called out in a piercing cry, and I was captivated by its striking yellow bill which stood out against its grey speckled feathers. I watched as it glided between heavy wing beats, just above the sparking water. It epitomised freedom and I revelled in mine. Even if I were recaptured, it would make little difference to my ultimate sentence. Colonel van Deventer and Inspector Rabie had already decided that my minimum term would be extensive, so I sorely needed a plan to get myself out of South Africa and back to Swaziland.

I trudged on and heard, in the distance, the muffled sound of engines. At first, I panicked thinking it might be armoured vehicles, but then by the tone of them I realised they were moving fast. I found a tall tree and climbed up as high in its limbs as possible and was rewarded with the sight of a dual carriage motorway in the distance. This had to be the main trunk route the N1 which traversed the country from Cape Town in the South to Louis Trichardt in the North, close to the Zimbabwe border. It went through Johannesburg and Pretoria, which is where I would want to divert towards Swaziland. I decided it was worth the risk of trying to get a lift along this busy route.

Within the hour I was able to negotiate my way along the side of the motorway without being seen by the passing traffic. I was extremely cautious as I knew they were patrolled by police vehicles, so I had to make sure that I was not foolishly apprehended as a 'hitch hiker'. I lay close to the ground watching the south bound side, until I was able to sprint across it and jump the central reservation and then get across the northbound carriageway. This was not as simple as it would seem as when there was no traffic visible on one side, there were always vehicles on the other side. But after much patience, I was on the northbound carriageway in the undergrowth.

Little by little I tentatively made my way north on the side of the motorway, until I came to a layby where heavy articulated trucks could pull in, either for the drivers to have a rest or occasionally sort out problems, and I found an articulated horse with a double trailer parked. I noticed the driver was busy re-tensioning the tarpaulins that secured his load. The air was blue with his expletives as he was struggling against the wind and could not keep the tarpaulins tight at the same time as securing the fastenings. I sauntered nonchalantly up and asked "Kan ek help Meneer?" (Can I help you Mister), presuming that no doubt he would be Afrikaans. Looking up, still swearing, he answered, "Ja, man hou die vervlakste tou"(Yes, man, hold onto this damn rope). I quickly grabbed the rope and hung onto to it with all my paltry weight. He brought the flapping tarpaulin under control and then told me to tie it to a loop welded under the side of the trailer. I tied it up in a thrice using a clove hitch. Going around the two trailers we did the same, until he was satisfied that the tarpaulins were now secure and would not flap loose as he drove along. Wiping his forehead with the back of his hand, he looked at me as if noticing me for the first time, "Vaar van daan het jy gekom?" (Where did you come from), he now queried. I had had time to think of an answer while we were busy with the tarpaulins so, glibly lied that I had been evicted from my girlfriend's car as we had had an altercation. He burst out laughing, "Wat sy het gestop en jou uitgegooi hier , ek het gun voertuig gesien!?" (What, she stopped and threw you out here, I didn't see a car). I told him that she quickly pulled up and told me to get out and he hadn't seen her because he had been on the opposite side of the trailers. "Ja nee, so wat gaan jy nou doen?" (Yes -now what are you going to do).

I shrugged and tried to look as helpless as possible, "Waarna toe was jy oppad?" (Where were you headed?), he asked. I told him that I lived in a small town, Benoni, on the East Rand, hoping to get to Dick and Sandy's who I hoped would be able to help me with some money. "Nou ja, ek is op pad na Johannesburg so jy kan maar saam ry" (Well I am on the way to Johannesburg so you can ride along with me). I needed no second bidding and hurriedly opened the truck's cab passenger door, just desperately wanting to get off the motor way.

The powerful engine throbbed beneath us and my new friend, who had introduced himself as Dries, changed up through the many gears. I told him my name was James and that I worked as a stores assistant for a well-known East Rand mine but had been on holiday with my girlfriend which unfortunately had not worked out and ended with her dumping me on the motorway. Dries found this very amusing and asked, "Gaan sy nie bekomered wees, nie?" (Is she not going to worry about you). I shook my head replying, "Ek glo nie, dinge het net erger en erger geraak" (I think not, things have been just getting worse and worse). "Ja neef," (Yes cousin), he chucked, "wie kan vrou mensa verstaan?" (Who can understand women). Thankfully, he then broke into a diatribe on the fickleness of women, saying that he had a wife and two young children, but that his wife was always complaining that he was seldom home, but did she not realise that the only way he could provide the lifestyle she desired was by him doing long distance trips. I nodded in sympathy and support, saying that I was sure he was doing his best. This spurred him on, and he chatted away happily about his family, which suited me admirably.

The truck rumbled on, and the comfort and hum of the engine was soporific, so having not slept in the last twenty-four hours, I nodded off. I was awoken by voices and rousing myself out of my slumber I noticed we were stopped at a toll booth and Dries was busy speaking to the assistant. I rubbed my face and apologised for falling asleep. Dries smiled and said it was fine, finished his business with the lady assistant and putting the heavy truck into gear we moved through the toll gate, but not far because just on the other side there were a considerable number of blue flashing lights, and my heart sank. It was a roadblock. I noted that this one was staffed by both the Police and the military. Dries moved along slowly till we came up to the Army Officer in charge of the operation. He looked up at us but then, seeing the livery of the well-known transport company on the door, said, "Julle kan maar aan ry , ons is eintlike opsoek na a klomp bandita wat ontsnap het" (you can drive on, we are looking for a group of escaped prisoners). I could feel my nails digging deep into my palms as I clenched my hands in dismay, but Dries told him that no, we had seen no 'swartes' (blacks) on the road and then going on up a gear we moved off. For once I was relieved that most white South Africans believed all miscreants were African.

Driving on through the day we reached Johannesburg in the late afternoon and as Dries was heading for one of the

Industrial estates in the Western suburbs, I asked him to drop me off in the small village of Eikenhof, which was both close to the motorway and to the Asian township of Lenz, where I hoped to contact my A.N.C cadre -leader. I was extremely grateful to Dries and told him so before alighting from the cab. Shaking my hand he said, "Wel ek wens jou geluk James en ek hoop dat jy n beter meisie kies volgend keer" (Well I wish you good luck James and I hope you choose a better girl next time) and then with a roar the pantechnicon moved off.

I left the motorway as quickly as possible and finding the road to Lenz I began hiking along it. It did not take long before I was picked up by a kindly Muslim gentleman who luckily was on his way there. He was a little puzzled as to why a European wanted to go to Lenz, but I allayed his curiosity by telling him that I was on my way to meet a friend at the cinema. The journey was not long and soon I was in the centre of Lenz and thanking him for the lift, I made my way to the cinema. On reaching it I went upstairs to my old accommodation, only to find that it was now occupied by a small family. I apologised to the young mother, who looked genuinely upset, but she said they had recently rented the flat from the owner, Mr Sadique, who was in my cadre. I assuaged her concerns, saying that it was my fault as I had been unexpectedly detained and had had no opportunity to contact Mr Sadique, but that I would sort it out with him. I went downstairs to the cinema and asked the manager where I could find Suliman-Mr Sadique. He recognised me instantly and said I would find him at the Mosque, as it was Maghrib (sunset prayers). I made my way as quickly as possible to the Mosque hoping to catch him before the call to prayer but unfortunately was too late, so I had to wait outside until prayers were over.

I watched as the men left the mosque and was finally rewarded with the sight of Suliman. I hurried over to him and was about to speak when he noticed me. He gasped and grabbed my arm, whispering to me not to say anything, and dragged me off to his estate car. Once we were cosseted inside and away from the bystanders, he cried out, "May Allah the merciful help us! How did you escape, we heard you had been captured and were in Prison?" I quickly updated him with what had happened on the road to court, and I could see he was hugely surprised. He responded, "We haven't seen or heard anything on the news about this, but if you are on the run, we must keep you away from your known haunts. I hope you haven't been back to the cinema and your old flat!" I sighed and told him that naturally I had, as I was looking for my clothes. He slapped his forehead and then said, "Come I will take you to a cousin of mine, what are your plans?" I told him that I needed to get to Swaziland as soon as possible and had hoped to contact some friends on the East Rand. Looking troubled he expressed his doubts, "Whatever you do you must not approach any of your known contacts, the security services will already be watching all your friends and known associates. They will be exceedingly put out by your escape!"

I dwelled on this. Was I putting other people's lives in jeopardy needlessly? I had gotten myself into this situation and had no right to compromise or endanger anyone else. I was now in a desperate situation; I needed funds and help to get to Swaziland. I decided that Suliman and the organisation owed me some sort of support and voiced this to him. Stroking his straggly beard, he replied "They will be watching all your cadre contacts and most certainly Solly and the roofing company, so you cannot go anywhere near there. Additionally, I don't believe the cinema is safe. There are many informants in Lenz!" "The best is for me to arrange some temporary accommodation until I can get some funds for you. But unfortunately, your escape will sooner or later be publicized." Suliman was not helping to calm me in the slightest and I was feeling increasingly vulnerable and told him so. "Right my boy" he said "let us get you to a safe house for now and I will do what I can to help you."

It was only a short drive to a luxurious two-story dwelling where Suliman, leaving me in the car, went in. I waited patiently for over an hour before he returned and I could see that he was not overly pleased, but he smiled and said, "Right, you can stay the night here. These are good people, but they don't really want to get involved so they are willing to help you but only for one night. I suggest you shower and have dinner, then get some sleep and I will call for you early tomorrow morning. In the interim, I will start putting things into place to get you funds and some clothes and essentials. Beyond that, I am not sure there is much else I can do."

The house was luxurious and my host, Mr Hussain, took me to a small annex that was attached to the main dwelling. Showing me into a room with an ensuite bathroom facility, he told me to make myself comfortable, but also added that I was please not to roam the house, as I was a 'non-believer' and there were women in the residence who should not be approached. I thanked him sincerely, as was I dead tired and no doubt smelt like a jackal that had been scavenging. Leaving me he disappeared, and I found the opulent shower cubicle and spent over an hour under the hot cleansing spray.

Early the next morning Suliman came round and supplied me with some funds and a collection of clothes. The clothes were a little big, but they were an improvement on what I was wearing, which sorely needed a wash. I thanked Mr Hussain and taking the small sports bag that Suliman had brought, I took a minibus taxi to the centre of Johannesburg. In town, I bought a cheap pair of sunglasses to try and disguise myself. I was not sure if there was an 'all points' security bulletin out about me, but suspected by now that all the police stations would have been furnished with my photo, close contacts, and last known whereabouts, so I was trying to alter my appearance as best I could. I went to a telephone box and dialled Sollys number at the Roofing company and using code words I suggested a meeting at Galoolies Farm, a local picnic area. I used another minibus taxi to get to the area and waited patiently for him to arrive. It took a couple of hours before he appeared and when he did, I could see he was significantly agitated. He wiped the sweat from his brow and indicated to me that we should stroll along the pathway next to the Jukskei River. Walking along he told me that he believed he was being followed but was sure that he had slipped out of the back of the warehouse without being seen. Firstly, he asked how things had gone so horribly wrong with the movement of Colonel Perez. I told him that due to the Colonel's inability to accept any instructions, it became a fiasco. He sighed and apologised, admitting that bombastic people could often be a big problem. I decided now to bring up the fact that when the M.K. comrades had rescued the Colonel, I had let them know that I was also an M.K comrade. and needed help, but they had simply ignored me, treating me like the other prisoners, with total disdain! Solly, shook his head saying "Well, I suspect their orders were simply to extricate the Colonel and get him away as soon as possible. I am sorry but obviously you were not a priority for those making the decisions." I grabbed his arm and hissed, "Have I now served my purpose and am to be abandoned!" Pulling his arm away he answered, "It's not that, but you have to understand that you are now an embarrassment to the security services and they will do anything to recapture you, and naturally Colonel Perez as well, so evidently any of your known contacts in the organization will be anxious to avoid you."

I mulled this over, while we meandered our way along the river. What he was saying was obvious and I was now on my own. No one had asked me to escape, and I could have gone to court and accepted my sentence. So why should they now put other operatives at risk! I was an unacceptable liability to the A.N.C. and a colossal embarrassment to the security services, specifically Colonel Van Deventer and Inspector Rabie, who would harness all available resources to recapture me. It dawned on me that I needed to formulate some sort of plan of my own. Solly exhaled audibly and said, "I can help you with some funds if needs be, but unfortunately as for transport that is plainly impossible! I suggest you get yourself back to Swaziland using as many back roads as possible. Your main problem will be getting across the border as I am sure they will have tightened their security, knowing that you will be heading home." I agreed with him and decided that every moment I wasted was decreasing my chances of staying at large. So, patting him on the back I left him, thanking him for the risk he had taken in coming to meet me.

I sat on a bench in the morning sun and watched as Solly nonchalantly bought an ice cream and made his way to the exit. I remembered the last time I had been here and seen Wendy with someone else. It seemed a lifetime away, so much had happened. I had gotten engaged, slipped across several borders and foolishly collected the disgruntled Colonel Perez, who with hindsight I should have left in Botswana, returned to S. A., and advised Solly of his intractability so that some other arrangement more to his liking could be formulated. I had been arrested, incarcerated, and learned to cope with my new life. I had unwittingly escaped custody and was a fugitive! I remained seated for a time ruminating that it wasn't all bad, I had met a few good people in prison and if the worst came to the worst, and I ended up back inside, I was a gang member and now knew how the system worked. I was free, the sun was shining, and I still had a chance to get back home.

I left the area and made my way to the East gate Mall, which was in the proximity, working on the assumption that being one of a crowd was a safe solution. I entered the Mall attempting to avoid all the CCTV cameras, which were positioned in several places, and found the newsagents where I bought a pocket-sized map of the Transvaal extending to Swaziland. I then went to the food court where I chose a table close to other diners and ordered myself lunch and coffee. I sat studying the map considering my options. I was sure that the main trunk roads to Swaziland, such as the N1 and N4, would be risky and therefore I needed to use obscure smaller roads. I was hopeful that using the African taxis would be a safe option, as most would avoid helping government law enforcement. I needed to do a lot of small trips heading east, moving from small town to small town.

I decided initially to try and make it to Oom Frik and Tant Marie in Carolina and so I went in search of a taxi heading for Benoni, a largish town on the East Rand. From there I hoped to progress to Springs, Devon, Leandra, Evander, Bethal, Hendrina and then onwards to Carolina. I hoped that there would not be many people on this route, but conversely these were small towns where strangers would be noticeable. But I intended to be transient, so I hoped not to arouse suspicion.

I made the short trip to Benoni and was sorely tempted to try and contact Sandy and Dick, as this was their hometown. But following Solly's advice, I pushed on for Springs where I arrived in the late afternoon. I now had to decide if I should search for a cheap guest house or move on to Devon. Springs was far larger than Devon and so would have more in the way of accommodation and I would attract less attention, so I strolled down the main street in the bright sunshine. The birds were getting ready to roost for the night and gathered in the tree lined avenues chirping to one another happily. I found an old farm style boarding house on the edge of town. It was not overly salubrious and the proprietor who showed me to my room wore a stained tea shirt and was moderately odoriferous, but even though the room was sparse with only a bed and a small side table it seemed clean. He told me that the bathroom was shared by several rooms but there was a sign you put on the handle to indicate you were using it. I thanked him put my bag down, then left to find a little something to eat.

I had an agreeable pizza at the local cafe and then headed back to the boarding house. On entering, I could hear the local news on the television and my scruffy 'proprietor' came out of his office saying to me, "Kan jy dit glo, n klomp bandita het ontsnap oppad na Bloemfontein Hof!" (Can you believe it a bunch of prisoners have escaped on the way to Bloemfontein Court). My heart skipped a beat, but before I could comment he continued, "Dus net hoe die Swartes is, hulle kan baie gevaarlik wees." (That's exactly how the Blacks are, they can be extremely dangerous). I nodded in agreement, once again relieved that Afrikaner logic believed all criminals were Africans.

I spent the night valiantly fighting off what I presumed were bed bugs, as no sooner had I been under the sheets than I suffered their first onslaught. I jumped up and put the light on and stripped the bed, but my enterprising tormentors were either too small or too wily. In the end, after a hot shower in the communal bathroom, I slept on top of the bed in my clothes.

I left early the next morning luckily getting a taxi to Bethal. The driver was young and exuberant and at first a little suspicious of me, as I presumed, he seldom had any European fares, but after I had chatted away to him in Zulu, he accepted me readily. I sat towards the back of the minibus on his side while we waited for other passengers so that his trip would be profitable. In the interim he played rap music, at full volume, through the minibus cassette player. I learnt from him that he had regular clientele who travelled to the power station in Secunda which was close to the town of Trichardt which was on our route to Bethal. In time we had a full complement, and he started the 'wheezy' Toyota's engine, and we were on our way.

The sun soon had the interior of the taxi hot and countless smells now permeated through the vehicle. My decision to be next to a window was vindicated as I was able to slide it open and breath in the joyous Eastern Transvaal air, which reminded me of the sun-bleached grassland of Swaziland. The minibus stopped in Devon and some passengers alighted, while others joined us. I was thirsty and longed to get an Ice-cold Ginger beer but was loath to leave my seat next to the window. Luckily, our flamboyant driver also needed some sort of sustenance. As he vacated the driver's seat and headed for the cafe, I called to him and asked if he would get me my drink and thankfully, he agreed. Momentarily he returned with the drinks and called me up to the front. I was at first hesitant to move but he assured me that if I left my bag on the seat, it would not be taken. I went up front and sat in the front passenger seat sipping my ice-cold drink. Putting his feet on the dashboard he told me his name was Dumisani and that the taxi belonged to his uncle who had quite a few. Smiling, he updated me with the fact that he had only been driving for nine months but that he enjoyed it immensely. Not only was it a well-paid job, but it also gave him the opportunity to meet many lovely 'izintombi' (young women). Winking he punched my arm lightly saying, "Uyazi ukuthi ngiqonde ukuthini" (You know what I mean right!?) I smiled in what I hoped was a lascivious manner. Laughing he asked where I was headed after Bethal and I decided that telling him could do no harm, so told him I was hoping to get to Carolina as soon as possible. "Aish umfowethu," (Ah brother) he said " namathela kimi futhi ngizokufikisa lapho ngemali ephansi" (stick with me, I will get you there cheaply).

The vehicle filled with sufficient passengers for Dumisani to push on and soon we were once again trundling down the road east, stopping once more in Leandra before pushing on to Evander. The day was hot, and I could smell the fumes coming from the overheated Toyota engine, but it struggled resolutely on. On reaching Evander, Dumisani told me that we would be in the small town for an hour or two, as we had to change vehicles, and would I please not seek out another taxi. I had developed a mild affinity to our driver and felt that it would be wiser to stick with him, so I wandered around the small town looking for lunch. I found a Chip Shop that was open and frying so, getting a decent size cod and chips, I sat on the pavement enjoying my repast. The Chip Shop had a radio blaring on a local radio station and the lunch time news came on. I listened intently and was dismayed to hear a report on the escape of several prisoners from a police transport taking them to the Bloemfontein High Court. The news reader said that a few of the escapees had been re-arrested but that three were still on the run, these included two white men, one a Cuban and another a European. The public were warned not to approach any of the errant prisoners as they were considered extremely dangerous, but to inform the police of any suspicious individuals. Thankfully, the broadcaster moved on to another news story, but I was now a little agitated and felt my stomach heave. Could I really be considered dangerous? It was disturbing and hard to accept that the broadcaster had been referring to me! I got up and putting the remains of my lunch in a bin, I walked down the road deeply despondent. I decided that to be best informed I needed to try to listen to the news as much as possible.

I found Dumisani in a battered Green Mazda minibus. It had seen better days, but Dumisani assured me that it was mechanically sound and not to worry. He told me to put my bag on the passenger seat and ride up front with him.

The Mazda set off with voluminous clouds of blue exhaust smoke, but it quite plainly was not short of horsepower. Dumisani whistled along to the in-vogue tracks on the 'Jurassic' looking car stereo. I asked if there was a chance to listen to the news when it came on. "Akunankinga nhlobo" (no problem) Dumisani replied, "Ngizoshintsha" (I will switch). Later that afternoon, as we approached Bethal down a steep hill, I noticed that the Mazda was gaining speed and looked at Dumisani to see if he had noticed, but he seemed unfazed. He was in his element and clung on to the steering wheel like a maniacal stock car driver. He pushed the vehicle even faster as we thundered down the hill towards Bethal. This was his undoing because we were approaching the junction with the R345 coming in from the North. I began to suspect that something was wrong when Dumisani began repeatedly pumping the brake pedal and he turned to me, his face now deeply concerned, and yelled at me to pull the hand brake that extended from just under the dashboard. I found the lever and clung onto it with all my might, while he wound his window down and started yelling, "Accident, Accident, Accident!" This chant was taken up by all the passengers and in a cataclysmic chorus we clattered towards the junction. I am not sure whether it was the cacophony that alerted the truck that was approaching the junction, or just a very observant driver, but with a squeal of tortured tyres and the deafening blaring of his air horn, he brought the massive articulated truck to a stop, just as it nudged the back of the minibus, which caused it to slew into a spin.

Round and round, we went until finally we ended up partly on our side in the ditch on the side of the road. Then there was silence, except for a ticking coming from the overheated engine. Dumisani sat for a moment not saying anything, but then in the characteristic manner of Africans he simply uttered "Aish!" Most of the passengers now realising they were not going to die, started laughing and congratulating each other, as if they had something to do with our good fortune. Dumisani asked if everyone was ok and luckily, apart from the odd possible bruise everyone was fine.

Fortunately, the exit sliding door was on the side of the minibus facing up, so without much trouble it was opened, and all the passengers started getting out. I climbed out of the front passenger door and was followed by Dumisani. By now the truck driver had pulled the vehicle up onto the side of the road and was storming towards us. I could see he was not in the best of humours. He was a burly European and on approach bellowed "Uyahlanya" (are you mad!?) Poor Dumisani started wringing his hands and obsequiously retorted in a small voice "Amabhuleki ahlulekile"(The brakes failed). The truck driver for some reason looked at me, thinking I was responsible for Dumisani. I shrugged and added, "Dis waar" (it's true). The truck driver, wiping his forehead with a soiled handkerchief, replied, "Wel ons sal most die polisie aanroep" (Well, we will have to call the police). This did not suit me in the slightest, the last thing I wanted was the police asking me awkward questions. But I simply nodded and walked back to the minibus and surreptitiously extricated my bag.

There were now a couple of cars at the scene and with the other minibus passengers there were several people milling about. In the distance I heard approaching sirens, and this made me even more desperate to disappear. I noticed a bushy area to the south and moving as quickly as possible I slipped into the brush and kept going, hoping that no one had noticed I had slipped away. I felt bad about deserting Dumisani, but I knew that if I gave the Police the opportunity to question me, my story would not hold up and I would be back in custody.

Walking as fast as possible I arrived at a small stream, which I later learnt was the Blesbok Spruit. I forded this easily and saw that there were houses not far off, so I made my way towards them. It was getting towards dusk, so I was able to move along the street into the town. I was looking for the minibus rank as I needed to put as much distance between myself and the town. I asked around, but it seemed that the earliest minibus out of town to Hendrina would be in an hour or so. I walked down the street looking for somewhere where a stranger would not stand out, as in these small towns everyone knew everyone else. I noticed that the small library was still open and would be for the next couple of hours.

I spent my time quietly reading some wildlife magazines and then, thanking the library assistant, I made my way back to the minibus rank and found that the minibus heading for Hendrina was already half full. I found a seat near the front. The talk in the taxi was mostly about poor Dumisani's accident. I was getting slightly anxious that one of my fellow travellers from Dumisani's taxi might turn up and then I would have a lot of explaining to do! I sighed with relief when we finally set off into the night heading for Hendrina. I sat back and tried to relax, but I reasoned that Dumisani, and the other passengers would have told the police about a small 'umlungu' travelling East and the Police would soon connect the 'dots' and realize that it was their escapee. I was now more vulnerable than ever.

Hendrina was once again a small Eastern Transvaal town, but I soon found a boarding house which unlike my previous evening was clean and comfortable. It was run by a kindly elderly couple who even cooked me a small supper. I listened to them as they talked about their children and grandchildren. Their son ran a farm close by which was the family farm. But it had become too much for them, so they had moved into town to run the boarding house, as it had been the wife's early home. I silently thanked the Lord for these kind people who had made me so welcome.

Chapter Nine

Desperation

Early the next morning I left Hendrina after thanking my hosts. I found a minibus heading for Carolina and hoped that I would make Oom Frik and Tant Marie's before nightfall. My concern was that by now the police would be aware of my destination and might install roadblocks on the routes east. I sat in the minibus watching my fellow passengers and any other traffic on the road, but everything seemed normal. The minibus pulled into Carolina just after noon and I quickly made my way out of the town heading for Oom Frik's farm. I walked along the small dirt by-roads but whenever I heard a car or tractor coming, I scurried into the bush on the side of the road. By late afternoon I was nearing their farm and felt that if I could just stay a night or two with them and then push on with the final leg to the border, I might make it. I was walking down the road feeling optimistic, when I heard the hum of a fast-approaching vehicle. I only just had time to secrete myself when a police van came hurtling along the road in a cloud of red dust. My heart sank, they would be heading for Oom Frik and Tant Marie's farm! I was disconsolate, once again amazed at their intelligence gathering.

After they had passed, I moved cautiously up the road listening intently for any approaching vehicles. Close to the farm I left the road and creeping along the under growth I approached the farm gate. The police van was parked outside, and the occupants had obviously gone inside to speak to Oom Frik and Tant Marie. I waited in consternation for what seemed forever, but was only ten minutes, and was finally rewarded by the sight of two policemen walking down the drive with Oom Frik and I could hear their conversation. "Wel as julle hom opmerk moet jy onmiddellik ons in kennis stel, he is n baie gevaarlik terroris" (Well if you see him, you must inform us at once, he is a dangerous terrorist). Oom Frik rubbed the stubble on his chin and replied, "Man, ons ken die okie, hey is definitief nie gevaarlik nie en ons glo nie hy is n terroris, my magtig hy is maar net n skraal Ier" (Man, we know the guy. He is not dangerous, and we don't believe he is terrorist. My God he is just a thin Irishman!) The sergeant didn't seem overly pleased and responded, "Wel as jy hom bystaan , sal julle n misdadiger koester en die wet oortree, wees versigtig goeie nag "(Well if you help him, you will be harbouring a criminal and breaking the law. Be careful, good night!).

The two policemen got into their van and with great aplomb sped off down the road. Oom Frik stood leaning on the big gate in deep thought, staring into the setting sun, Leeu the massive Boerboel dog nuzzling his hand, intuitively sensing his master's mood. I could see he was in a quandary, but I was also desperate, so I whistled. Leeu reacted, with a small growl, "Wat is dit dan Leeu"(what is it Leeu?). I stood up and walked towards the gate and Leeu gave me a welcoming bark. "Wat die joos, is dit dan jy Irish" (What, is that you Irish?)

I walked up and told him straight away that I heard all the sergeants had said and it was all true, I was on the run. For a second, he just looked at me, then he burst out laughing saying that if I were all that the A.N.C. could recruit, they were in trouble! Opening the gate and still chuckling he led me up the drive and into the house saying "Hy Marie kyk net wat nou uit die hemel geval het, net die okie wat die polisie opsoek is" (Hy Marie, look what's just fallen from the sky, just the guy the police are looking for).

Marie came and hugged me so hard I thought my ribs would be fractured, then looking at me she said, "My kind ons is so bly om jou te sien, en ons glo nie dat jy gevaarlik is" (my child we are so happy to see you and don't believe you are dangerous). I felt warm all over and almost broke down. I had been living on my wits for so many days and dreading what could happen that this first bit of compassion shown to me was deeply overwhelming!

Oom Frik now confirmed that he believed I could never be considered dangerous and whatever I had done, he was sure I could not have harmed anyone. Tant Marie took my hand and asked when last, I had eaten. I told her I had a meal at lunch time, but I didn't want to cause them any trouble. If they could just help me with some advice and a plan, I would be grateful. I also was worried that the police might return and then they would be liable to be charged with aiding and abetting. Oom Frik shrugged his shoulders and said, "Hulle sal nie weer terug kom nie , ons het hulle vertel dat dit lang laas dat ons jou gesien het en as ons jou teekom sal ons hulle onmidelik in kennis stel" (They won't be back, we told them that it is a long time since we saw you and if you contact us, we will notify them!). Tant Marie asked if I would like a shower while she cooked me some supper. I accepted the offer gratefully and made my way to the bathroom.

I stood under the hot shower, and felt my muscles relax and considered the absurdity of the apartheid system. These were people that should undeniably despise me for what I was, but instead they were giving me succour at no small risk to themselves. Yet my organisation, that had gotten me in the situation, just wanted to distance themselves from me because I was now a risk. I finished my shower and made my way to the kitchen where Tant Marie was cooking a couple of chops and frying chips, she smiled at me. Setting a place at the table she said she had taken my clothes from my bag and put them in the washing machine, so thanking her I began to eat! Oom Frik came in and getting a cup of coffee from the stove he chuckled and said, "Wel Irish hoe kan ons u help" (Well, Irish how can we help you?)

I sat at the table enjoying the chops and chips and decided that these people had my best interests at heart, so between mouthfuls I told them everything, from the time I first obtained a conviction for terrorism and the consequences. They both sat staring at me as they tried to assimilate everything. Oom Frik, shaking his head, asked if I had had a good lawyer. I replied that yes, I had had representation, but it hardly mattered as I was guilty. I knew that it was illegal to take photographs of the police actions in the township and not only had I broken the law, but I had exacerbated my felony by selling them to the international media. Tant Marie asked me in English, "So because your life was unavoidably altered by one mistake, you joined the A.N.C. knowing they posed a danger to the European population by bombing malls and restaurants?" I nodded but explained that I had made it clear that I would not be involved in harming anyone. "So Irish" Oom Frik added, "your choices were limited, and we are not stupid enough to deny that there needs to be change in this country, but violence will never be the answer!" Tant Marie asked in a quiet voice, "Prison must have been frightening. How did you cope?" I explained that in some way I had been lucky by meeting Spike and a few decent warders, both European and African.

Oom Frik, sat quietly for a bit, then suggested, "So what we need to do is to get you across the border back into Swaziland, but I imagine the police will do everything in their power to prevent that and re-capture you. I am sure by now all the border posts will have heightened security and your picture will have been circulated". I nodded "So the only option is to get you across somehow," he continued. I told them that was my plan and that I had done it on a couple of occasions. "Ja" (Yes) but that was not like now, where they will be on full alert and will make use of defence force personnel to patrol the border. Do you have an idea where you might cross?" I thought for a moment then decided that I needed help from Swaziland. "There is a small river just north of Sandelane border post, called the Metfulo, and I know someone who would help me cross." I told them about Dr Dlamini. "Ah Irish" Oom Frik remarked "that would be the best, I am sure. Will we be able to contact him?"

I considered for a moment as to whether Nhandla – the Isangoma- would help and recalled how he had said that if ever I needed him, I was just to call. Tant Marie filled my cup with coffee and took away my empty plate, commenting, "Do you have a way of contacting him?" I sat in my chair, pondering if the security services were aware of my connection to him and if so, was their reach that extensive? I asked Oom Frik if they were on a private telephone line or a 'party line' as many of these outlying farms still relied on a shared line through an exchange. This would be dangerous as the operators made a habit of listening in on calls. Tant Marie confirmed that they were on a 'party line' and it was certainly unsecure, saying that she believed the operator in Carolina listened in on most of the calls.

I sighed, it was unsettling that the security services had known about Oom Frik and Tant Marie. No doubt they would be using their unending resources and internal agents in Swaziland to keep track of Grand-pere Jacques and the Faulkner's as well! The situation was not looking optimistic, but I had to try to think of something. Oom Frik was silent for a while but then mooted a solution. "We have a young Siswati worker here called Sfiso, who helps me with the plants. He often returns home to Manzini, he could carry a message to your 'Witch Doctor'?" I considered this and believed it would be possible, as Nhandla was well known in Swaziland. The only drawback was that I would have to wait for him to return with information and this would endanger Oom Frik and Tant Marie's lives, as well as mine. I voiced this concern but they both made light of it saying that they believed the police had gone around all the local farms warning them to be on the lookout for me and that they had not been singled out. I was not so sure about this but thanked them. "Wel dis nou slaap tyd," (Well its now bedtime) Tant Marie said getting up. She disappeared returning with bedding and Oom Frik pulled out the sofa bed, which she made up for me They then retired, with Oom Frik commenting that it was likely I would have Leeu for company. I crawled into the bed and Leeu's large bulk curled up next to me.

The following day Oom Frik introduced me to Sfiso who was characteristically a tall Swazi, and I asked him in Siswati if he knew of Nhandla Dlamini. He nodded saying, "Yebo, uyiSangoma esinamandla futhi kufanele esatshwe" (Yes, he is a powerful iSangoma and one to be feared). I relaxed as it was obvious that he knew Nhandla. Oom Frik now told him that he wanted him to go home and take a message to Nhandla . Sfiso looked uneasy, saying one just did not approach a powerful iSangoma without reason. I allayed his fears by telling him that Nhandla and myself were old acquaintances and all I wanted was for him to pass on a message. Looking slightly doubtful he asked what the message was? I decided to keep it short but told him he was to tell Nhandla where I was and that I needed help urgently. Oom Frik now added that he was not to worry, as he would pay for his bus or taxi fares and that he was to leave at once.

Oom Frik said he would drop Sfiso in Amsterdam, the closest town to the Sandelane border post. Just before leaving Sfiso addressed me, looking worried, "Isangoma esikhulu sizokwazi kanjani ukuthi umyalezo uvela kuwe" (How will the Witch doctor know the message is from you?) I reassured him, "Mtshele ukuti iSikhova sisenkingeni enkulu futhi sidinga usizo"(Tell him the Owl is in danger and needs help!) He looked at me and I could see he was still unhappy about approaching Nhandla, so anxious that he would not deliver the message. I asked if he knew my 'brother' Mandla who was a minor chief. "Aish, kodwa-ke uyindoda yethu eyinhloko"(Ah, but of course he is our headman!) I sighed with relief and told him not to worry about approaching Nhandla, but to ask Mandla to do it. He smiled, saying, "Impela mfowethu ngizoya kuye ngqo"(Certainly brother, I will go directly to him). Oom Frik drove around with the pickup, and they left. I closed the gate and locked it, with Leeu next to me. I rubbed his large ear and he looked at me with his typical big dog 'smile.' I patted his head as we walked back up the drive feeling more at ease.

Tant Marie suggested that I try to keep to the house, as she said one never knew when a visitor might arrive, and it would be best if no one saw me. I happily agreed to this and spent the rest of the morning and early afternoon helping her make Apricot and Peach Jam. I never realized just what an involved process it was.

Later, in the afternoon, Oom Frik returned and sitting down with a cup of coffee updated me "Well Irish, Sfiso got a minibus to Manzini, and I am sure he will deliver your message to his headman. So, all we can do now is to await his return or better still the arrival of your friend." I thanked him and then we discussed how long that would be. Oom Frik allayed our fears a little by telling us that he ran into his friend Manie in town who had told him that the police had been around to his farm as well and cautioning them to contact the authorities if they saw any strangers around! Tant Marie smiled and patting my hand said, "See they are going around all the district and didn't come directly to us." "Ja (Yes) Irish," Oom Frik commented, "in a way that is a good thing, but also a little unwelcome news as this is a small community and its best you are not seen by anyone until we can get you back home." I nodded, and Tant Marie said, "It's not important as our farm stretches almost five hundred acres, so if you keep away from the front entrance, we should be fine."

I spent the next couple of days helping Oom Frik with the plants in the Greenhouses and plastic tunnels. Once or twice, I had to hide in them when visitors arrived, but I always had the faithful Leeu with me and it was not usually for any length of time. On the Sunday Tant Marie and Oom Frik went off to the 'Kerk' (church). They both agreed that it was worth the risk leaving me alone with Leeu, as they were regulars at the service and if one of them didn't go, their friends might ask questions. Additionally, they said that they would hear all the local gossip at the 'Kerk'.

They returned from church in good spirits and as I helped Tant Marie prepare for Sunday lunch, Oom Frik told me that the police visits to all the adjacent farms had been commented on profusely. The consensus amongst the farmers was that the police were 'barking up the wrong tree' as why would any escaped 'bandit'(prisoner) come to this area. He would more likely go to a district close to the border where he had a chance of crossing. One of his friends whose son was a policeman said that several of the elite Police squad called 'Koevoet' had been deployed along the border, claiming that there was no way any 'bandit' would outsmart them as they were trained in reconnaissance and tracking down terrorists on the borders. I swallowed and was dismayed as I had heard of this elite group who were ruthless. Oom Frik patted me on the back, saying, "Not to worry Irish, they won't be there forever. But apparently you were identified by a minibus driver who was involved in a collision. You were to be his prime witness, but you disappeared!" I nodded and told them about the crazy Dumisani who had started shouting 'Accident, Accident' long before it happened. Oom Frik found this extremely amusing! "Well Irish, that was a bit unfortunate because your disappearance aroused suspicion and then the police began showing your picture around and he and a few of the other passengers identified you." I sighed but there was nothing to be done about it now. So, we sat down to Tant Marie's delicious lunch and then I helped with the dishes before we all gravitated to the ' voorkamer' (front room) to watch the S.A.B.C. news broadcast. I was dreading seeing my face all over the television, but thankfully there was no mention of me or the escape. Oom Frik fell asleep in his chair while Tant Marie watched an ancient film that had been 'resurrected.'

Oom Frik woke up and rubbing his face, suddenly declared, "Hey Irish, I just had an idea while thinking on your situation. We should colour your hair and you should start growing a beard and moustache." "Ja," (Yes) "Tant Marie enjoined, "that is a brilliant plan, I will go tomorrow and get some peroxide and hair dye from the chemist, and you must stop shaving!" Oom Frik looked at her and warned, "Be careful, you know how nosey the people are in town. How will you explain it?" "Ag Ja" (Oh yes), "I am not stupid; I will say you want to see how I look like as a blond and you will just have to back me up when I change my hair colour." She replied. I gasped and begged her not to go to the trouble, but Oom Frik snickered, "Ja nee (Yes/No), that's an excellent plan and you will make a gorgeous blond." "Vent" (idiot), she replied good naturedly, throwing a cushion at him, "I bet you always wanted a blonde." "Nee(no)," he smiled chortling, "but if we can get his appearance altered a little it might help, it's just the ears that are a giveaway!" "Sies man" (Sis man), leave him alone, there is nothing wrong with his ears." She said. "Well not if he was an Elephant," Oom Frik chucked. I agreed with Oom Frik, my 'lugs' were unmistakable but changing my hair colour and trying to grow a moustache and a beard seemed a good plan.

The following day Tant Marie went to Carolina and returned with enough peroxide and hair colour to open a small hair salon. In no time at all both of us became 'blonde'. I don't think it did much for me except to enhance my already rodent characteristics. Conversely, I thought Tant Marie looked fetching and even Oom complimented her. The beard and moustache that I grew were straggly, wispy and once dyed, were hardly noticeable, but both Tant Marie and Frik agreed that they did change my appearance.

The days went by, and I continued do my best to help where I could on the farm, hoping that every day I would hear some news of the return of Sfiso or a plan that would somehow get me across the border to safety. I feared that eventually I would be discovered and then not only I, but Tant Marie and Oom Frik, would be arrested. Late one evening Sfiso returned and updated us on what he had accomplished in Swaziland. He had gone straight to see Mandla, who initially wanted to leave right away to rescue me. But after speaking to Nhandla, he had told Sfiso that he was to return to us and let us know that we were to wait for the new moon in a weeks' time. Then I was to be ready to leave at a moment's notice as the iSangoma would come for me. I felt more positive because arrangements were being formulated and now Nhandla knew of my plight I might have a chance.

The days dragged but Tant Marie and Oom Frik tried their best to keep my spirits up and Leeu was a great comfort. Finally, the moon waned until it was only a sliver of the letter C and late one night close to midnight a heavy truck drew up outside, it was a timber logging vehicle fully loaded. Oom Frik went to the gate to investigate and came running back to say that the driver had asked for me and I was to go at once. Tant Marie hugged me and Oom Frik shook my hand saying, "Baie geluck Irish, last ons weet dat jy veilig is (best of luck Irish, let us know when you are safe). I took the small bag that Tant Marie and myself had prepared, patted, and hugged the faithful Leeu and then hastened down the drive.

The truck was a fixed axle low-bed and loaded with timber. I approached the cab, but the driver simply pointed to the rear and the load, so I walked round a little bemused but then heard a voice say, "Ngapha isikhova (over here owl)!"

I stared at the massive logs and was just able to discern the face of the iSangoma peering down at me. I scrambled up the logs and found a gap to squeeze through. Once through I discovered a small niche amongst the logs which had a couple of thick sheepskins.

"Make yourself comfortable," he motioned and then banged on the rear wall of the truck cab with his thick staff.

The trucks massive engine thundered, and we set off down the road. Nhandla looked at me and grinning commented, "Well, you have changed a bit and look a little like a dwarf mongoose, but it is good to see you. I was afraid they might have caught you!"

I shook my head saying that I was fortunate to have friends like him and Oom Frik and Tant Marie. He sat down on one of the sheepskins, leaning against the back of the cab and patted the other skin next to him for me to sit down. I made myself as comfortable as was possible, as the truck bumped and shook along the dirt road.

"Well, we have a way to go, and I am sorry we must travel this way, but I am afraid the security forces are extremely active along the border, and I suspect they are desperate to get you back. This truck is returning to the Lazy Bend Sawmill near the Westoe dam. We are travelling via Crissiesmeer and Lothair along the small gravel roads and it is the way we came because all the bigger roads have check points or roadblocks." He grinned and added, "I remember once telling you that you should take care that when you poke the anthill you are able to get away before being attacked. You have well and truly poked the wrong anthill."

I felt sheepish and apologised for all the trouble I had put him to. "Ah akunandaba (Ah it is no matter)," he replied, "I expected this day would come so let us not worry about it." Looking amused he said, "Come we have time, so it is best you update me as to what has been happening to you since our last trip across the border?"

The truck rumbled on into the night over the rough corrugated road, throwing up clouds of dust behind it now and some of it permeated our small 'cranny' and made us gag. But I slowly and meticulously told him everything. Now and then he asked pertinent questions, such as why Colonel Perez had behaved so foolishly and shaking his head he commented, "Ah, you'll find that in life arrogance and self-importance are one of the most dangerous aspects of a person's character, I now understand why they are determined to recapture you!"

I nodded and Nhandla shaking his head remarked, "You have walked a difficult path, but you have also had some extraordinarily good fortune. Let's hope it continues. When we reach the Westoe dam we will follow the river that flows into it back into Swaziland. The river crosses the border just north of the border post and when I left, I noticed that it is being patrolled by both army and police personnel. They are also making use of tracker dogs, but no matter we will cross that bridge when we come to it."

The truck slowed through the streets of Chrissiesmeer and then ominously stopped. We could hear voices and Nhandla motioned for me to be quiet. The driver was being questioned and we heard him being asked where he had come from and had he seen anything untoward. My stomach clenched, but the driver replied that he had simply been collecting timber from the Belfast area and he had not stopped or seen anyone as he was on a tight schedule. "Ek sien" (I see), his interrogator responded and then we heard footsteps along the side of the truck, around the back and then up the other side to the front of the vehicle. Once again, he came to the driver's side and then instructed the driver, "Nou goed, as u iemand agterdogtig sien meld did aan" (All good if you see anyone suspicious report it). He then slapped the driver's door and the truck slowly moved off, meshing through its many gears.

Nhandla grinned and said, "Well they are determined to clip your wings to put up road blocks at this time of night in out of the way little towns." I agreed with him and apologised for involving him in my misadventures. He laughed aloud and responded, "No it is not a problem, I was beginning to get bored with the normal requests of our people to sanction life partners, promise prosperity or divine the future, the only excitement being the annual circumcision with the 'izinyanga(healers), in the mountains." I replied "But many rely on you, and I have dragged you away from helping them." " Avume(agreed)," he responded, "but as I have told you on several occasions, you interest me, and you have unintentionally become like a Tsetse Fly to this countries law enforcement and need 'swatting'! "Don't worry these, things happen and even the darkest night has a dawn." I accepted this and looking at him, reflected on just how fortunate I was to have such a wise friend.

It was an hour or so before midnight when the truck pulled up and we heard the driver get out and approach the side. He then called out, "Silapha Omkhulu (we are here)."

"The iSangoma replied, "Wenze kahle Thabiso futhi Siyabonga (you have done well Thabiso and thank you)."

Getting up we squirmed our way out between the logs and Nhandla shook the obsequious Thabiso's hand.

I too thanked Thabiso who, after saying to us that it was nothing, jumped back into the driver's side and putting the bulky truck back into gear moved off down the road.

"Well, Isakova, we are now on our own and must make our way to the dam to pick up the river. I don't imagine anyone is around but if you could be as quiet as possible it will help." Without waiting for a reply, he strode off and I hastened after him.

We reached the dam and skirting around the south side found the small river and struck off following it in a south easterly direction.

"We will need to enter the river closer to the border to keep the dogs off our scent," he mentioned, as he strode on at a furious pace with no let up.

On and on he pushed, now and then looking back, making sure I was still behind him. We surprised a couple of grazing Bush Buck who went crashing off into the Bush, and an Eagle owl called out 'Hoo Hoo hooo' and Nhandla remarked, "That is a good sign Owl, your 'spirit guides' are out and aware of you." He called out in an almost perfect reply. It was so perfect it made me think one was close! Straight away the Owl reciprocated with vigour. I was astounded at his skill.

Hours later, he stopped, saying, "We are close to the border now and must be extremely careful, because even if police or army personnel don't hear us their dogs will pick up our scent."

I drew in my breath and tried to slow my now pounding heart, as he slowly edged forward closer to the river. Creeping along I did my best to watch where I was placing my feet, in an attempt not to break stalks or sticks underfoot. Little by little we inched our way then Nhandla stopped and stood dead still, he stood erect and sniffed turning his head this way and that. Then turning to me, his voice a soft guttural growl, he said "Ngizwa iphunga lezinja (I can smell dogs)," adding, "the border is over there," he pointed, "but so are they! Whatever happens you must run as fast you can along the river. Do not look back or stop on any account. I will find you on the other side!"

I was a little disconcerted, but he was adamant and slapping me on the back he hissed, "Balekela Isikova, gijima (run away Owl, run)!" I didn't wait for further bidding but set off as fast as my now tired legs could manage. A cry went up, "Daar is iemand, stop ons sal die honde laat los (There is someone, listen, stop or we will release the dogs)." This spurred me on, and I ran like I had never ran in my life. I heard dogs barking and baying and their handlers urging them to 'vang en hou vas' (catch and hold). I ran on crashing through the vegetation and then heard behind me the furious growl of a leopard. There was a bright flash and a resounding bang, followed by the yelping of dogs and a couple of gunshots. But I did as Nhandla had ordered and ran on into Swaziland.

Chapter Ten

Respite

I am not sure how long I ran but inevitably I had to stop to get my breath. Was I across the border? I hoped so but was so exhausted, I was getting to the stage where I was beyond caring! I stood trying to catch my breath and between rasping gasps tried to listen if I was being pursued. But all I could hear was the rustle of the river, so struggling on at a stumbling pace I followed the river.

The sky began to lighten in the East, and I knew dawn could not be far off. I was distraught thinking on what might have happened to the iSangoma. Had he been apprehended, or worse still shot and injured? I staggered on into a brilliant early sunrise as it rose magnificently over the mountains. The birds celebrated the new day, but none of this registered because I felt drained, and grief stricken. Had I sacrificed a great man to save myself? Trudging on until I could walk no more, I came to a bend in the river where it had formed a small oxbow like pool. I sat at the side of the pool and after having a rest I removed my boots, dabbling my feet in cold refreshing water and reflected on what had happened. I had escaped the clutches of the army and police and was safe for the moment, but at what cost? I held my head in my hands, thinking that I should have handed myself in and been returned to prison. I had managed to survive previously, so would be able to again but instead, I had involved other people in my dramatic escape. It was as Nhandla had said a matter of pride; mine to thwart the security services; theirs, their determination not let me get away. I was a nobody, just a ridiculous insignificant cog in a mighty machine and now I had robbed many people of an influential, respected and much valued man! I sat and watched as juvenile Tilapia fish examined my toes, suspecting they were edible. I was exhausted and ravenous and had no real idea where I was but reasoned that eventually if I carried on along the river I would come to a road. I was musing on this when a soft voice came from behind me, "Well done Owl, you did as I requested, and it all worked out perfectly." I jumped up and there was Nhandla. I noticed that his cloak had been torn but otherwise he seemed in good form. I greeted him enthusiastically and asked a deluge of questions. "Enough!" he exclaimed. "Come, we have much ground to cover before explanations and we need to eat as I am very hungry.". Setting off once more, we headed away from the river. Thankfully there was no urgency to his pace, so I was able to keep up on my fatigued legs.

It was mid-morning when we came into the small village of Mangcongco and the head induna ran out to greet, us overjoyed at seeing Nhandla.. Leading us through the village he inquired how he could help us. Nhandla thanked him and replied that some fresh food and drink would be very much appreciated. Several of the villagers now appeared, most in awe of Nhandla, but some wondering why he was accompanied by a slight, strange 'umlungu'. Sitting outside the headman's house we were offered mugs of delicious hot coffee. Nhandla turned to me and said quietly, "Don't say much, I will do the talking. There are many informers, even in our country." I was astounded, did the sinister reach of those I opposed penetrate even a small Swazi village? I tacitly sipped my coffee and munched on a delicious freshly cooked 'ummbila wommbila (corn cob). Nhandla and the headman, who was called Sibusiso, talked and little by little more of the esteemed villagers arrived, not wanting to miss a visit from an iSangoma. I sat pleasantly in the sun and after the exertions and emotional tumult of the previous night, dozed off.

I was nudged awake by Nhandla, who said, "Come Isikova, Sibusiso has kindly arranged transport to Mbabane. "An aged but serviceable minibus drew up and after many salutations on behalf of the small villagers, we embarked with several of the locals, heading for Mbabane. I was still half asleep and struggled to keep my eyes open, but Nhandla seemed unaffected by our previous night's exertions. He chatted away to the other passengers about mundane things. Turning to me he said, "We will drop you in Enzulweni near 'izwe Lokuduma kwezulu' (the voice of Thunder-Grand-peres) office, and then in a few days I suggest we meet up." I agreed and thanked him for everything. He simply smiled and answered, "Later Owl, we will talk."

The minibus pulled up close to the small road that led to Grand-pere's office, I got out, and it trundled off on its way to the capitol. I walked slowly up the road to the office, exhausted and drained. I entered the offices and Nosibusiso gasped and jumped up from behind her desk exclaiming, "Sean, I thought you were in prison?" I found it difficult to respond, as how do you tell someone that you don't really want to confide in, that you are a fugitive. So, I simply said, "No not anymore." "Aish" she responded, " Lokuduma is up country, but I can get him on the radio immediately and tell him you are here!" I held up my hand saying no it was fine, but could I use the phone. "Ah" she replied, "yes of course, and I will organise you some coffee. You can go through to his office and use the phone in there." I thanked her and made my way into the office. I phoned the house in the valley, and Hetty answered. I said hello in a hushed tone, and she replied in amazement, "Sean, is that you? Are you phoning from prison?" I simply said, "Could you come and collect me from the office?" "My kind" (my child), but of course" she replied, "I am on my way" and I heard her calling out to Nolwesi that she was going out and then she put the receiver down. I sat in one of the chairs in the office while Nosibusiso brought me a tray with my coffee and a plate of biscuits, saying, "Lokuduma will be pleased to see you. It's really a shame that he isn't here."! I thanked her and assured her not to worry, as I would see him when he got back and that Hetty was on her way to collect me.

Hetty arrived before my coffee cup got cold and rushed into the reception asking after me. Nosibusiso told her I was in Grand-pere's office. She crashed through the door then simply stared at me, before blurting out, "My Hemel," (my heavens), it is you. I can't believe it. We thought you were in prison!" I got up and said "can we go home please?" "Of course," she said and started for the door. I thanked Nosibusiso for the coffee and followed Hetty out to her car. On the way I told her that I would tell them all as soon as I had had a shower and a sleep, as I was desperately tired and, in the meantime, it would be best to keep my presence at the bungalow quiet. "Naturally," she replied, "leave it to me. I will tell Nolwesi. We are expecting Jacques later this evening, so you can have a good rest this afternoon." I nodded and expressed my gratitude at her understanding. On reaching the bungalow Nolwesi greeted me with a massive hug and like Hetty, wanted details. But Hetty told her to let me shower and sleep and then when Grand-pere arrived, I would explain everything. "Ah Isikova esimpofu (Ah poor Owl) Nolwesi said, "I will get your bed made up while you shower, but it is wonderful to see you!" Nolwesi bustled off and I made my way to the shower.

I woke to the calling of Hadada Ibis as they came into roost in the trees in groups. I dressed in my own clothes, that Nolwesi had found and quickly freshened up while I slept, then made my way to the kitchen where I found not only Hetty and Nolwesi, but Grand-pere as well. Nolwesi said that supper was about ready and would I like coffee or something else to drink. Grand-pere observed casually that since 'the prodigal son' had arrived we should celebrate with a bit of champagne. I laughed and answered that, a drop of red wine would be appreciated, but I didn't think I could handle champagne. "Absolutely, "he responded and asked Hetty and Nolwesi if they would like a little wine? Hetty accepted but Nolwesi said she would have coffee and that the supper was ready. Hetty helped her serve and we sat down to eat.

I could see they were all bursting wanting to know how I had managed to get back home. So, beginning with how Nhandla had helped me leave Swaziland, to my journey back to Johannesburg and then my mission to collect Colonel Perez, I began my narrative.

The dishes were taken away and coffee brought as I came to the end of my account. They were dumbfounded and the only comment made was by Nolwesi, who uttered "Iowo Mthakathi uDlamini uyesabeka"(That Witch Dlamini is awesome)!" Grand-pere and Hetty asked about the prison, the escape and why I had not contacted them, and I could see they were a little upset. I explained that I believed that from the moment I had escaped with the others from the prison vehicle, the police and security services would have monitored all means of telecommunication. Hetty exclaimed, "But surely, as you were surviving in the prison system, it would have been better not to run but to do your sentence?" I took a moment to refute her argument saying, "I had no idea what sentence I would have received or where I might have ended up serving it, because they might have transferred me anywhere or put me in with the white inmates where my life would be difficult. "Ah," she gasped, "that's dreadful!" "Ja nee (Yes), I would imagine it would be a simple proposition for the authorities to make your life unbearable. No, you took a significant risk, but it was the correct decision." Grand-pere observed, "I don't think we should let your mother know any of this as she was really upset when I told her you were in prison." I sighed; I had forgotten how badly she had reacted after my first conviction.

Hetty now took my hand and asked, "And what about your fiancée Suzanne, what are you going to tell her and her family? When the catholic minister contacted us to tell us where you were, Jacques did go and see them." I groaned, as this was another matter I hadn't considered. "Well," I replied "I will tell them everything. It is best that she knows so she can move on with her life with someone who is not on the run." "Ai my kind (Oh my child)," Hetty remarked, "it is upsetting but you are doing the honourable thing by not holding her to any commitment." Grand-pere shook his head saying, "Life is strange, don't make any decisions until you have had time to think things through and discuss them with Nhandla. He has been wise counsel and an incredibly good friend to you and knows many things that we don't." "Yebo (Yes)," Nolwesi intoned smiling, "the iSangoma can see into the future and knows things. Lokuduma is right, he will have a plan for you. Don't worry Isikova." "Certainly," Grand-pere added, "but it's late and tomorrow is another day. We are simply happy to have you back and owe Nhandla our gratitude, but for now I think a good rest and sleep without worry is what you need!" Hetty and Nolwesi concurred, and we all retired.

I woke up just before dawn and wrapping a soft blanket around me, crept out to the veranda and perched on an old wicker chair. It was very still, and I watched as a lone Black Backed Jackal skirted around the edge of the garden where it merged with the bush. He looked at me having picked up my scent or movement. I laughed aloud and called out to him, "Don't worry ' Ujakalasi', I too am like you, hounded and hunted, so I wish you no harm." He hesitated a moment and then calmly walked off. I smiled and considered how life fluctuated. Only days ago, my main worry was how to do best by my students, then just avoiding the police and security services had been my main preoccupation but here I was now calmly sitting and deliberating with friend Jackal.

A Secretary Bird flew in on heavy wings and began stalking around like a disgruntled clergyman, on its tall spindly legs, and I decided not to offend its contemplation and went in search of coffee which I smelt. I wandered into the kitchen where I found Nolwesi who, having 'induced' the stove back into life, had the coffee percolating. "Ekuseni (Morning)," she greeted me, "I hope you slept well?" I greeted her and sat at the table while she got the coffee sorted, then handing me a mug she sat down and I followed the polite custom of enquiring about her, her family, her health and life in general. Smiling she updated me with all the intricacies of her family. This took some time, as apparently her sister's hen had hatched a one-winged chicken which was of utmost significance, according to her, and a portent of sorcery by an enemy, so she planned to consult our iSangoma about it. I almost burst out laughing but knowing how important these things were, I nodded gravely. Eventually she asked if I would like some breakfast, just as Grand-pere and Hetty came into the kitchen.

Grand-pere asked what my plans for the day were. I replied that I hoped to go to town and see Nhandla's secretary to make an appointment and then possibly later visit my brother Mandla at his home, after he had finished with his day's affairs, as I needed to thank him for his help and update him on what had happened. "Oui (Yes), that is the right thing to do, but I have to say that you look very strange with blonde hair and hopefully it will help a little. I will do my best to keep your presence here at home a secret until we know what best course of action to take but let me assure you, you have many friends here who will stand by you." I thanked him saying, "I have no doubt caused a fair amount of apprehension to all of you. I know there have been occasions over the last years where you have often wondered what next calamity would overtake me." He smiled and replied, "It is as your iSangoma says, 'there are people who attract controversy, and I am afraid my boy you are one of those, but no matter."

After breakfast I asked Hetty if I could use her car but before she could reply, Grand-pere suggested that it would be better if I used one of the plantation pickups. I agreed and said that any old vehicle I could use would be appreciated. I went into the office with Grand-pere and in no time was behind the wheel of a Datsun pickup that although aged was serviceable. I drove out towards Mbabane in the glorious morning sunshine.

I found an unobtrusive loading zone and parked the pickup. I strolled into town and found Nhandla's building. A trim, sophisticated lady greeted me with a big smile and asked how she could help? I told her I needed an appointment with Dr Dlamini as soon as possible. She smiled and asked my name, so I simply said it was 'Owl.' "Isikova (Owl) yes, he told me to expect you and not to worry, but that he will find you and you will understand." I nodded and left the office. I decided that hanging around town would not be advisable, so on the off chance I drove to Dr Toms surgery and found him getting ready to tackle the mornings surgical operations. He greeted me enthusiastically and asked what had happened to me, as he thought I was going to pop around on a regular basis to help and by so doing keep my hand in. I grinned diffidently and said that unfortunately I had had to go back to South Africa, to sort out a few things. "Ah, well no matter, you are here now, and I am sure James would like a hand with the inpatients and prep. There is also a Bassett Hound in need of a dental, so I will be on hand while you anesthetize it. Then once it's on the dental table you can carry on with it, try and save as many of the teeth as you can" he suggested. I was surprised that he was so confident in my abilities but didn't question it. Instead, I went to the kennels and found James who, though surprised to see me seemed happy, that I was there to help.

I spent the morning cleaning cages, walking in-patient dogs and just enjoying myself. It was late afternoon when I left and drove back to the bungalow, where after having a coffee with Nolwesi I left and took the path towards Mandla's 'khaya'(house), as I had done on so many occasions as a boy. I met an old mama heading my way with a load of forest wood tied in a bundle on her tired twisted back. I stopped and after the exchange of customary greetings I asked where she was headed and why her children or grandchildren were not helping her? "Aish," she replied, "you know how it is with today's youngsters, they are too busy!" I was surprised because in eSwatini culture the aged are revered and I took the bundle from her and slung it across my shoulders. "Ungumlungu onomusa(you are a kind white person)," she said and with her hands now free she delved into her shirt pocket and retrieved a bit of newspaper and tobacco and rolled a thick cigarette. Lighting it she puffed out clouds of blue smoke, with a beatific expression on her face, and proceeded to tell me that in fact it was not necessary for her to go foraging in the plantation for 'izinti'(sticks), as she lived with her son and his wives, and he looked after her well enough. But from an early age, it had been her job to collect wood and she didn't see why she should stop now. I agreed with her as I couldn't fault her logic. She said looking at me "You are a strange 'umlungu', "you speak our language and show respect to an old lady as our 'sons' do, how is this?" I smiled and told her that that was one of nicest things anyone had ever said to me. "Ah" she replied and asked, "and where are you headed now and what is your name?" I told her I was called Sean, but mostly in Swaziland I was simply 'Isikhova' (owl). "Well, Isikhova," it is good to have met you I am Futty, usually called old Futty, but my old legs could do

with a little rest so could we find a place to sit for a while?"
"Impele(certainly)," I said and finding a large log I suggested we make use of it.

We sat in silence for a moment or two, Futty happily enjoying the last of her cigarette. Then she nudged me and said, "So Isikhova, you didn't say where you are going?" "Ah" I replied, "sorry!" I am on my way to my bother Mandla's house." Puffing away happily, she asked who Mandla was and who were his antecedents. People were usually defined by what family they belonged to. I acquainted her with his family and connections. "Ah, ah," she uttered surprised, "yes, I know him. he is well respected. You are fortunate to have a 'brother' like him." I agreed saying that without good friends I might not be sitting with her! "Really?" she wheezed, coughing a bit, "how is that? Are you involved in an extremely dangerous job or pastime?" I laughed and said no, as in truth I was just a doctor of animals. "What sort of animals," she asked, "you mean like 'I Izinkomo nezimbuzi' (cattle and goats)?" "Yebo (Yes)" I confirmed. "Oh, then you are important, because cattle are very valuable. Are you a good 'udokotela wezilwane' (doctor of animals)?" she queried, looking at me searchingly. I was at a loss for words, as I had never thought much about it and now, faced with the question, I had to consider if I was a good vet. On reflection, I felt that I couldn't class myself to be anything near such a competent a practitioner as Dr Tom, but then I had not had much chance to practice. I shrugged and told her that I really didn't know. "Isikhova" she said with conviction, "if that is your destiny to be an 'umphilisi wezilwane' (healer of animals), it is important that you do it with all your heart, just as I am a humble 'umqoqi wezinkuni' (wood collector). These are our obligations to the world."

I looked up into the sky, now ablaze in a brilliant orange glow and marvelled that this simple old woman had so eloquently put things into perspective. A lot of money and effort had been spent to get me prepared for a career helping animals and I had gone astray. "Uhlakaniphile Ma (You are wise Mother)" I said. Futty now rummaged once again amongst her clothes and finding her old leather tobacco pouch, she put a pinch of it in another crumpled piece of newspaper and with her gnarled fingers rolled it into a cigarette which she lit. I asked where she was going and through a haze of blue smoke, she told me it was close to 'umuzi kaMandla' (Mandla house) so were going in the same direction. I helped her up and then once again, balancing her bundle on my shoulders, we continued our journey.

Darkness was just beginning to descend in earnest when we approached Mandla's house. Futty now made to retake her bundle from me, but I resisted and said that I was happy to carry it to her house which was not much further on, so she happily agreed to this. On our arrival we were met by several small children who came running up but then seeing their 'ugogo'(grandmother) was accompanied by an 'umlungu' became bashful. Futty called out to them, but they ran back into the house only coming out with their father. Futty introduced him as Thabiso and, he seemed as surprised to see her with a white man as the children had been. I put the bundle of sticks down and shook his hand saying in Siswati that I was happy to meet him and complimented him on having such a wise mother. This pleased him no end and at once he relaxed and thanked me for helping his mother. Futty now told him that I was going to Mandla's house as he was my 'brother'. Thabiso looked me over obviously wondering how a strange white man could be the 'brother' of an induna, saying that undoubtedly, he knew Mandla and how was it that I knew him, a hint of suspicion creeping into his voice. I laughed and suggested that he go with me back to Mandla's house as not only would it prove that I was telling the truth, but I also wanted to get some tobacco from Mandla for him to give to Futty. He readily agreed to this and so I took Futty's old hand in mine and thanked her for the company, telling her that I hoped to meet her again. She smiled broadly replying "'Kunjalo' (of course), you know where I live Isikhova, so you will be welcome."

It wasn't far off, so we arrived within fifteen minutes and were met by Senti, who made us welcome, saying that they expected Mandla any minute. Thula offered us coffee which we gratefully accepted. I watched as their little Sophie crawled around the floor exploring and I imagine she was nearing the stage where she would start walking. She reached my boots and explored them with her stubby little fingers. I picked her up and she smiled which spread from her small mouth to her dark Olive eyes and I was captivated. The door opened and Mandla came in and Sophie cried out in joy and reached for him totally, forgetting me. Taking her, he threw her up in the air, catching her as she screamed in delight. Sitting down he cuddled her and looking at me said, "Ah Isikova, it's good to see you in one piece." I laughed and then, seeing Thabiso, he frowned and asked if there was a problem at work?" Thabiso shook his head and replied, "Cha Mnumzane(No sir), I came with Isikhova as he asked me to." It was obvious that Thabiso was one of Mandla's employees. I told Mandla that I had asked him to come with me, as I wished to give him some tobacco for his mother. Mandla relaxed and said of course, they had plenty in the house and asked Senti to get me a few pouches. Senti returned with the tobacco which I gave to Thabiso, telling him to thank his wonderful mother and he happily took his leave.

Thula and Senti then served supper and the children told their father how they had spent their day, with their mothers adding small snippets. Mandla gave them his full attention listening intently, which pleased them. Supper over we migrated to the sitting room where the children watched their television programmes, then their mothers took them off to bed. Once they left Mandla turned to me saying, "Aish mfowethu" (Wow brother), when Sifiso came to me to tell me that I should contact the iSangoma at once as you were in trouble, I was ready to go to your aid. But Nhandla said it would be best if he went to you on his own, so I trusted his judgement." I told him I appreciated his help and that the iSangoma had been more than adequate and without him I would either be back in prison or even have been shot! He looked at me in amazement and said I better tell him everything. I sat back and related all that had happened. I finished my story, and he shook his head adding, "Ah brother, that's amazing!" I agreed but said that I now hoped to lead a more settled life, as I couldn't cross the border again any time soon. Clicking his tongue, he said, "Well thankfully it's over now and even though you are wanted across the border, you have friends here and we will do all we can to help you."

Senti and Thula returned and refilled our cups, and I spent an enjoyable evening listening to all the local happenings before taking my leave and heading back to the bungalow.

The night was dark, and a storm was brewing, lightning flashed, and the accompanying thunder shook the ground. The bush was in a 'hush' as it awaited the impending downpour, and I hastened my steps hoping to reach the bungalow before it broke. But I was still away off when the rain began to fall in heavy drops that soon soaked me to the skin. I was soon sloshing along the muddy path my boots soaked, but it was a warm night, so it didn't bother me. A muffled beat of wings flew past my ear and as the lightning flashed, I saw the tawny plumage of a large Verreaux Eagle Owl. It hooted in a loud deep base 'gwok, gwok,gwonk,gwokwokwok,gwokwokwok,gwonk,' when it noticed me, very put out at my intrusion, but regaining its composure it flew off hooting in disgust. I burst out laughing feeling admonished at having intruded on its nights hunting, but had it not been for the discord of the storm it would have heard me. I got to the bungalow totally wet through, but over the last months I had seldom had the pleasure to experience hot warm rain, so it did not dampen my good humour at all.

I ran to my room and after disrobing and drying myself off I changed and made my way to the kitchen where I found Grand-pere and Hetty in quiet conversation over a bottle of wine. Getting a glass, I joined them and asked how come they were up so late. "Eh bien Sean (Well Sean)," Grand-pere answered, "I only got in late, and we were just relaxing before retiring and I also have a message for you from Nhandla." I sipped my wine feeling it warm my body and inquired, "Oh when did you see him?" "I didn't actually, he replied, "he left a message at the office saying that he will meet you at the falls tomorrow mid-morning. I imagine that you know which falls he means?" "Ah yes," I responded, "we have met there once or twice, and it is quiet." "Oh," Grand-pere conceded, "he is a total enigma. You are fortunate that he took an interest in you all those years ago." I agreed and then saying goodnight, I went to bed.

The following morning, I awoke feeling positive. Futty had, in her straightforward way put things in perspective. I knew that in some way I should endeavour to use my education and limited veterinary talents as best I could. I found the family enjoying their breakfast and joined them.

"So," Grand-pere queried, "what are your plans after seeing Nhandla?" I shook my head and replied, "It all depends on what he suggests, obviously I have been poor at making any decisions, so I am now going to be guided by him. I know a lot of Europeans cast aspersions on the abilities of 'iSangomas' to make predictions about the future, but in my case Nhandla has been correct." "Iqiniso"(True) Nolwesi exclaimed, "many things have no explanation, but if anyone can guide you it will be him!" Grand-pere sniffed and I wasn't sure if it was in derision or just his normal habit, but I suspect his long association with Catholicism made it hard for him to accept any type of mysticism. Looking over her cup at Nolwesi, Hetty commented, "I agree with you, not everything is 'black and white' in Africa," then she giggled and clarified her observation saying, "and I don't mean in the literal sense." Grand-pere burst out laughing and patting her hand said, "I am sure across the border, that's exactly what it's all about, as Sean has discovered, but who knows Sean, if you are comfortable with your 'Witch Doctor, 'so be it.'" I smiled and replied, "Well life is strange, and I will accept any guidance now, in fact last night I met an incredibly wise old mother who in a matter of minutes simplified a few things for me. "I then told them of my encounter with the aged Futty. Nolwesi clicked her tongue and commented, "The old ones have lived many years and so become wise." Hetty, looking at me said, "Well, you are here and free so that is something." Grand-pere getting up remarked, "Well I hope you have a successful day, but don't forget that sooner or later you have to face the problem of your fiancée." "Yes," Hetty observed, "it is only right that you let her, and her family know that you are no longer in prison." I sighed and told them that as soon as I knew what the future held, I would contact them.

I set off just after breakfast in brilliant sunshine and wandered eastwards, walking along the well-trodden path. The morning air was alive with bird calls and buzzing insects. A mother warthog trotted across my path, snorting as she called to a bunch of piglets. I stopped giving them time to get on their way then continued. I reached the falls around mid-morning and because it was now hot, I sat in the shade at the side of the pool. I scanned the bush to make sure Nhandla had not arrived and then leaned back against a convenient tree, thinking that he could very easily be next to me, and I wouldn't know.

I sat watching as two Nyala antelope came to drink, first the one slaked its thirst while the other stood alert on watch, then they changed positions. They moved off and were replaced by a small group of tiny Duiker antelope who were more skittish as they were more vulnerable. They were still busy drinking when they were surprised by a troop of baboons, who like rude adolescent boys were boisterous and loud. The Duikers made way for the troop and a large grey male positioned himself at an advantageous position so he could watch for any predators and yawning showed off his fearsome canine teeth. The troop then settled down to drink, some of the females having small young clinging to them. I didn't move a muscle and was genuinely surprised that I hadn't been seen, but I had no intention of disturbing them. Another smaller male joined him and began grooming him, trying to ingratiate himself. I was struggling to keep still as flies were buzzing around my face, some settling and being extremely irritating, so I shook my head as surreptitiously as was possible without alerting the sentinel male. The situation was deteriorating by the second, as now a black wasp settled on my arm poking his proboscis around and I was almost sure if I didn't dissuade it, I was going to get stung. I had about made up my mind to move when suddenly the sentinel male gave a harsh bark and jumped up in great agitation, something had alerted him, and it was something he feared. He barked a few more times and the troop gathered, the males facing the danger, whatever it was. It was then that I heard a voice. This spurred the baboons into action, and they loped off in a panic, the males defending their retreat. I swatted at the wasp, and he took flight, and I wiped my face with my hands, ridding myself of the flies!

I stared at the bush hoping to see any movement and began imagining that I had heard a voice. I held my breath for what seemed an age trying to decide what would be the best course of action, and finally decided to call out, "Ukhona lapha(is there anyone here)?" The bush simmered in the heat, and I was beginning to think that I had imagined it, when a deep raucous laugh came from the bush and Nhandla strolled out nonchalantly and motioned for me to follow him. We climbed up the side of the falls without much trouble and Nhandla led the way till it seemed that we could go no further, as it ended in a megalith rock. He moved to the left side of it and unexpectedly disappeared. I was puzzled but then detected a small fissure that led into a small cavern. It had a soft sandy floor and I noticed it had been used by someone, as there were the remains of a fire. "Make yourself comfortable and I will get a fire made for some bush tea." He got some dry grass from the corner and in a matter of minutes had a small fire going and produced two tin mugs from the corner and asked me to go out to the falls and fill them with water.

The bush tea made we sat on the soft sandy floor me with my legs straight out, but Nhandla crouched on his haunches. He removed a thick black pipe from his robe and filling it, set it a light then drew heavily on it, blowing out a thick cloud of smoke. "So, it's good to sit here and take time to consider what's to be done. Do you have any plans going forward?"

I told him of my meeting with Futty the previous evening and how our chat had affected me.

"Ah," he said, sucking again on the pipe "I know Futty, she has a wise head and I think could easily have been a 'umelaphi' (healer) or an iSangoma, but I think her priority has always been her family which I understood."

I sipped my tea and replied, "I do think that it's time that I do what I planned to do from the start, to help animals in some way, whether in a conservation capacity, veterinary or a combination of both would be ideal."

Nhandla, removing the pipe from his mouth and pointing with it responded, "It is genuinely a shame that things have worked out the way they have, but in some infinitesimal way you have played your part, which was occasionally perilous. But know this, a mother giving birth experiences much pain, but the joy of the new-born far outweighs the pain."

I thought this over, then remarked "I understand, but it seems to me that I have only brought danger, anguish and embarrassment to all. Even you have been put at risk by my stupidity."

He chuckled and peering at me through a haze of blue smoke said, "I have faced far worse dangers I assure you and the poor soldiers, and their dogs were at a far greater peril. Are you not aware that it exceeding difficult to scare or kill 'abathakathi'(witches)?"

I had no inkling how to answer that, so countered with a question, "Do you think I will be safe in Swaziland?"

He pondered this for a moment before replying, "Owl, to them across the border you are an embarrassment. To have been able to bring you into their court and sentence you to a lengthy term was their plan. No doubt your conviction and that of a foreign Military Colonel, would have been highly publicised, and they would have made an example of you as a deterrent for others that might be thinking of attempting change."

It was a sobering thought and I sat quiet for a while. Nhandla got up and walked to the small entrance before walking back and refilling his pipe, asking. "What is it you want from life?"

I simply answered, "Just to be normal."

The iSangoma burst out laughing, "And what 'umuntu wami' (my man), what is normal? Normal is an abstract concept. What may be normal to one is abnormal to others. Anyway, you are not and never will be a normal, and will always be an 'aberrant'. But to answer your question no I don't think Swaziland will be safe. Those across the border are like 'e-octopus' and have many tentacles spread around!" Pulling on the pipe and then gesticulating with it, he added, "Cha mngani wami (no my friend), I think we should do what they least expect! You want to do what you have trained for, and I have a solution, but it will mean crossing into Mozambique to the Port of Maputo. You are a keen sailor and I know a 'person who knows a person' who is looking for someone who can help him sail back to Holland. He unfortunately damaged his back crossing the Indian Ocean and needs a crew to help him get back home. Would you be interested?"

I was astounded, but before I could comment he continued, "From Holland you can cross to the United Kingdom where with a new identity, which I will ensure that the A.N.C. provide, you can then hopefully fulfil your wish to practice as a vet."

I looked at him in amazement and responded in a small voice, "But it will mean leaving Africa."

He nodded sagely, then said sympathetically, "That is true, but it will not be forever. You and I both know that change must come across the border and it is not far off. I have connections with many who are positive that things are going in the right direction."

Getting up he took my mug off me and said, "I think it is a workable solution because it will get you out of harm's way until you are no longer a fugitive. I know now I cannot guarantee your safety here, even though you have many powerful friends. Your adversaries have a record for dealing underhand, even when the people they want are in neighbouring countries. They have assassinated people in Botswana!"

I nodded in agreement, as I also knew that they had had some off the original Soweto rioters eliminated in Botswana and Zimbabwe.

I got up and dusting the sand off said, "Can I discuss it with Izwi Lokuduma – Grand-pere and Hetty and I must sort things out with my fiancée, which I don't think will be a problem. I suspect once she heard I was in jail for an extended period, she changed her opinion of me."

"Ah," Nhandla commented, "that may be so. But as far as Lokuduma is concerned, I believe he and his wife will just be happy to know that you are safely out of harm's way."

Going around the small cave he secreted the small tin kettle and tea making paraphernalia and then threw sand on the small fire to make sure it was out. Leaving, we once again climbed-down the side of the falls. It was now just past midday and very warm as we walked along the path. Nhandla said, "I will leave you here. You will need to let me know of your decision as soon as feasible, as I need to plan." I thanked him saying that I would contact him within a few days.

Chapter Eleven

Disengagement

I watched as he disappeared into the bush then carried on my way back to our bungalow. I entered the screen door and found Nolwesi squeezing lemons to make lemonade, smiling she asked if I would like some. "That would be lovely 'udadewethu' (my sister)," I answered. "The 'Nkosikazi' (Madam) is on the veranda. Why don't you join her, and I will bring it out to you.". I went out to the veranda where I found Hetty in one of the comfortable wicker chairs. "Ah, you are back then," she greeted me, "did you meet with the doctor?" I told her that yes, I had met Nhandla and we had had a long chat. "Oh" she replied, "and did he have a solution for you?" I was saved from answering by Nolwesi bringing the lemonade. I was perched on the veranda banister, so Nolwesi handed us our drinks, then taking a glass she sat on the top step of the veranda. I sipped my drink and watched as a small group of russet ground Woodpeckers used their beaks and sticky tongues to peck away at the dead wood at the bottom of the garden. Putting my glass on the floor I said, "Well, it's relatively complicated and I think it would be best if we waited for Grand-pere, so that I can go through it with all of you." "Of course," Hetty agreed, "he should not be long, as he phoned a little while back to say he was leaving the offices." Finishing her drink Nolwesi left to begin the supper. Hetty said she was going to freshen up, so I was left on my own to watch the Woodpeckers. They fussed about pecking and poking until they were rewarded with what they were looking for, an ant's nest with eggs and pupae.

I sat cogitating. On the face of it, it appeared that I would have to leave all this behind for the time being but reasoned that hopefully it wouldn't be for too long and sailing a yacht on the sea could be an attractive adventure. Yes, I decided, it was time I did something useful with the 'talents' that had been instilled into me at great expense by my family and a reasonable effort on my part. I needed to see if I was really any good at it. I finished my drink and leaving the ground Woodpeckers to their task, I went to my room and thought I might compose a letter to Suzanne.

I had begun a rough draft when I heard Grand-pere's land-rover pulling up, so leaving my missive incomplete I made my way to the kitchen. He was sitting at the table chatting to Hetty while Nolwesi busied herself with our supper. "So, Sean," he beamed, "Hetty tells me that you had your 'tete-a-tete' with Dr Dlamini." I laughed a little self-consciously and pulling a chair out told them of Nhandla's plan. Grand-pere remarked, "I also didn't think you would be safe here but didn't want to alarm you and was trying to consider how important it is for the authorities across the border to lay their hands on you. You are quite unimportant to them as you are no longer a threat, but your Colonel Perez is another matter. I suspect it was a great coup capturing him and they were going to make much of his trial in the media, to show their prowess at keeping the European population safe. Unfortunately, his rescue by dissident forces and your escape has changed that and I surmise that the hierarchy of 'umkhonte we sizwe' will have spirited him out the country and harm's way. You are a different proposition; they know full well about all of us sitting at this table and about the Faulkner's and I believe Nhandla when he says that it will be difficult to keep you out of their clutches."

Nolwesi,who had been listening, gasped and said in an angry voice, "But we can keep iSikhova safe here. We have our own police. They cannot just come here and do as they please, as they do across the border." Grand-pere agreed but explained, "We do have a good police force here, but this country has no military force anywhere near as sophisticated as theirs. Also, we are a small land-locked country! We are dependent on them for telecommunications and other technology, so they have a big advantage." Hetty paled looking worried and exclaimed, "But surely that is illegal. This is a sovereign state, and they have no right to try and kidnap Sean."

Once the meal was over and after coffee we continued with the discussion. Grand-pere said "Nhandla's plan has merit, not only does it get you out of the way but also, if he can supply the right documentation, you might gain valuable experience in your profession." Hetty asked, "but surely it could be dangerous, he has no experience of sailing across oceans?" Grand-pere smiled at her saying, "The boy has done plenty of sailing, admittedly no ocean crossings, but with mentoring I am sure he will be fine!" "Aish," Nolwesi cried, "are there not 'Oshaka abayingozi' (dangerous sharks) in the sea?" I giggled as I remembered once, in a discussion with Mandla and Sambulo, they had been adamant that 'Oshaka' didn't attack Africans only Europeans, when it was simply the fact that most Africans didn't take part in many water activities. Consequently, they seldom had opportunity to encounter sharks. Nolwesi glared at me and remarked, "It's true, there are all sorts of dangerous things in the sea, and it will be better for you to be here with us, where you have friends to help you. At least we might know where the danger is coming from!" Hetty agreed, with her remarking, "there must be someway of you living a normal life here surely?" Grand-pere shook his head saying, "I think we must take Nhandla's warnings seriously as he knows this country and its infrastructure intimately, and if he believes that Sean is still at risk then I believe him. We must consider the possible alternatives if he is betrayed and handed over. He will be returned to prison, and they will certainly make an example of him, which could mean an extended time in custody either until he completes his sentence, or more likely until finally there is change, which is inevitable. I think a period overseas either in the United Kingdom or Eire will be the best thing and he will be able to gain practical experience." Looking at me he continued, "But it is not our lives but yours and you must make the choice, we can only offer advice."

I sat back in my chair and tried to weigh up all the alternatives. Was I prepared to take the risk of being returned to prison, where I would be doing a lengthy sentence? I considered that I would then have no control of my life or decisions and would have to hope for the Apartheid government to finally capitulate and hold free elections, which would end in a new government and inevitably my release. Alternatively, I could take the opportunity to experience crossing an ocean on a yacht, which was an attractive proposition, plus the chance to practise in either Ireland or the United Kingdom. I got up and refilled my cup then walking around said, "I think eventually the constant worry of being 'nabbed' would make my life fraught with anxiety, so as much as I am going to miss all of you, it will be even worse if I am incarcerated for an indeterminate period. I trust Nhandla's guidance implicitly, as but for him I would not be a free man today, and you may laugh but he knows things." Nolwesi said, "Ah, ah, he is incredibly wise and of course he can divine future events and if he has a plan for you, I think it might be the best if you follow it." I chuckled and replied, "But 'udadewethu', a moment ago you were against me leaving?" Nolwesi clicked her tongue and said "Aish, am I not a 'owesifazane'(woman)!?" Hetty laughed and concurred saying that it was a woman's prerogative to change her mind.

Grand-pere getting up said, "Well then, I think if you are able to come to terms with living overseas, until there is some sort of resolution across the border it may be the best solution. Do you want me to contact Nhandla, by private messenger, to tell him that you will be happy for him to make all the arrangements?" I sighed but nodded in compliance. Hetty now asked "What about Suzanne and the rest of your other family? What are you going to tell them?" I groaned as I was still mulling over what to say in my letters to them. I envisaged that Suzanne had already ended our engagement and would be relieved at my decision. I said that I was busy trying to compose letters to them, but it was not an easy task. "Uum , I would think not," Hetty replied in sympathy, "but at least it will put their minds at ease and even though it may be painful, time heals all."

The rest of the evening was spent with me trying to glean as much information on Ireland. Grand-pere was able to describe the southern counties well as he had lived there, but because he had never lived in the UK, he was unable to comment. On reflection he said it might be a promising idea to contact some of my father's family in county Clare and he would ask my mother, without revealing any details why he needed the information. I felt a little better, as knowing someone in a foreign country would be a significant help. "In fact," he said, "they will be waking up in Queensland in a couple of hours, so I will do it tonight." I got up and told them I was going to try and finish my letters for Grand-pere to take in the morning and post and left them still discussing the 'old country'.

In my room I sat down and tried to write first to Suzanne and then to the rest of the family, but it was very problematic because they believed that I was still being held in prison. I sat chewing the back of my pen, trying to draft a suitable letter. Since leaving all those months ago my life had been in a state of upheaval, and I had seldom thought of Suzanne. I reflected that there was no question that I was not the ideal prospective partner, but conversely ours wasn't a normal relationship. I decided that the best was just to lay down the facts. Firstly, in the eyes of the law across the border, I was on the run for crimes that they wished to punish me for and according to Nhandla they could try to 'kidnap 'me. Additionally, my prospects of practicing as a vet were severely limited in Africa.

I finally expressed my sentiments in the two letters, one to Suzanne and the other to Mia and the rest of the family. I suggested that we meet up at the Phophonyane reserve the following Sunday. I sealed both letters and took them to Grand-pere, who took them and said that he would use one of his staff to personally deliver them to the Faulkner's House on the hill. I nodded my thanks, then feeling a little tired went to bed.

The following day I considered going to Dr Tom's practice to help and was getting ready to leave in the van when Grand-pere, also on his way out, mentioned that it might be a risk not worth taking and it was best that I didn't visit places that I had habitually frequented. "I don't foresee them trying here at the bungalow as Hetty, Nolwesi or myself are usually here and they would prefer not to have any witnesses. I will also from today use some of the plantations 'Abalindi'(watchmen) to be here all the time till you leave. They can act as gardeners. I nodded and thanked him. He simply shrugged and replied, "I also spoke to your mother early this morning and she has given me several contacts for you in Ireland, she was incredibly happy to hear that you are planning to go to Europe. I will try to contact them telephonically, after I have had a chat with Nhandla as regards your documentation. I think the best thing for you to do for now is to stay close to the bungalow and start brushing up on your veterinary knowledge." I concurred and after seeing him off returned to the house and asked Nolwesi if she needed help with anything. She smiled broadly saying if I was up for helping her, she would appreciate it. I readily accepted and in no time was up to my elbows in flour.

The day wore on and after helping and eating copious amounts of 'vetkoek' I went and dug out my old veterinary textbooks and started trying to pummel my befuddled brain with disease aetiologies and surgical procedures. Grand-pere returned early that evening and we all sat on the veranda watching the sun slowly sink under the western horizon. Grand-pere, leaning back in his wicker chair updated me. "I had your letters hand delivered and spoke to Nhandla personally, he is satisfied that going overseas is the best possible solution for you. He will expedite your passage with the Dutch yachtsman, and he is approaching his contacts to organise your documents, so there is no going back now." I thanked him. "My messenger reported back to me that he had handed the letters to the 'intokazi yomuzi' (the lady of the house)," "Ah, that would be Mia," I remarked, "I hope that my letters don't upset them. Hopefully Sven will bring Suzanne, if she is in country, to see me on Sunday. I would really like to clarify things face to face." Hetty asked, "what do you think Suzanne is going to say?" I shook my head and admitted that I was dreading it, I had been a poor choice of intended partner because I had been so absorbed in my own affairs. "Well, it can't be helped," Hetty said soothingly. I agreed saying, "There were times, when I was in prison lying on my bed, that I did think of her and the family. But I thought and was told, that I would be there for an extended period, so rationalized that in time they would all forget me." Hetty looked at me sympathetically and asked in a quiet voice, "Was it particularly horrid?" I took a moment to think, yes initially it had been both scary and uncomfortable but with the help of Spike and the gang it had become bearable. I spent the evening, and late into the night, telling them of my experiences and I could see that it surprised them and at the end of my narrative Grand-pere simply commented that help often came from unexpected sources. Then we all went to bed.

The following days I spent helping Nolwesi and Hetty around the house and on the Friday, on returning from the office, Grand-pere said that he had had a visit from Sven and Mia at his office and they confirmed that they would all meet me on the Sunday at the reserve. In a way the news was welcome as I would be able to see all of them, but on the other hand it was a little daunting.

Sunday morning arrived and I dressed with care and then set off on my bike. It was a glorious day and I whizzed along the empty roads. I 'snaked' my way through Forbes reef and pushed on happily feeling remarkably free. It was exhilarating and I was able to put my apprehension about the upcoming meeting aside. Unfortunately, I was soon throttling back and 'burbling' my way through Piggs Peak with the falls resort close.

I left the bike and made my way to the restaurant area and found a good table under a substantial Waterbessie tree. I was at least an hour early and had planned it that way, so that I could compose my thoughts before they arrived. I ordered breakfast and coffee and then sat happily watching life go by. I was just finishing my second cup of coffee when a voice behind me said, "Well Sally, you are looking good for a fugitive." I jumped up as they approached the table feeling awkward, not sure of what sort of reception I would receive. Mia came up and hugged me and then putting me at arm's length inspected me. She smiled as only she could, her eyes reflecting her smile. "My God, Sean," she exclaimed, "we honestly thought it was going to be a long time before we would see you again." Jenny and Suzanne now came walking up, both looking cool and attractive. I smiled sheepishly and asked who wanted drinks, hoping to delay the upcoming interrogation. Sven said, "Come on Sally we will go and order, then we can sit down and hear your unbelievable story."

We sat in the sunshine around the table, and I looked at their expectant faces, not knowing where to start but strangely it was Suzzanne who began vehemently. "We are your family!" she exclaimed and asked, "do you think that when we heard that you had been arrested it didn't affect us? We were hoping, well especially me, for at least a telephone call, or a letter to say how you were and what was happening, but when we spoke to Jacques, he told us that he was not getting much information and what he was getting was only second hand via the Chaplain. How is that possible, surely it was your right to write letters to your family?" I nodded and replied that yes, I could have written letters to them, but was so worried about the scrutiny that these letters would have undergone and that they might have compromised their safety. Suzanne glared at me her eyes flashing and responded, "Surely that would have been for us to decide, and I would far rather have had news from you. For all we knew you were being abused or even possibly tortured, as you had been previously, it was very thoughtless of you!" Mia interrupted, "Now Suz, relax we are here now, and we have no idea what sort of pressures he faced in there."

I took a deep breath just as their orders arrived and then suggested that they let me relate all that had happened. I watched as Suzanne struggled to control her impulsiveness. I slowly and meticulously told them everything, noticing that at certain stages of my narrative they all wanted to question aspects, but Mia held up her hand so that I could continue. They were finishing their cups of tea when I finally came to the end. I sat back a little hoarse but satisfied that I had covered most of the salient points. At first, they sat in silence waiting for Mia to ask the first question which she did, and it surprised me, "Why did you not just tell Colonel Perez to make his own way to Johannesburg when he refused to obey your instructions? The man is obviously a pretentious idiot, you were there to advise him and help him to get to Johannesburg, you should have ditched him as soon as he refused to accept your help." I didn't quite know how to respond but said, "I thought it was my mission to deliver him to Solly as I had done on all previous occasions, but you are right I should have been more assertive, and things might have been different. But who knows?" Sven looked at me and shaking his head said, "Blimey Sally, you do get into some binds, not only did he get you both arrested but then when 'your crowd' decide to rescue him they abandon you." I shook my head and replied, "Those that rescued him were not told about the rest of the prison truck's occupants, so I imagine they believed we were just 'common criminals', I was the only other political detainee." Jenny remarked, "So really you were not actually convicted, so why are they so determined to recapture you." Sven chuckled and answered for me, "It's obvious Jen, they couldn't lay their hands on the 'organ grinder', so they were desperate to catch 'the monkey', but they hadn't reckoned on Sally's numinous Witch doctor. I have to say he is not someone I would want to tangle with on a dark night."

Suzanne, I could see, was not pleased and emphasised that even if I had ended up for an extended period in jail, I should have contacted them no matter what! I tried exonerating myself but, in the end, agreed that I could have made more of an effort. Sipping her coffee, she said in a mollified tone "Family support each other and I am your fiancée. Did you think we didn't care what happened to you or where you would end up? I can understand you had greater concerns, but we were worried". Sven shook his head and observed, "Well that's all in the past and we can't change what's happened, but what now Sally?" I sighed and told them of the plan for me to help the Dutch sailor to sail to Europe and then to move on to Ireland. Suzanne slammed her cup down and protested, "Good grief, are you serious? You have never sailed any ocean and you would be better off in the hands of the S.A. authorities, at least you will be alive." I had no idea how to respond because I couldn't refute her arguments.

There was silence at the table, then Mia asked, "So when you finally get to Ireland, hopefully in one piece, how are you going to survive as you will be a stranger in a foreign country?" I explained that I had some of my father's family who I was hoping to contact and that Nhandla was going to provide me with the necessary documentation for me to practice my profession. "Ah," she smiled, "and then you may lead a normal life?" "Bloody hell Sally," Sven laughed, "you never do things the straightforward way, but it might be a lot of fun." Suzanne stared at me and then asked, "How big is this yacht you are planning to leave on from Mozambique and what is wrong with the owner?" I shook my head saying that I wasn't sure of the size of the boat but only that the owner, who was not young, had damaged his back while trying to cross the Indian ocean. "I see," she said pensively, "and how long do you think the trip will take?" Again, I had to admit that I didn't know but a month or two at least.

"Ok" Mia said cheerfully, "well let us all have a walk up to the falls and then when we come back, we can have a lovely lunch." "Yes" that's a great idea," Jenny said, getting up and taking Sven's arm. The day had become hot, so it was pleasant walking along the heavily wooded path to the falls in the shade. Mia and Suzanne walked on either side of me, and Mia took my arm as we strolled along and said, "You know the whole idea is not bad and sailing the sea might just be fun." Suzanne asked, "You will have to stop on the way to get food and water surely?" I hadn't thought of that but now that she mentioned it, we would have to stop at some ports. I gasped and then replied, "Well it better not be in any South African port, otherwise, it will be problematic!"

"How awful it would be," Mia said concerned, "if you are caught at the last moment. It would be heart-breaking." Suzanne asked, "What if you get seasick?" I hadn't considered that either but reasoned that I had been on sailing catamaran start lines and sometimes had to bob around for ages before the start gun went off. Admittedly they had been on lakes and dams which could not be compared to a rough ocean swell.

Reaching the falls, we dabbled our feet in the cool water and Jenny remarked, "Are you not going to miss Africa, Sally?" I nodded replying, "I hope it's not too long before I am back. Things have to change, and I am sure I will be able to return sooner or later. Sven asked, "why don't you just fly out from Swaziland instead of sailing with an unknown man from Mozambique, surely that would be safer?" I admitted that I was just going along with what Nhandla had suggested. Mia agreed with me, "To have developed this elaborate plan he must be aware of things we don't know about, and from what you have told us he has not let you down yet." Amazingly Suzanne agreed with her mother and then looking at me unexpectedly announced, "Well if you are going on an adventure sailing the high seas, then you must count me in!"

I was astounded but it was Mia who cried, "What, you want to go with Sean!?" Suzanne simply replied, "Why not, he has never sailed the ocean and even though the captain is there he is quite plainly not a hundred percent fit, so will only be able to give instructions and advice and I am sure an extra hand would be welcome." Jenny was surprised and asked, "But what about your contracts, the agency will not be pleased!" Mia added, "And anyway you haven't been invited and additionally Sean doesn't have the details of when this is going to take place. Also, you have no sailing experience, and the owner may not want you on board."

Sven got up from the rock he was sitting on and went over to his sister and clapped her on the back saying, "I don't often compliment you Sis, but for once I am genuinely proud of you. You are prepared to make sacrifices and take risks to help Sally and Lord knows he needs all the help he can get!"

I sat watching the water tumble into the clear pool, wondering if I had heard Suzanne correctly. It was not as if we had even had any sort of relationship or closeness, yet she wanted to go with me on a perilous sea voyage. I decided not to comment until she had explained her motives fully. It didn't take long before she asked, "Will you approach Dr Dlamini and ask if he would consider asking the Dutch Captain to consider my proposal?" I took a moment before replying, "I am not sure you are grasping the full impact of what you are planning. I am wanted and anyone helping me could be charged with aiding and abetting. I am only resorting to these arrangements because I have limited options to leave to get to Europe. You on the other hand are free to travel where you will and do so frequently to both America and Europe. You have a career which you have been nurturing for years, yet you intend to risk life and limb on an enterprise that could end in disaster?" Suzanne smiled then replied, "Yes, I have a career, which for girls like Jen and myself has a limited lifespan, as the fashion world thrives on youthfulness. But I have been working for several years and the endless flights and hotels become very mundane. I want something else from life, don't you understand that even though your veterinary career was cut short you were doing something constructive by helping both the animals and the people.? What Jen and I do is vanity! In no way would the world be affected by our absence from the fashion merry-go-round, believe me no one would even give us a second thought! I just want to do something positive, where I feel that I have contributed instead of just being "frivolous." "Wow," Sven said, "that's really deep Suz, you are full of surprises." Mia looked at her daughter with admiration and then said, "You know Sean, I am beginning to think that it would be a good idea for you to approach Dr Dlamini, maybe he will agree to her request and being at sea will give both of you time to evaluate your lives." Again, I was unable to think of a reasonable retort. Things were moving too fast, so I merely agreed to discuss it with Nhandla saying that it would be up to him and the Dutch Captain.

The day was like most Swazi days, sunny in the mornings with the steady build-up of cumulus clouds with an electric thunderstorm brewing. With this in mind Mia suggested we return to the restaurant before the storm broke. Strolling slowly back down, my mind was in turmoil, but Suzanne took my arm and smiling up at me said quietly, "Don't look so worried, I am a big girl and have done loads of dangerous things and I am not easily breakable." I looked at her and thought why would any girl who had just about everything that any girl could want from life, decide to risk it all on a foolhardy trip with a semi cripple and a man on the run. It was mind boggling, but who was I to judge. I had minimal experience of the female psyche.

Migrating into the restaurant to avoid the upcoming storm, we all sat around, and the talk naturally was all about Suzanne's little 'bombshell', and I mostly listened, as I didn't want to douse her enthusiasm. I sat back after my meal and watched my 'family'. They might in most instances make fun of each other, but when it came down to being there for each other they never stinted, and I was unbelievably lucky that I was included. Jenny had now come round to Suzanne's thinking, and they sat discussing how and what a girl would take on an ocean crossing trip. It was vaguely amusing.

The time finally came when we had to part and as I walked them to their car Suzanne said, "Please try and contact your 'Witch doctor' and ask him about my proposal. I will come to yours in the valley in a day or so." I gulped and replied that I would do my best to get hold of him as soon as I could, but that there were many things she needed to think about and after a day or so she might reconsider her decision. Her eyes flashed and she snarled, "Oh how little you know me. Believe me, when I say I intend to come sailing with you, I mean it and whether you like it or not, you are still my fiancé." All I could do was open the car door for her and meekly agree. Mia hugged me again and said that she too would come with Suzanne to the bungalow. Sven and Jenny said that they would see me before I left, either with Suzanne or without. Sven added before driving off. "Take it easy on the way back to the Enzulweni valley Sally, the roads are bound to be a bit slippery." I nodded and then made my way back to my bike. I rode slowly back home, my thoughts on anything but the wet roads, but more on the day's events.

I updated Grand-pere, Hetty and Nolwesi on my day out and Suzanne's decision of hopefully going with me. Unbelievably none of them seemed overly surprised. Hetty said, "She seems like a girl who knows her mind and has decided that the only way to know what's happening to you is to be with you!" Grand-pere agreed and said, "I think you have underestimated her, so I will again contact Nhandla and set up a meeting for you." Nolwesi laughed and said, "'Nina besifazane' (us women) know what's best, I think it will be good for you to have someone watching over you." Hetty nodded in agreement adding, "I'm looking forward to meeting her, when is she coming?" I shook my head saying it all depended on how soon I could meet with Nhandla and how long it would it take to get a reply from the Dutch Captain. Grand-pere left his chair saying, "As time is of the essence, I will personally go to his office first thing tomorrow morning and if he is not there, I will leave an urgent message." It took a long time that night for sleep to invade the turmoil of my confused thoughts.

In a day or two, as the light was fading and the crickets and frogs were beginning their nightly chorus, the iSangoma came to the bungalow. Nolwesi was getting ready to go home to her family when she came bustling back, out of breath, and in a high state of excitement. "'Usefikile' (He has come)", she breathed and behind her came Nhandla. He was dressed in a smart business suit and Nolwesi was obsequious to the extreme, at once serving him the strong red bush tea that he asked for. He settled into the old deck chair on the veranda next to Grand-pere and sipping the tea commented, "Ah Lokuduma it's good to see you so well and I presume this is your 'good wife'. Grand-pere introduced Hetty who mused "I must admit you are not what I expected." Nhandla chortled and smiling replied, "I am glad, that is what I aim for. It is good to keep the people guessing, as it is part of the essence of being a' umthakathi'(witch)." I sat on the steps and waited as they all chatted about everyday things and Nolwesi plied Nhandla with scones, jam, and cream, which he said were the best he had tasted, since he had been in England. This compliment pleased her no end. Finally, he got down to the purpose of his visit, "Isikhova, I was undoubtedly surprised when Lokuduma told me that firstly, you had a fiancée and additionally, that she wishes to go with you. But after consideration I thought it a particularly innovative idea, not only will it throw off those across border as they will be checking airports and ports for a single person, but her help might prove invaluable." With Scone debris decorating his smart suit he proceeded, "I have also broached the subject with Captain Dirk who is ambivalent, as he is extremely happy to have any assistance to return home, and I have acquainted him with your circumstances." Grand-pere asked when he expected the captain to leave Maputo. In reply Nhandla said, "I think it will be entirely dependent on how soon I can accompany Isikhova and his young lady to the port. I know he is desperate to leave and return to Holland. He has tried to get some sort of crew locally but thankfully he has had little response, so it is the ideal situation for us."

He relaxed in his chair, obviously in no hurry to leave saying, "I have engaged with my contacts across the border and if you supply me with an updated photograph of yourself for the false passport, I will make the necessary arrangements. Unfortunately, you will have to accept a new identity till you reach Europe. I suspect your young lady will have her own valid passport." I confirmed that as she travelled regularly, I didn't envisage any problems. "Excellent!" he uttered. Well then, we are getting there. I would advise both of you to be ready at short notice and try to keep your luggage to the bare minimum!" Grand-pere said, "The photograph will not be a problem as we have facilities at the office which we use to take photographs for our employees ID cards, so we will take his picture tomorrow morning and send a messenger with it to your office." "Well, that will be ideal," Nhandla said, getting ready to leave, adding "as soon as I have the passport, I will use my influence to get a flight booked to Maputo so I will need your fiancées name." I was a little hesitant at first as I thought it would be best to consult Suzanne, but Hetty said that it wouldn't matter, as if she changed her mind, they would bear the flight cancellation fee. So, I gave Nhandla her details. Grand-pere and I walked with him to his luxury sedan, after he delighted Nolwesi by saying that after eating her scones he would be a regular visitor.

In the house, before going to bed, I asked Grand-pere if he could let Suzanne know as soon as possible, but Hetty volunteered to go up to the Faulkner's home the next day to meet them and tell her what was planned. I lay in bed that night listening to the evocative call of a lonely Civet trying to contact another Civet and knew no matter what happened

I would do my utmost to return to Africa as soon as possible.

Straight after breakfast the following morning Hetty left for the house on the hill while I started rooting through my sailing gear.

Hetty returned in the early afternoon and said that she had lunch with Mia who told her that she would bring Suzanne down that evening for supper, so Nolwesi and Hetty sprang into action preparing dinner. I spent the afternoon with my two 'minders', Wandile and Sipho, the two plantation security personnel that Grand-pere insisted watch the bungalow. I wasn't sure they were entirely necessary, but things were now out of my hands, so I had to comply.

Mia and Suzanne arrived early evening, both dressed exquisitely and strangely excited. Hetty and Nolwesi cosseted them in the small sitting room. Grand-pere arrived and suggested we migrate to the veranda where it was cooler, so I was dispatched to bring more wicker chairs from the small summer house in the garden, which had become the 'home' of Wandile and Sipho since their arrival. I brought the chairs and then helped to serve drinks. I found the situation slightly surreal as in all the time I had lived with the Faulkner's, they had never visited the bungalow. Mostly Sven had dropped me off, or I had taken a minibus taxi before I had got my bike. This was due to Grand-pere spending a lot of his time at the Marble Hall farm with Hetty.

"So," Suzanne said, with a self-satisfied smile, as soon as I sat down in my usual place on the top step of the veranda, "it appears your mentor is happy for me to go with you." "Yes," Hetty said, "he thought it was a promising idea, but I must admit Sean doesn't seem overly enamoured with the plan." I frowned and said in a small voice, "It's not that you are not welcome but honestly, neither of us have any ocean sailing experience and will be relying on a semi-incapacitated skipper. I am not sure that you realise the risks that you are taking, in my case I have limited options, but you have a successful career and a future." She was undaunted and replied, "Life's all about living and if you don't take risks you will stagnate. I have travelled and been 'wined and dined' and had numerous affairs, a couple of proposals but, ended up engaged to you. Have you not wondered why?" Everyone was silent and looked at me expectantly. I was at a loss for words and just stared at her, so she continued, "It's quite simple, I have known you a long time and you are an unassuming, kind and empathetic person, your ego is almost non-existent, and, in my world, it is something I rarely encounter. Unfortunately, you are also easily led, influenced and make poor decisions, but I am sure we can work on that." Mia tittered and said, "I agree, you can't change the past, but I think with Suzanne's help things will be better."

Grand-pere remarked, "I don't think it's going to be easy for either of you, but no doubt Suzanne's help will be invaluable and if she is prepared to risk all why should you object!" I assented without further comment, if Suzanne hated it, she could always 'jump ship' at the first convenient port.

Dinner was an elaborate affair with Nolwesi and Hetty doing their best to impress, and afterwards we sat with our wine glasses charged and talk drifted to other topics. I sat listening, my thoughts of nothing but how I was going to cope, not only with learning new sailing skills but also living with Suzanne, who I knew from experience had a mercurial temperament and often acted irrationally. I was so lost in my own thoughts I scarcely noticed her 'plonk' herself down next to me on the floor and I caught a whiff of her apple scented hair, which I had experienced before. Quietly she whispered in my ear, "It won't all be bad. Just think, you will have me all to yourself. Well, apart from our skipper, how old is he anyway?" I almost jumped up and ran as I hadn't even considered the fact that we would be in close proximity all day, every day! I gulped and replied, "I am not sure how old he is, but I am hoping he will be able to teach us quickly about ocean sailing! You are a little insane, this is not going to be a pleasure cruise by any means." She glared at me and murmured, "You know I think that maybe you don't even like me!" I shook my head assertively and replied, "That's just so untrue but you are sophisticated, and I am not. I have a big nose, am a little short and know nothing at all about women, apart from you and Wendy, and you are the only girls I ever even kissed, and I am sure I did that correctly." Suzanne burst out in a paroxysm of laughter, her slight body shaking. "Oh Lord," she said still giggling, "are you worried that I am going to corrupt your morals!"

I now noticed that everyone was looking at us. I felt foolish and when Mia asked Suzanne what was so amusing, I prepared myself for further embarrassment. But Suzanne only shrugged and said that I was just naive. Thankfully, she became engaged in a conversation with Hetty and Mia about shoes and I was left to my thoughts. Later as Mia and she were leaving, she took my hand and whispered, "Don't worry Sally, it will all work out and never stop being you. Let me know as soon as you have any news about our flights, I am all packed and ready." Mia hugged me and said she hoped to see me before we left.

I spent the days close to the bungalow, until one night Grand-pere returned to say that Nhandla had contacted him confirming that my documents were now in order and that the flight to Maputo was booked for three days' time. Hetty said that she would go the following morning early to update Suzanne and the rest of the Faulkner's.

Chapter Twelve

New Adventures

The day finally arrived, and I had packed my dunnage, clothes and toiletries and a larger waterproof duffle bag, which Hetty had bought, with a few veterinary books and sailing paraphernalia. I said a tearful goodbye to Nolwesi who said, "'Ungakhathazeki' (don't worry), you are safe if the iSangoma has planned this. You will be fine and soon return to us from 'ngaphesheya kwamanzi' (across the water)." I hugged her and agreed that I hoped to be back soon. I hardly noticed the trip to the airport and was surprised when we arrived that not only was Mia there to see us off, but so were Sven, Jenny, Luke and his girlfriend Carmel. Nhandla was dressed immaculately in his suit and Suzanne, a seasoned traveller in designer jeans and sweater. I noticed she only had a small hold-all with her and over her arm an expensive sailing jacket. "Ah," Nhandla greeted us, "and so the party is complete. Our flight leaves in an hour or so, so we can all have refreshments in the Departures coffee shop."

The coffee shop was a little rudimentary but both Jenny and Suzanne used it, so in no time we had put a few tables together, drinks had been procured and we settled down in quiet conversation. Jenny sitting across from Suzanne was slightly emotional and said to her, "I can't believe you're off on an adventure without me, we have been together for years now. So, after talking it through with Sven, I too am going to take a sabbatical." I could see Suzanne was genuinely surprised and asked what she was going to do with her time. Jenny replied, "I am going to sign up for a correspondence University course in law and move in permanently with Sven." Sven and Mia were undoubtedly pleased, and he said, "I think its brilliant, as not only will I know she is safe but also Mum will have a 'replacement' daughter."

Mia smiled smugly and remarked, "I know that Sean and Suzanne's trip is not going to be without risk but at least I know they will be there for each other, and Suzanne will keep me posted. I am used to Suz and Jen being away, so having Jen for company is going to be lovely." Nhandla chuckled and said to Suzanne, "I don't think you are going to have problems with Sean. With your direction, he may stop going from one debacle to another." "Oui," Grand-pere agreed, "I think we will all sleep easier knowing that he is out of the way and Hetty and myself are grateful to you." Sven snickered saying, "Oops Sally, I think you are in a bit of a predicament, our Suz doesn't take 'any prisoners' and if I was you, I would get ready for a few 'squalls'!" Suzanne glared at him and tutting retorted, "You are an idiot." I sat quietly while they squabbled good-naturedly as siblings do.

Nhandla got up and said, "Well I think you all need to say your farewells, as our flight has just been called." Hetty hugged me and said, "I am sure you are going to be fine. Please call as and when you can." Grand-pere nodded and said "A Bien Tot Suzanne et Sean, Dieu vous accompagne (See you soon Suzanne and Sean, God go with you)." Mia hugged us both and whispered in my ear, "You will be fine together. She's a tough cookie and if nothing else you have proved that you are a survivor, so in no time we will be welcoming you both back." Sven and Jenny wished us luck and a tearful Jenny, holding Suzanne's hand said, "You are and always will be my 'bestie' so take care of yourselves." Luke and Carmel wished us the absolute best and then with Nhandla, we passed through the departure gate.

The fight to Maputo was short and uneventful and after landing we got a taxi to the harbour. Our first sight of 'Meermin' was in the late afternoon. She was around thirteen metres or forty-two feet L.W.L., her hull blue with a white deck and a single mast, sloop rigged. Walking along the dock Nhandla called out "Kaptein Jansen, can we come aboard?" A tall gaunt bent over sunburned man climbed out of the companion way and smiling, shouted "Welkom (Welcome)!" Holding on to the wheel of the boat to steady himself, he shook our hands as we introduced ourselves. I would say he was in his mid- fifties and had the wrinkled complexion of one who has been in the sun his whole life. Using the steps on the 'tumble home stern' we all climbed on board, and he suggested we go down the companion way with our dunnage to the saloon.

The yacht was a lot 'roomier' than I had expected, with a decent sized table surrounded by comfortable seats. Suzanne and I dumped our bags down on the cabin sole while Nhandla helped Captain Jansen down the few stairs of the companion way. We stood hesitantly waiting for instructions. "Wel sit, sit," "the captain uttered in a thick Dutch accent. The three of us sat down while the captain slowly levered himself onto a chair on what I presumed was the chart table. Once seated he said, "So my name is Dirk, and I am happy to finally have you on board. Nhandla has told me that you are both happy to help me sail back to Rotterdam." Suzanne and I both told him our names and I thanked him saying that we were happy to help in any way, even though we had no sea going experience. "Ag," he exclaimed, "that is not a big problem. Sean is an accomplished catamaran sailor, so the basic principles of sailing are the same. Do either of you understand any navigation?" Shaking our heads, we said that unfortunately we didn't, but I added that I was eager to learn. He smiled and said, "No it's not a problem, you both look fit and capable and because of my back injury that is what I need, as I am unable to get around the deck to do sail adjustments. 'Meermin' is quite easy to handle and is as sweet as a nut on most points of sail, so with you two it should be fine. I have the aft cabin so you two can have the large forepeak double. I have cleared the lockers out so you can put your gear in them."

I coloured and remarked, "I think Suzanne would be more comfortable in the forepeak on her own, I am happy to find a berth anywhere." Suzanne giggled but said nothing. Dirk looked at us quizzically and said, "But Nhandla told me you were an engaged couple?" Nhandla smirked and commented, "Sean is a good Catholic boy and feels it might be inappropriate." At this Suzanne burst out laughing and then in quick precise narrative explained our relationship so far. Amazingly, the way she described it somehow made sense. "Ah," Dirk said, "well that's not a problem, the seats you are sitting on convert into berths and there is also a small pilot berth here," he said pointing to a small hammock that was folded up next to him, which I think will suit you." I nodded saying that would be ideal.

Nhandla stood up and said "Well I must be getting back to the airport so as not to miss my return flight. Thank you, Kaptein Dirk for helping Sean out, I hope you have fair winds and a good trip back home." Dirk tried to get up, but Nhandla said, "No don't trouble yourself, Sean will see me off." Dirk sat back down and replied, "No, thank you Dr Dlamini, I think that it will be a case of it being mutually beneficial to us and now we have the additional bonus of an extra crew member." Nhandla nodded and shaking Suzanne's hand said, "Well goodbye my dear, I am happy that you decided to accompany Sean, your support and experience of life will be a great asset to him." Suzanne I could see was genuinely touched and taking his hand replied, "I think this trip will not only serve the purpose of getting Sean to Europe but will also be a great learning curve for both of us."

I went on deck to see Nhandla off while Suzanne asked Dirk if there was anything she could do for him before she went forward to put her gear in the forepeak cabin. Nhandla put his hand on my shoulder and looking at me sternly said, "So Isikhova, it is goodbye for now. You will need to start thinking of those two people in there. Captain Dirk although a very experienced sailor is physically incapable of handling this boat, so it will be down to your ability to learn all you can as soon as possible to help him and keep that loyal, young lady safe. I know you have been a 'loner' for a long time but now things will be different, you have a responsibility to both!" Please stay connected, when and where possible, with all of us but for now 'hamba ngokuphepha' (go safely)." he added, climbing down onto the dock and walking off.

I watched him go and it suddenly dawned on me that what he had said was sobering. I had never even owned a pet that was dependent on me, but here I was getting ready to cross oceans with no experience and had to consider that failure to learn quickly could have dire consequences for all three of us. I went back down the companion way, to find Suzanne sitting across from Captain Dirk, having opened a bottle of wine, in amiable conversation and with a note pad in front of her. Captain Dirk smiled and said to me, "Bring a glass Sean, I am just making a victualling list so that we hopefully won't need to put into port until Durban." I found a plastic wine glass and asked diffidently if it was entirely necessary to put into any South African port? He grunted, as he shifted his position, obviously feeling uncomfortable, saying, "Unfortunately we won't have enough sweet water on board to miss all the S.A. ports, so it will have to be Cape Town. I understand your concern, but Nhandla assured me that your 'new passport' will hold up to scrutiny and if you stay on board, I am sure it will be fine, we will only go in to victual. Now I will need to start teaching you navigation as soon as possible, but first let's all get to know each other better."

I could see that Suzanne and the Captain already had a rapport and she updated him on her career and how many countries she had visited. Captain Dirk had also been to a lot of the cities and towns she mentioned so they conferred happily, he then told us all about his life at sea. It had begun as a humble deck hand and ended up with him being a first officer on tankers. I was impressed, you needed to be a master mariner to be in control of a colossal tanker! In time he had married and had two children, a daughter who was a physiotherapist in Utrecht and a son who had gone into politics and lived with his wife in Amsterdam. Unfortunately, his wife had passed away tragically which had made him re-evaluate his life and he had decided to buy Meermin and travel the world's oceans. Regrettably he had run into a cyclonic storm off Madagascar where he had damaged his back, but he was optimistic that in time it would heal, as the doctors he had seen in Maputo claimed that he had damaged a disk, but it could be repaired with surgery. Captain Dirk felt that he would rather have the surgery in his home country, so consequently he needed help to get home. He had, at first, thought to recruit crew in South Africa as sailors were rare in the port of Maputo but then his doctor, who was a friend of Nhandla, told him of my predicament, which resulted in our presence. "So, I am happy to have you on board," he said in conclusion.

Sitting back, he looked my way and then commented "Don't worry Sean, Dr Dlamini has advised me of your situation and as a humanitarian I was extremely pleased to comply with his suggestion that you be the person to help me and now you have brought an added benefit of this young lady." Suzanne simpered and patting his hand got up and suggested that she start looking to get some sort of supper on the go. This surprised me as I had never previously seen her doing anything domestic. "Ja Ja,"

Captain Dirk said, "there are some fresh vegetables that were delivered this morning and a cooked chicken that is still edible." Suzanne found the chicken in the small freezer chest, and I began to peel the vegetables. I had a feeling that this was going to be a happy boat.

The next few days went by in a haze. I studied charts and navigational books on how to calculate longitude with use of the chronometer and then Captain Dirk tutored me in the use of the sextant and how to 'shoot' the sun at noon to obtain the azimuth and then using trigonometry calculate latitude. Captain Dirk did have satellite navigation as well, but passionately believed that knowing the rudiments of determining a vessels position was paramount.

Suzanne had morphed into a slight blonde girl with a ponytail, a tee shirt and shorts and looked the accomplished sailor. She went about shopping for all the requisites that Captain Dirk had listed, and she was always ready to help him. I was often on Meermin alone while they went into town or the chandlery, buying cordage, spare anchors etc. Suzanne and myself shared the cooking and cleaning and I began, under the supervision of Captain Dirk, servicing the winches and blocks and checking the standard rigging. There was no doubt that Captain Dirk ran a well-maintained yacht.

Finally, the day dawned for us to slip the moorings and put to sea. Suzanne was as excited as a toddler at its first birthday party and in all the time I had known her, I had never seen her so effervescent. Captain Dirk and she left to go to clear us at the harbour master's office and phone Mia, Hetty, Grand-pere and Dr Dlamini to tell them we were finally on our way. I stayed on board checking the met office weather and trying to organise everything I thought we might need. Suzanne and Captain Dirk returned and telling me to fire up the motor he wedged himself in the cockpit, taking the wheel. Then Suzanne and I slipped the moorings and we motored into Maputo Bay, heading east towards the Indian ocean. I raised the main sail as we had a steady force three south westerly wind. I set the fore sail on its roller furling and showed Suzanne how to sheet it in using the self-tailing winch. Meermin gained momentum and became alive under our feet. Suzanne was overjoyed and joined Captain Dirk in the cockpit hugging him and thanking him again for letting her join the trip. I smiled, thinking that she wouldn't be so effusive when the weather turned, or she suffered sea sickness, but I too felt a little euphoric.

Meermin dipped her prow into the blue green Indian ocean, and we left Ilha da Inhaca, to port and Captain Dirk steered a Sou Sou Westerly course straight into the wind but this only increased our speed as he 'pinched' close into the wind and I showed Suzanne how to trim the sails for close hauled beating. Using the winch, she soon had the sails drawing to their optimum. She grinned and squeezed my hand saying, "I so love this, I can see why you became so addicted." I suddenly felt a twinge in my gut and looking at the horizon felt queasy, then without out further warning I knew I had to get to the weather side of the boat to be sick. I hurled my breakfast over the side and then heard Captain Dirk laugh aloud, "Ah, so my only semi competent crew is suffering a touch of the 'Mal de Mer'(Sea sickness) never mind 'Mijn Zoon'(my son), many of the world's most illustrious sailors including Lord Nelson suffered sea sickness, so you are in good company and I suspect once you gain your sea legs you will be fine." I looked through watery eyes at Suzanne who looked worried, came to me and asked if I was all right. I was gutted, I was supposed to be the sailor while she had only once come out with me on the catamaran, but here she was as happy as I had seldom seen her, and I was as sick as the proverbial dog.

Captain Dirk didn't seem fazed at all and told Suzanne to get a can of cola and some plain biscuits. Suzanne went below and returned with the cola. Captain Dirk took the can and gave it a good shake then just popped the tab slightly. The cola fizzed out of the small aperture, and he added that I was to leave it to go flat and then drink it with the bland biscuits, while he asked Suzanne to sort out their lunch. They sat in the cockpit affably enjoying their lunch while I 'fed the fish' intermittently over the weather side. Suzanne asked if I was all right, but the captain told her not to worry and that I would be fine if I stayed hydrated. I had to admit that I felt awful and was not having much fun, but I managed to make slight sail adjustments to keep Meermin moving quickly through the sea. Suzanne busied herself with making sure the captain was comfortable and sorting out our meals, happy in her newfound domesticity.

I spent the first night at sea on deck as I thought that I might as well be on deck where I could not only be sick over the side, but also watch the Furano radar screen and check for other vessels' navigation lights. I had spent days studying the marine lights of trawlers, merchant vessels, tankers and pleasure craft, but even though we were now in the Indian ocean and in a shipping lane, I couldn't pick up anything on the screen or by looking out to sea.

The night was dark with an infinite array of stars overhead, Captain Dirk had left me a course to steer which I adhered to conscientiously keeping Meermin as close to the Sou Westerly wind as possible. I knew that going down into the saloon would be futile as the dissipating fumes from the diesel motor would aggravate my nausea. Suzanne came on deck with a cup of hot coffee laced with condensed milk, which I thankfully kept down. Looking up into the stars she said, "My God it is so exquisite. Never have I seen the stars like this, where have they all come from?" I was surprised, as living in Swaziland with little night lighting the night sky was visible, so I asked "Have you never been in the bush at night at home?" "Not really," she lamented wistfully, "I stupidly assumed that in life all that mattered was success and approbation, so seldom took time to look at the stars!" I made a slight adjustment to the wheel as Meermin had strayed slightly off course, and then said, "I think what you have done and achieved has to matter to certain people and is not a waste, you have at least seen most of the world." Sighing she said, "That I have, but are cities like Paris, London, New York and Milan really the world when you have that?" She asked, pointing to the illuminated milky way. I had to agree as there was no question that the sky littered with illuminating pin pricks was awesome. "Well, I have settled Dirk down to get a bit of sleep and he and I will take over at midnight." she informed me. I asked if she would be able to cope with trimming and doing sail changes. "I am sure with his instructions I will be fine." she replied, and I must do it eventually. So, I am going to see if I can get a bit of sleep. If you need anything, please just call down." I nodded as she climbed down the companion way.

At midnight she helped Captain Dirk up and settled him at the wheel. I updated him on our course and boat speed and told him that as the wind had increased, I had been able to sail closer to the desired true course. "'Goed Goed' (good good)," he responded, "try and get some rest as we will need you in four or five hours." I swallowed but said I would rather try and sleep on one of the cockpit cushions as I still felt rather queasy. "'Ja ja' (yes yes), probably a good idea, he replied. So, I settled on the starboard cockpit bench, stretching out, and tried to relax.

I dozed intermittently while Captain Dirk gave Suzanne sailing tips about helming and how to gage the sea swells so as the sails didn't luff. It was obvious that they got on so it was decided that they would share watches while I was to do mine on my own as Captain Dirk affirmed that I was plainly capable, I felt both happy and sad at the same time but was glad he acknowledged my abilities but also felt a little left out.

The following morning, we left the Port of Richards Bay to port, it was only a smudge on the horizon, but Captain Dirk told us that on his way past he had stopped in the St Lucia Estuary, which he said had been beautiful. "Well, if the wind holds, we should be able to make Cape Town in a week or so." he asserted. Suzanne asked how long we would be in Cape Town for as she said she had several friends there. I personally hoped that it would not be too long as any contact with South Africa was risky for me. "Only a day or two," he confirmed, "and I suggest Sean stays on board, but you will have an opportunity to go ashore." He was still speaking when we heard the VHF radio blaring in the saloon. He shouted to me to slip down and get the hand-held radio, I jumped down into the saloon and quickly found the small handheld radio then jumped back up into the cockpit and handed it to him. Switching on the universal channel we heard, "Sailing yacht, please identify yourself, your port of departure and your destination." The captain acknowledged with our call sign and the information requested and he was still speaking when I spotted the S.A. Air Force Shackleton high up in the Eastern sky. It buzzed around us in a loop and my stomach lurched as I thought they might request crew information, but they seemed satisfied and wished us happy sailing and then flew off to the North.

The wind strengthened and was now blowing force five, Meermin revelled in it, skimming along at an exhilarating pace. Suzanne was overjoyed and went forward up onto the pulpit and stood with the spindrift soaking her. Captain Dirk shouted to her to connect a static line in case she slipped and fell into the sea. I took a harness to her and connected it to the running lines that ran along the deck. As I helped her into the harness she was beaming and exclaimed, "I love this, why did you not insist that I go sailing with you before? This is just unbelievable!" I watched her as she clung on to the pulpit, Meermin dipped and rose in a splendid action, obviously built for this type of sailing.

I felt a lot better, still having the occasional twinge, but thankfully was able to keep some food down. So, leaving Suzanne to enjoy the sailing. I made my way back to cockpit where Captain Dirk sat at the helm. I asked if he needed anything and he suggested coffee all round, so going down to the galley I made the coffee and carefully took it back up to him, handing him his cup. He thanked me and commented, "That is a delightful young woman, who is obviously a natural born sailor." I agreed saying, "Well she has certainly surprised me, as in all the years I have known her I found her to be a little self-centred." Captain Dirk coughed in derision and countered, "That girl, since coming aboard, has made my life bearable. Nothing is too much trouble for her. You are truly fortunate to have such a special fiancée. I thought back on the times that Suzanne had treated me with contempt but decided that he was right. She was now a different little person. He called to her to get her coffee and she came aft balancing easily to the motion of the boat and I had to concur with him, she moved around the boat as if she had been doing it for ever.

The wind remained constant from the southwest, backing a little but not overly much over the next few days and we made satisfactory progress. Passing the port of Durban and turning more westerly, we headed for the Wild coast. The pattern of watches remained the same, with us all usually being on deck in the early part of the night and then me doing the dog watches with Captain Dirk and Suzanne taking over just before dawn. Every night Captain Dirk helped with my instruction in Astral navigation. He offered to teach Suzanne as well, but she said that as her mathematical skills were poor, she would leave it to us. She was comfortable marking down positions on the chart after getting them from one of the small satellite devices. Captain Dirk didn't push her but complimented her.

My solitary watches gave me much time to contemplate my life. I realised that I would have been hard pressed to help the captain had Suzanne not volunteered to come along, as there was no way he could manage a watch on his own, he was just incapable of moving around the deck safely. I smiled to myself ruefully, she was more of an asset to Meermin than I could be in the situation, even with my experience. I was pondering this late one night just after the 'bewitching hour', when Suzanne came and asked if I wanted a drink before she went to her berth. I thanked her saying that no, I was fine as if needed I would put Meermin on the auto helm wind vane and then nip down and make a 'brew '. "Ok," she responded squeezing my hand. Adding" Thank you for letting me come along, I couldn't have wished for better shipmates" I was left alone on deck with my thoughts.

At around four o'clock in the morning, Suzanne helped Captain Dirk up into the cockpit and he took the wheel. I updated him on our course. The wind had strengthened, and the captain stared up at the mast head and exclaimed, "Verdriet (Grief), the mast tri colour light is out, when did that happen?" This took me by surprise as I had not thought to check it. "We need to get that sorted at once," he asserted, "otherwise other traffic may not see us. Not everyone has radar and there are many sailing dhows in the Indian ocean. Go down below and get a new light from the locker and then you will need to go up the mast and change it." I gaped at him, it was not far off dawn and then we would no longer need sailing lights and we would have all day to replace the bulb. I suggested this. Captain Dirk shook his head and was adamant and commented, "By then we may have been run over by another vessel in the dark, no it must be done as soon as possible. You can use the harness and Suzanne can winch you up with the deck winch." I sighed and went below to get the box of spare bulbs to show him, so he could find the replacement bulb.

Captain Dirk now explained what had to be done. I had to attach a new rope to the end of the topping lift and then thread it through the mast head block and down to the deck to the deck winch. I was then to attach the one end to my harness, while the other would go around the deck winch so Suzanne could winch me up the mast. He said he would bring Meermin 'into the wind' to keep the mast as steady as possible to avoid it healing. Once I was able to reach the tricolour glass, I was to twist it anti clockwise as it was a bayonet fitting, but to be sure not to drop the glass as we had no replacement. I looked at Suzanne and could see she was apprehensive, but I was blatantly petrified! I had no head for heights and there was a heavy swell running, so the boat was pitching even though the captain had her head into the wind.

Captain Dirk said to Suzanne, "You will need to make sure you keep a steady pull on the rope from the winch and use the winch handle to slowly get Sean up to the mast head. Then once he has changed the bulb you will need to let him down again." Suzanne grimaced but said she would do her best. "Now Sean," he continued, "you must wrap your legs around the mast and when you reach the cross trees be careful not to stand on them to gain purchase, as they will not withstand your weight. 'So ja' (so yes), once at the mast head and having changed the bulb, give us a flash with this torch so that Suzanne can begin playing out the rope for your decent." I put the bulb in one pocket of my sailing jacket and the torch in the other, zipping both up and then went to the foot of the mast and told Suzanne I was ready, and she should begin winching.

The assent was extremely harrowing as the mast was swaying like a reed and once or twice, I nearly lost my grip and had to flail my legs to get them around the mast again. To say I was terrified was an understatement. Slowly but surely, I made it to the mast head amid encouragement from Suzanne below. Once there I had difficulty removing the glass, I could only use one hand as I needed the other to try to keep myself close to the pitching mast. Finally, I removed it and worrying that I might drop it onto the deck, or worse into the sea, I unzipped my jacket and stuffed it down the front. I removed the defunct bulb and replaced it with the new one. At once it flashed into life which made putting the glass back on a little easier. I made sure the glass was tightly fitted, then using the torch flashed down to Suzanne to start playing out the rope for my decent. Inch by inch I descended and had just navigated my way past the first set of cross trees, when I lost my grip on the mast and swayed out on the end of the rope across the dark churning sea. I heard Captain Dirk yelling instructions to Suzanne to cleat the rope. I swung like a pendulum first one way and then the other across the deck and the sea, my arms and legs flailing like a tipsy spider. Until luckily, I was able to hook my foot around a shroud and hang on for dear life. The pitching boat was doing its best to dislodge me, but I had my legs now firmly around the shroud. Even though it was cutting into my leg there was no way I was going to let go.

I heard Captain Dirk shouting to Suzanne and then she slowly resumed playing out the rope and I slowly but surely managed to make it back to the deck. Captain Dirk put Meemin back into the wind to stop the sails flogging and once again the boat had an easier motion. Suzanne asked, "Are you ok, it looked pretty scary up there?" I was just so relieved to be back on deck, it took me a while to get my equilibrium back. The calf and the back if my leg were bleeding, but it was only from the chaffing from the stainless-steel shroud. I managed to reply, "I thought I was going to end up in the dark in a lumpy sea, and without a Dan buoy light you would never have found me." Suzanne suddenly noticed that there was blood on the white deck and cried, "Oh no, you're bleeding, come quick," and grabbing my hand she dragged me to the cockpit, where with the light that came up from the saloon, she could inspect my leg. Captain Dirk, worried, asked if I was injured, so I assured him that no, it was only multiple grazes. Suzanne disappeared below and returned with the First Aid kit and then fussed, disinfecting my leg, and even suggesting that it needed a bandage, which I strenuously refused. I placated her by putting a couple of swabs behind my knee and keeping my leg bent, which helped to stop the bleeding.

I sat in the cockpit as dawn broke, Suzanne plying me with strong black coffee and Captain Dirk thanked me saying "I know it wasn't easy in this swell, but you did an excellent job." I instantly felt a lot better. Suzanne now organised our breakfasts and we all sat around as the sun rose over the Indian ocean, as we headed ever south.

In the late afternoon of our ninth day at sea we weathered Cape Point where the Indian ocean met the Atlantic. Captain Dirk told us that we were now leaving the Augulas current, which had been beneficial by adding to our boat speed as it flowed south westerly at a rate of four knots. Suzanne sat next to him at the wheel totally captivated, seldom had I ever seen her so happy in all the time I had known her. The port of Cape Town was just breath taking and undoubtedly, I would have found it more so had I not been anxious! Once we had been directed to moor on the international dock and the medical officer had completed his examination of us, the captain could go ashore with our passports to have us cleared. I went below trying to be as unobtrusive as possible. Suzanne was going ashore with the captain to help him so she was getting her makeup on, but she said, "Don't worry, the Captain and I will facilitate all the shopping and victualing as speedily as possible." She could see I was apprehensive, so smiling came up and squeezed my hand and added, "Don't fret we will be out of here in no time."

They left with the captain doing his best to walk without Suzanne's aid and I began getting Meermin ship shape. I tidied up below deck and got all the dirty clothes ready for Suzanne, as she said she planned to take them to the marina laundrette, and then went on deck. I coiled all the sheets and cordage neatly and swabbed the deck. I was throwing the dirty water over the side, when I was hailed from the dock. I looked up and my heart froze, it was a harbour police officer. She was stout with an ample bosom and a cheerful ruddy complexion, "van waar af het julle gekom (where have you come from)," she enquired in a pleasant manner. I smiled obsequiously and shrugged incomprehension. "Oh," she acknowledged in English, "sorry, I asked where you have come from?" "Ah," I managed in an almost normal voice, "our last port of call was Maputo." "Well, your boat is certainly incredibly beautiful, where are you headed?" she asked. I put my deck squeegee aside and decided to take 'the bull by the horns' and invited her aboard. She accepted with alacrity, clambering up into the cockpit with a skill that surprised me. "So," I explained, "I am only a deck hand, the captain -the owner, and other crew have gone ashore to sort things out." "Ah," she responded, "I hope you won't be in any trouble for inviting me aboard."

Sitting by the wheel she surveyed the freshly swabbed deck and then asked if she could see the rest of the boat. I relaxed a little, taking her down the companion way and showing her. I could see she was hugely impressed and going back on deck she asked wistfully, "Where are you all headed?" I took a moment or two but then replied, "We are Europe bound with ports of call on the way for victualing I imagine, but I am not sure which ports." I was still speaking when the Captain and Suzanne came along the dock, the captain now leaning heavily on Suzanne's slight frame, and she with both hands full of shopping bags. The trip to town had plainly taken its toll on his injury and he was grimacing in pain. "Ah, here they are now," I said getting ready to jump down to help them. My guest amazingly beat me to it and jumping on the dock and going to the captain's aid.

"Magtig jou arme man" (Lord you poor man), "she exclaimed supporting the captain and helping him on deck. Captain Dirk sank thankfully down on the cockpit bench and then he and Suzanne looked to me for an explanation.

I was at a loss for words as I had not even bothered to ask her name or check her credentials, so simply shrugged saying I had invited her aboard. I was saved from further embarrassment by the lady herself, who sitting down opposite the captain said, "Don't blame him Kaptien, he was just showing me around and this is a magnificent boat. You are all so fortunate. I am Alida Duvenhage and just patrol the marina to stop any petty pilfering from the boats." Captain Dirk, now having caught his breath, shook her hand and introduced himself and then Suzanne and myself. Suzanne smiled and said, "Thank you for helping us, it has been a been a trying day for the captain, would you like a coffee?" Alida's face lit up and she responded with a smile that spread right across her round face saying, "Oh that would be lovely if it is not too much trouble." "Not at all," Suzanne replied. Looking at me she continued, "Come on Sally, come help me."

Once in the galley Suzanne looked at me and then burst out laughing saying, "Dear Lord you should see your face. Relax she is only a junior constable, not a security agent and anyway she seems really pleasant." I smiled wanly then getting the kettle, put it on while Suzanne got the cups and produced a freshly bought lemon cake. Once all was to Suzanne's liking we went back on deck where we found Alida and the Captain in deep conversation. "So, Sean," Captain Dirk smiled, "Alida has been telling me that you have been the perfect host." I frowned, thinking that I had only tried to obfuscate Alida by being as amenable as possible but said nothing as I helped Suzanne with serving the coffee and cake. The captain now asked Alida, "Do you enjoy your work and your life?"

Surprisingly her face fell, and she replied, "No! It's very boring and I have little chance of promotion because unfortunately my education is lacking." "Oh no," Suzanne commiserated, "how awful. If you don't mind me asking, what about your home life?" Alida sighed and replied, "That's not much better, I live with my parents and my four siblings who really drive me crazy! You people are so lucky to be able to sail the world. I have never even been out of the Western Cape." Suzanne looked at her with genuine concern and asked her, "So what are your dreams?" Alida, wiping the lemon cake crumbs from her chin replied whimsically, "I would just love to have an adventure and see some of the world." Captain Dirk, settling back into his plethora of cockpit cushions smiled and said, "So you would like to see the world, do you even have a passport?" Alida surprised us all with her rejoinder, "Ag Ja (Oh Yes), because I work in the harbour and marina I sometimes must go on foreign commercial ships and so I must have a passport!" The captain looked suitably impressed and looking at Suzanne and myself and asked, "What say you shipmates? Should we invite this lady to come with us?" I was surprised, but Suzanne seemed unfazed and smilingly said, "Oh definitely, there is no doubt we are shorthanded and with four of us we could split into two complete watches and, not being derogatory," she added looking at Alida, "this lady looks very able and will be a significant help to you Captain. As long as it won't delay us, I think it's a fantastic idea." I sat, completely speechless not knowing where this was going.

Alida's face was picture of pure bliss and she exclaimed, "What! Are you genuinely asking me to come with you?" Of course," the captain confirmed, this is a sizeable yacht, and you may need to share a cabin with Suzanne or myself. But don't worry if you choose to come into the aft cabin with me, I assure you I will make no amorous advances towards you! It is a big cabin and there is plenty of room."

I sat dumfounded but agreed all the extra help would be an advantage. But this was an agent of law enforcement, so I tentatively asked, "Have you ever sailed Alida?" It took a moment for her to reply as she was still trying to come to terms with the captains offer but then she replied, "Are you serious Captain, please don't get my hopes up needlessly!? Captain Dirk replied by looking questioningly at us, "Well if it's fine with Suzanne and Sean, I see no problem, if your documents are in order welcome aboard."

Alida jumped up and embraced the captain and then after he managed to disentangle himself, she hugged Suzanne's small frame and then me. "Goeia Hemel (good Heavens), I can't believe this. I am going straight home to pack and resign from my position. It's a dream come true!" I still had no answer as to whether she had any sailing experience but mused that neither Suzanne nor myself were seasoned sailors and Suzanne had become surprisingly proficient. The captain said, "Well Alida we plan to leave within a day or so and obviously we will need to get extra stores on board, so we need you to make your arrangements as quickly as possible." Excitedly Alida replied, "Oh don't worry, I will hopefully be back this evening with my stuff. What should I pack?" Suzanne quickly apprised her what she had found most useful so far and then Alida, with some dexterity, was over the side and hastening down the Dock.

Suzanne began clearing up and then looking at the captain and myself said, "Well Dirk, I think you have made a wise decision; she is going to be an asset." I was still a little uneasy, but he was the captain so said, "Well Captain you are obviously a good judge of character. I am just thankful that you are helping me, so if you think it's for the best, I am happy."

Alida returned within a couple of hours, flushed and out of breath but looking extremely pleased with herself. Handing her passport to the captain she said she would be more than happy to join him in the aft cabin. Suzanne helped her with gear, and they went below to stow it. The captain looked at me then sniggered saying, "Don't worry, it will be fine. She has already resigned her position with immediate effect and anyway she didn't seem overly inquisitive. I think she will be a great help and if not, I will take the responsibility of making sure she gets back here." I nodded and replied, "I will just be a lot happier when we are out of S.A.territorial waters." "Ja (Yes), I can understand that but once we leave Cape Town, we have to go up the coast of Southwest Africa which is relatively hazardous, before we reach Windhoek, which will be our last port of call under South African control," he confirmed. "All good," I said getting up and making for the companion way "I'll just see how the ladies are getting on below."

Alida settled in and helped the captain in getting around, nothing seemed too much trouble and over dinner that night we learnt that she lived with her mother and stepfather, who she was not overly fond of. In her job as harbour law enforcement, she had always hankered on one day sailing away on one of the vessels in the harbour and now she was doing just that. She was beaming. The following day we completed the victualling of Meermin and then the captain, aided by Alida, made the trip to the Harbour Master and cleared us for departure the following morning.

The day dawned bright and blustery, and we slipped the moorings and motored out into the harbour and into the Atlantic Ocean. There was a sizable swell running and even though we were making good headway with a force four south easterly, it wasn't long before my sea sickness re-emerged. Miserably I began heaving over the leeward side of the yacht, but again Suzanne seemed unaffected, and neither was Alida. This peeved me as I was supposed to be the sailor. I spent my time trying to stay hydrated and hoped that as before my 'mal de mer' would pass.

The sailing was perfect, and we made steady progress up the West Coast of South Africa. Alida surprised us with some delicious baked cakes. I had to limit my intake but the Captain, Alida and Suzanne sat in the cockpit enjoying them.

Three days out, off the West coast of Southwest Africa, which is aptly named the 'skeleton coast', the barometric pressure dropped, and Captain Dirk warned that we were in for a 'blow', recommending that we secure everything below and batten the hatches.

Suzanne and I who had the watch attached ourselves to static lines and harnesses and clipped them on to the running lines that ran from fore to aft. The sea now had deep troughs and crests and we were taking them on the port bow. The captain shouted that we should start reefing in the mainsail, secure the foresail roller furling and attach the storm jib to the forestay.

We obeyed him explicitly and even though it was now drizzling heavily Suzanne was unfazed. Meermin was now beginning to heel and Alida came on deck with our wet weather gear, which we quickly changed into. I took the helm and Captain Dirk gave us our instructions, "Sean, I want you to bring the helm up, so we are taking the waves head on, but just keep her slightly into the wind so that we have way."

I brought Mermin up just into the wind. Captain Dirk now told Suzanne and Alida to go up and reef the main to the boom and go forward and 'hank on' the storm jib, securing the sheets along the running lines back to the cockpit.

The boat had settled into an easier motion and Suzanne and Alida had returned to the cockpit and secured the jib sheet starboard. Captain Dirk, with the help of Alida, secured himself in the cockpit and told me to slowly lay Meermin off on a close reach, head out to sea and put as much distance between ourselves and the dangerous lee Skelton Coast.

The wind howled through the rigging. Dirk told us all to make sure we had our safety lines securely attached and we sailed on into the dark gloom. Captain Dirk told Alida and Suzanne to check the lashings on the life raft canister, below the mast, in case it was needed in an emergency. The wind had now strengthened, to force six and a lot of scud from the crests of the large waves stung our cheeks. I hung on to the wheel as it bucked under my hands and shouted to Suzanne, asking if she still thought it was such fun? Her small oval face, streaming water, smiled and she re-iterated that she was fine and that sailing, like life, was not always fair winds and calm seas. Alida was making sure Captain Dirk was ok, but he tutted, assuring us that he had experienced worse storms.

Night fell and with it squalls and spectacular fork lightening that illuminated the dark thunderous clouds. The captain told Suzanne to go below and disconnect all the electrical navigation systems because if we took a strike the conductor in the mast would diffuse it into the ocean, but anything with wiring would be destroyed. The noise was deafening, and the wind shrieked through the rigging. The waves were now enormous as Meermin buried her bow into them, and a deluge of water came streaming down the deck, but fortunately most ran down the scuppers. Dirk told the girls to totally reef the main sail so that we were only running on the storm jib.

Meermin and her crew, with their hopes and dreams, sailed on into the vast Atlantic night!

www.ingramcontent.com/pod-product-compliance
Lightning Source LLC
Chambersburg PA
CBHW070636170726
48291CB00003B/1040